The Chocolate Kiss-Off
Book Three
The Persephone Cole Vintage Mysteries

Heather Haven

The Chocolate Kiss-Off © 2015 by Heather Haven

This book is a work of fiction. Characters, names, places, events, and incidents either are the product of the author's imagination or are used fictitiously, and any resemblance to any actual persons, living or dead, events, or locales is entirely coincidental.

The Wives of Bath Press
5512 Cribari Bend
San Jose, CA 95135

http:// www.thewivesofbath.com

Cover Art © 2015 by Heather Haven and Robert Goldberg
Edited by Baird Nuckolls
Layout and book production by
Heather Haven and Baird Nuckolls

Print ISBN 978-0-9892265-7-8
eBook ISBN 978-0-9892265-6-1
First eBook edition

Testimonials

"Percy is a great character, and I found myself smiling and laughing at her antics throughout the story. Anyone looking for a fun, fast read should certainly give this book a try. I know I'll be on the lookout for more about Percy and her adventures."
Long and Short Reviews

"Another Hit Series for Ms Haven. Set in the 1940s, this new series is about a female Private Investigator, something unheard of in those days. Hats off to Ms Haven for another fine series. I couldn't put it down."
Roseanne Dowell, Author

"As a Heather Haven fan, I couldn't resist leaving an encouraging word to those of you who love your genres mixed with a heaping of humor. I read her first series and absolutely loved it, so I was really excited to see this debut of her new heroine and series. Her spunky leading ladies are realistic, determined, and inspiring and her secondary characters are colorful and so well described you'll swear you'd recognize them on the street. I'm thinking of running for president of the Heather Haven Fan Club, so after you read her work and leave your own positive review, you can vote for me." :) *Ginger Simpson, Spice up Your Life With Ginger*

"If you like to take a chance on a book, you won't be disappointed with this one. I am looking forward to reading her next book about Persephone Cole." *Amazon Reader*

The Persephone Cole Vintage Mystery Series:

The Dagger Before Me – Book One
**Iced Diamonds* – Book Two
The Chocolate Kiss-Off – Book Three

*Formerly *Persephone Cole and the Halloween Curse*
**Formerly *Persephone Cole and the Christmas Killings
Conundrum*

Dedication

This book is dedicated to my mother, Mary Lee, an original thinker if there ever was one; husband, Norman Meister, who loves strong women; and gutsy broads everywhere who get out there, do what they love, and blaze the trail for the rest of us.

Acknowledgments

Thanks to Mary Wollesen, a generous friend, who was willing to read the first shi--y draft of this novel. As a non-writer but avid reader, Mary made suggestions that were extremely helpful. Bless you.

I could never do what I do without my writing group and buddies, Myra Strober, Carter Schwonk, and Jerry Burger. Each one a talented author, they are always willing to share their knowledge and love of the craft. It's an honor to share a round table with them.

Thanks, too, to Robert (Bobbo) Goldberg for assistance with the cover art from the beginning of this series. I get by with a little help from my friends. Actually, a LOT of help from my friends.

Last but never least, I want to acknowledge Baird Nuckolls, fellow writer, co-publisher, visionary, editor, and friend, whose expertise in nearly everything holds me in good stead. And on top of everything else, she's a pastry chef. Yum, yum.

Thank you. I love you all.

The Chocolate Kiss-Off

Chapter One

Dear Diary,

July 15th, 1941. I will always remember this date. This is the day I found out her name, who she is. When I come face to face with her, will she know who I am? Will she be sorry? I will make sure of it, if it takes years.

Chapter Two

"Persela! Persela!"

The banging on the front door merged with the crying of a familiar voice. The sound shot through the thin walls of the apartment like a police siren blaring across forty-second street.

Though it was four forty-five a.m. on a Friday morning, Persephone "Percy" Cole sat bolt up-right, wide awake, and mind alert. She threw back the covers, leapt out of bed, snatched her robe from the end post, and raced out of the room. No time for slippers or pushing long, flaming-red hair out of her face.

The bedroom was the largest of the four in the railroad apartment, but no one else in the family wanted it. Day or night you could hear every noise in the hallway. But Percy Cole, one of Manhattan's first female detectives, liked being the first to know what was what. It suited her.

Reaching the front door within seconds, she grabbed the knob, just as the thumping and calling increased in volume. Without hesitation, Percy flung the door open wide. The only person in the world that called her Persela was Mrs. Goldberg.

The long-time family friend and neighbor froze at the door's opening, a fisted hand drawn back midair. More than a foot shorter than Percy, the older woman threw back her head and looked up, open-mouthed. Words formed on the woman's lips but no sound came forth.

Fear or something closer to horror tracked itself across her face, and came to a stop in pale blue eyes. Percy's own green ones became sharp and searching.

"You'd better get in here, Mrs. Goldberg, and tell me what's wrong."

The five-foot eleven-iinch woman stepped aside to allow the rotund one entrance to the apartment. But instead of moving, Mrs. Goldberg picked up the two bottom corners of the long, bibbed apron she was wearing and chucked them over her head.

Bursting into tears, she stood weaving in the doorway. Percy reached down and wrapped a strong arm around the hooded woman, guiding her into the most cluttered room of the lower east side apartment, the parlor-slash-office.

Fast movements returned the detective to the front door, where she gave a quick glance in both directions to see if any neighbors came out into the hall, curious about the commotion. Satisfied the answer was 'no', Percy shut the door. Another glance down the hallway of the apartment showed the doors to her son, sister, and parents' bedrooms all remained closed.

Good. I don't know what the hell's going on, but I don't want to be interrupted yet.

Mrs. Goldberg was where she'd been left, sniffling in the center of the parlor. With gentle fingers, Percy lifted the apron from the top of the weeping woman's head, causing tufts of salt and pepper hair to stick out every which way in the process. She studied the round face, red from crying.

"Sit down, Mrs. Goldberg. You don't look so good."

"How can I look good? My boy's in jail."

Shock colored Percy's voice. "Who's in jail? Howie?"

"How many boys do I have?" Mrs. Goldberg's exasperation overrode her fear.

"What happened?"

"He's been arrested!"

"Howie? Our Howard Goldberg? There's got to be some mistake."

Percy stifled the urge to laugh when she saw the older woman's distressed expression. She waited for Mrs. Goldberg to say more. But instead, the woman let out a wail. It ended in a screech similar to a beginner's violin being played by one of the neighborhood kids.

Percy hurried to close the parlor door, hoping the rest of the family would remain sleeping, although things were getting dicier by the minute. She turned back to the wobbly woman.

"You need to sit, Mrs. Goldberg, before you fall down."

When she got no response, Percy took the woman by the elbow and led her to the faded brocade sofa dominating the section of the room nearest the door. She repeated the command in a tone usually saved for the family dog.

"Sit." Percy gave a gentle push.

Still sobbing, Mrs. Goldberg fell on the sofa, let out a hiccup, and wiped her nose on the edge of the apron. Percy eased into the matching overstuffed chair, and leaned forward.

"You look like you could use something to calm your nerves. Mother's sherry? Sweet but soothing." She gestured to a half-filled bottle of sherry perched on the radio console at the end of the sofa. "Or Pop's whiskey? Strong but numbing." She studied her friend and neighbor.

"Whiskey it is."

Percy patted the other woman's hand in an encouraging manner, stood, and disappeared behind a gold and cobalt blue screen covered with strutting, iridescent peacocks. As far as Percy was concerned, the screen was an unwelcomed legacy from a deceased great-aunt, but her mother loved it. As it served to separate the Cole Brothers Detective Agency from the family parlor, Percy chose to ignore the tasteless addition to an already crowded room.

Mrs. Goldberg let out another sob before the words tumbled out. "He called me from the police station. My Howie! Arrested for murder! *Oy vey iz mir!*"

"Murder? In that case, I could use something, myself. You take a couple of deep breaths while I'm pouring," Percy said from behind the screen. The sounds of a drawer opening, a top being unscrewed from a bottle, and a quick pour into two glasses could be heard. "Start at the beginning."

"What beginning?" Mrs. Goldberg's voice trembled on the other side of the barrier. "Who knows the beginning? He calls and tells me he found a dead woman in the chocolate this morning when he gets to work and when he tells the police, they arrest him, my Howie, for murder."

She was silent. Even her breathing seemed to stop.

Percy returned from behind the screen carrying two full shot glasses. She shoved one in Mrs. Goldberg's hand, who sat in a daze.

"Go on, drink that," Percy said, swallowing about half of the amber liquid in her own glass in one gulp. "Good stuff," she muttered in appreciation.

She sat down again opposite Mrs. Goldberg, who took a tentative sip of the alcohol and coughed. But the woman's color returned and Percy was satisfied. She leaned in again.

"Okay, so Howie found a dead woman?"

Mrs. Goldberg nodded vehemently. "Yes. Persela, he says the police, they think he killed this woman he found in the chocolate. But you know my Howie; he wouldn't hurt a fly, such a gentle boy, such a good boy, always remembering my birthday and so kind to animals. All the ones he would bring home to doctor and take care of, years and years of them. You remember those pigeons, flying all over the apartment. Such messy birds, pigeons. I was covered in pigeon droppings for weeks."

"At the chocolate factory, right?"

"The pigeons?"

"The body."

"Yes, yes. *Oy*, those pigeons. Remember?"

"Forget the pigeons."

Mrs. Goldberg wiped her eyes and went on, not hearing Percy's comment.

"But could you tell that boy anything? No. Three baby birds he carried with him wherever he went for nearly a month. He nursed them back to health no matter what anybody said," Mrs. Goldberg added, with a touch of pride.

The memory of Howie as a nine-year old boy flashed through Percy's mind. Howard Goldberg - Howie to his friends and family -- was a true *mensch*, Yiddish for an all-around good guy. He was not only a dear friend, but also godfather to her son. As far as Percy was concerned Captain America had nothing on him.

"When did Howie call you from the police station? What time?"

"Who could know the time? I was making the *Challah* for the store, like I do every day, that's all I know. He said he didn't want me to hear it on the radio. Who plays the radio? All I hear about is that Hitler and Benny Goodman. Then he said I was the only call he could make, so to be sure to run up and get you."

"That would be Howie who called you."

"Who else? Hitler?"

"Just clarifying, Mrs. Goldberg." Percy took the nearly full shot glass from Mrs. Goldberg's hand and placed it on the side table, while the woman continued talking.

"And what does that mean; I'm the 'only call'? Are they charging money to make these phone calls? I told him to always carry a dollar on him, always, but does he listen? No, I'm just his mother. You never know when you're going to need money for an emergency, like now." She started to sob again, and picked up the corners of her soggy apron, dabbing at her eyes.

Percy's mind raced, paying little attention to Mrs. Goldberg's chidings of her son's disregard for a mother's golden words.

"Did he say which station he was at?"

Mrs. Goldberg didn't answer, but shook her head. She became distracted and over-wrought again, her face taking on a pleading look. Her hands clasped together in a prayer-like manner.

"Persela, help my boy. You're a detective with a badge --"

"A license," Percy murmured, deep in thought.

"A license, a badge, who cares, and so what?" Anger and indignation flared up in Mrs. Goldberg, replacing the fear. "You know he didn't do this. Him! As if he would put somebody in his vat of chocolate like a bon-bon. Not my Howie. It takes him hours and hours to make his chocolate. He's so proud of it. Why just the other day --"

"Forget the chocolate."

"Forget the chocolate, forget the pigeons. Such fuss."

"Right now we need to find him. If we're not careful, he could get lost within the system for days. You're sure he didn't say where he was?"

Percy stood and looked down at her neighbor. The woman stared back, unblinking.

"He lives and works in Brooklyn." Percy answered herself. "Let's see." Percy scrunched her forehead in thought. "He's probably being held at the closest precinct to the factory. That would be the Ninetieth. Did he mention Williamsburg? The Ninetieth?"

"I don't know. Maybe." Mrs. Goldberg looked startled. "The Ninetieth? There are ninety police stations in Brooklyn? It's just a little burg. What kind of dangerous place is that, there should be so many police stations?"

"Forget the police stations."

"Oy, so much to forget, who can remember?"

"I'll start with the Ninetieth," Percy said more to herself than Mrs. Goldberg. "With any luck, he's there. Then I'll phone Jude." Percy noticed the terrified look returning to the other woman's face. "Don't worry. It'll be all right. We'll get him out of this."

It was a large promise, but even without any facts, Percy knew one thing. While anyone is capable of murder given the right circumstances, the Howard Goldberg she knew would never kill someone and put them in a vat of chocolate. To him chocolate was sacrosanct. Percy looked down at Howie's mother.

"You okay? You want to lie down for a moment?"

Mrs. Goldberg shook her head, caught up in her thoughts. Percy studied her with sympathy.

That's how I'd be if my son got arrested for murder.

"Here's an idea." Percy leaned down and stroked the woman lightly on the shoulder to get her attention. "Why don't you go to the kitchen and rustle us up some coffee? I'll make a few calls to see what's going on. You know where everything is, right?"

Mrs. Goldberg rallied, stood, and smoothed out her apron. "Better than your mother, Persela. How she can find anything the way she keeps that kitchen of hers, I'll never know, but I'm not one to complain."

"You? Never."

"Of course, this room has so much gold paint it's enough to wake the de..." Mrs. Goldberg broke off speaking as suddenly as she'd started. "What am I doing, talking about paint when my son..." She brought one hand to her face, pressing fingers against quivering lips.

"Easy, Mrs. Goldberg."

Percy put a sturdy arm around the short woman's shoulders again. Mrs. Goldberg leaned into her, looking small, fragile and old. Percy hated seeing her like that.

"We'll find out what's what and take care of it. You go make that coffee. Mr. Goldberg still out of town?"

"My Seymour comes back from sitting Shiva tomorrow. Seven whole days he's been in the Bronx. How will I tell him?" Mrs. Goldberg's entire body began to tremble. "First, my Seymour's brother dead from cancer and now this! Our Howie!" She shook her head sadly, moving with heavy steps toward the door. "I'll go make with the coffee."

Percy watched her go out the door then turned. She headed again to the corner of the room where the Cole Brothers Investigations office resided. Behind the screen, two small dark oak desks sat, one belonging to her, the other to her father.

Sitting down, she opened her desk drawer, pulled out the phone book, looked up the Brooklyn police station in question, and dialed the number. Even though it was barely five o'clock in the morning, the phone answered on the first ring.

"Ninetieth Precinct. Officer O'Hara speaking."

Percy heard a world of attitude in those few brief words. Officer O'Hara sounded young, yet already jaded. The low-income residential and factory district had high crime and little love for coppers. It turned even rookies into worn-out cynics fast.

"Good morning." Percy tried to make her voice sound business-like but polite. "I'm looking for a Howard Goldberg and wondered if he was brought there this morning? Maybe an hour or two ago."

"Who wants to know? This his wife?"

If I say I'm a private detective, there's going to be twenty minutes of crapola and then he'll only hang up on me.

"Yeah, I'm his wife. Is he there? He called his mother but didn't call me, the louse."

"A real mama's boy, huh? Yeah, we got him."

"What's the charge?"

"We're holding him for questioning on suspicion of murder."

"On what grounds?"

"On the grounds of the victim got found in a big bowl of his chocolate with a rope around her neck pulled tighter than my mother's girdle. You'd better get a lawyer, lady. It don't look so good for him."

"If he's around, I'd like to talk to him."

"Naw. He's in his cell by now. It being Friday, he won't be arraigned until Monday morning. He'll be spending the weekend in the slammer. Don't worry, we'll treat him right, honey." Officer O'Hara left off with a laugh indicating just the opposite.

"Thanks." She hung up then muttered, "And don't call me honey."

Percy reached into the top drawer and snatched a stick of Doublemint gum from a pack. Opening it up, she folded the gum into a wad and shoved it in her mouth, chewing absentmindedly.

It was an old trick her father showed her years ago to keep Mother from knowing he 'tipped the bottle' from time to time. Mother tipping the sherry bottle never seemed to count.

She dialed her brother, Jude, and looked around at the cramped quarters as the phone rang. Two file cabinets, worn but cared-for, were crammed against the wall into a space too small for the amount of business they were currently doing. She let out a sigh.

Percy grew up with the room functioning as the office for the detective agency started by her father and uncle. Uncle Gil's sudden death and Pop's recent broken leg had taken their toll on business. Cole Brothers Investigations – once thriving – had receded more and more into a corner of the parlor.

When Percy got her investigator's license six-months earlier, she assumed the lost partnership position. Despite many people's initial scorn of a female detective, the business was resurrecting itself.

Pop was gone on a big case in New Jersey, and she was juggling two other cases, one arriving only the day before. Percy wasn't sure how she'd fit Mrs. Goldberg in, but she'd do more than that; it would take precedence over the other jobs she had going.

Shame to toss them aside, though. Good money. And they're both mostly legwork. Time to spread out and make some changes.

Her brother, Jude, finally answered on the eighth ring. He didn't sound as wide awake as Officer O'Hara, but he didn't sound as jaded, either.

Chapter Three

Dear Diary,

February 5, 1942. This monumental day has come and gone. It took over a year of waiting and planning, but the deed is done. She didn't deserve to live after what she did to me. Let others make of it what they will. I am vindicated.

Chapter Four

Dressed in her dark gray, Marlene Dietrich knock-off pants suit, Percy pulled her long red hair into a ponytail. She grabbed the ever-present bag of pistachio nuts from her bureau, crammed it into a 'kangaroo' pocket of her slacks, and headed for the kitchen. It was probably too much to hope no one else was up; Mrs. Goldberg had been loud, especially when wailing.

Percy cracked open the kitchen door. As usual, the smell of Percy's least favorite breakfast food, oatmeal, filled the air. Just once Percy would like to push at the kitchen door and have the aroma of eggs and bacon assail her nostrils. No such luck, with the war's rationing. She paused, listening to the conversation on the other side of the door.

"Don't you worry, Rachel," said Mother. "Everything's going to be just fine. Persephone and Adjudication would take care of this. Serendipity will help, too. Between the three of them, they'll get this straightened out."

"Uh-uh. Not me," said Sera. "I don't know nothin' about birthin' babies."

"Now, Serendipity, this is no time for an imitation of Lana Turner, even though you do a lovely one," Mother added as an afterthought.

"That was Butterfly McQueen. Honestly, Mother, don't you know anything?"Offense riddled Sera's voice. It didn't take much to offend Sera.

Fifteen years younger than Percy and seventeen years younger than Jude, their kid sister had been a change-of-life baby. From the beginning, she'd been treated like everyone's child, causing her to rebel by age thirteen. At twenty, she was still rebelling.

Opening the door fully, Percy saw her mother seated at the kitchen table. Mother's white-blonde hair was even wilder than usual, lying on her blue and green chenille bathrobe like a fur collar. Percy watched as her mother reached across the table to pat Mrs. Goldberg's chubby hand.

Sera stood at the stove. With her dyed blonde hair, heavily made-up face, and pink satin pajamas, she seemed out of place stirring the never-ending bubbling pot of oatmeal.

Mother looked up and noticed Percy's entrance. A questioning look came to her face.

"Is everything all right? What did you find out?"

Percy put on a small smile and pulled out one of the empty spindle-back chairs surrounding the rectangular kitchen table. Spinning it around, she straddled the seat, facing the two older women. She leaned her elbows on the back of the chair.

"Okay, first of all, Howie *is* at the Ninetieth. I also made two more calls. We'll start with the last. That was to my friend, Detective Hutchers --"

"You remember him, Rachel," Mother interrupted. "Such a nice man. He took Persephone to the Policeman's Ball for New Year's."

"Oh, yes." Mrs. Goldberg nodded, trying to be agreeable but heavy with worry. Both women looked expectantly at Percy.

"Unfortunately," Percy went on, still chewing gum, "Hutchers doesn't know anyone at the Ninetieth, but is going to make some phone calls; see if he can get the inside scoop. Jude is on his way there right now and --"

"And there you are," Mother interrupted, with a self-satisfied grin, slapping the palms of her hands on the kitchen table. Mother stood, relief cloaking her body like wool jersey. She crossed to the stove and took the large spoon from her daughter's hand.

"You go sit down, dear. I'll do this. We don't want to burn the oatmeal again, do we?"

"Thank you, Mother," said Sera. "I find making oatmeal quite gauche."

"Serendipity, I will not have you using that kind of language in my kitchen."

Mrs. Goldberg was taken aback by her friend's shift in demeanor. She turned to Percy. "You mean everything's all right? My son's --"

"Not exactly, Mrs. Goldberg." Percy's voice was quiet but firm. She spit the gum out in the palm of her hand then tossed it into the sink. "Mother's jumped the gun a bit on this."

"Oh, have I, Persephone? How silly of me. Here." She thrust the spoon back into Sera's hand. "You keep stirring this, dear. I'll tell you when to quit. And lower the flame."

"Aw, gee." Sera took the spoon with reluctance. "I have to curl my hair before I leave for work. I got a big date tonight. It's important," she added.

"Hush, Serendipity." Mother crossed the large and homey but well-used kitchen, returned to the table, and sat down. "We'll be nice and quiet until Persephone's done, won't we, Rachel?"

"Yes, yes," Mrs. Goldberg stuttered.

Percy returned her attention to Mrs. Goldberg. "Okay, to continue –"

"I can't go with my hair looking like this," whined Sera.

"So wear a hat," Percy said over her shoulder. She turned back to Mrs. Goldberg.

"Jude is on his way over to the Ninetieth Precinct right now. His hope is to discover just what the charges might wind up being; in other words, why they're holding Howie at all. In order to arrest a person, the police have to have something called Probable Cause. Over the phone, the cop mentioned an arraignment. If that's the case, Jude hopes to speed up the process --"

It was Mrs. Goldberg's turn to interrupt. "Arraignment? What means this word, 'arraignment'?" Confusion clouded her face.

"What she meant to say was 'arrange'. They're going to arrange to let him go, right Persephone?" Mother's dark brown eyes sparkled, looking from her daughter to her dearest and oldest friend. "And they'd better say they're sorry for frightening all of us like this."

"Not exactly, Mother." Percy's voice took on more of an authoritative tone. "Listen, why don't you let me tell it my way and if either of you have any questions afterward, I can answer them. Okay?"

Both women nodded and Mother, to add to her part of the agreement, raised her fingers to her closed mouth, mimed locking it and throwing away the key.

"Let's see how long that lasts," Sera murmured from the stove.

"Serendipity, you behave," Mother said. "And stop interrupting Persephone." She turned back to her elder daughter. "You go right ahead, dear. Tell us what you've learned about this misunderstanding between Howard and the law."

Percy turned back to Mrs. Goldberg. "To answer the question about what an arraignment is, it's a formal reading of a criminal complaint in the presence of the defendant stating the charges against him or her. From what I understand, no formal charges have been made yet. Jude hopes to have them do it sometime today, so we can post bail, and not have Howie spend the weekend in jail."

Mrs. Goldberg took in a long breath, coupled with one of her small wails of despair. She clasped her hands to her bosom, her gold wedding band glinting on hands that were chapped and much-used from decades of hard work.

"My son in jail. My Howie spending the weekend in jail. And for killing someone!"

Bursting into tears, she turned to Mother's outstretched arms. Mrs. Goldberg buried herself in her friend's thin, concave chest, sobbing uncontrollably. Percy stared.

"Nice going, Percy. Sometimes you can be so gauche." Sera crossed to her sister's side, pointing the oatmeal encrusted spoon in her face. A small drop of oatmeal landed on Percy's thigh.

"I was just explaining --"

"Maybe explanations are not what we need right now, Persephone." Mother interrupted in a whisper over Mrs. Goldberg's shaking shoulders.

"Right." Percy stood and shook out her large frame like a dog after a bath. "I'm going to get Oliver up then head on down to Brooklyn. See if I can get in to talk to Howie and --"

"Still too much explaining, dear. Off you go." Mother gestured with her head toward the door.

"Right."

* * * *

Percy opened the door of her son's blue and yellow bedroom, and peeked inside. There the child who gave her life meaning lay sleeping on his side, head resting on his pillow. Tousled blue-black hair and a cherub-like face made Percy marvel once again at how a child could look so much like an angel in sleep and be so 'all boy' when awake.

She tiptoed into the room and the short-legged, long-bodied dog that slept at the foot of the bed raised his head and wagged a furry tail. Named after Oliver's best friend, Freddie, the dog was her son's constant companion since arriving as a Christmas present.

Percy had been surprised and delighted at how Oliver took on the responsibility of the care and feeding of his pet. With an eight-year old son, she'd expected to do the bulk of the work herself. Such was not the case. Oliver walked him at least twice daily and made sure his water bowl was full. The family watched every evening as the boy solemnly gathered leftovers to be mixed in with the dry meat-meal dog food he insisted they purchased from a feed and grain store in Queens. It wasn't surprising when he announced one day he wanted to be a 'dog doctor'.

While listening to the dog's tail thumping on the mattress, Percy stroked Oliver's forehead and cheek. Her son began to stir.

"Hey, sleepy-head." She crooned to him, as she leaned over and kissed him on the cheek. "Time to get up and get ready for school."

Eyelids fluttered open and he looked up at her with a smile. "Mommy! Is it morning already?"

"Yes, it is, sweetie." He struggled to a sitting position, as she half-embraced, half-pulled him up. "Come on. There's a good boy." She watched him yawn and stretch for a moment then stroked his rumpled hair.

"Oliver, Mrs. Goldberg is sitting in the kitchen. She's a little upset over something somebody *said* Uncle Howie did, but I want you to know he didn't do it."

"Then why is she upset?"

"Sometimes mothers get upset when our children are in trouble. So I don't want you to bother her this morning. I'm going out now to make sure these people know they're wrong about Uncle Howie. Okay?"

"Okay." Oliver rubbed sleep-filled eyes. "What is it Uncle Howie didn't do?"

"I'm not too sure myself, sweetie, but we know him to be an upright kind of guy, right?" Oliver nodded. "When I get home I'll tell you all about it, I promise. Meanwhile, I want you to walk Freddie, get ready for school, eat your breakfast, and not ask any questions of Mrs. Goldberg or your grandmother, okay? I'll explain everything when I see you later today."

Oliver nodded. "Okay, Mommy."

"There's my good boy. And Aunt Sera made the oatmeal this morning, so if it's a little burned, try not to say anything."

Oliver wrinkled his nose. "She always burns the oatmeal."

"I know, but you're going to let it slide this morning. If it's burnt, eat around the edges. But be sure to get to school on time. And take your lunch. Don't forget it like you did yesterday."

"I didn't forget it, Mommy. I didn't want it. Grandmother made me a mashed potato and grape jelly sandwich. And then for dessert, strawberry potato pudding."

Oliver wrinkled his nose again.

"Yeah, we seem to be having a run on potatoes." Percy let out a sigh. "I'll speak to her about it. You like Spam, don't you?"

He nodded.

"I'll see that Spam is in your lunchbox from now on."

"And an apple? I like apples. But not strawberry-potato pudding. Yuk."

"Is that so, young man?"

His mother reached out and began to tickle him under his arms. A giggle burst forth from him, sounding more like the tinkle of a wind chime.

She repeated her words and tickled him again. He giggled again, slightly louder. Percy laughed and looked down at her son in mock severity.

"Remember, Oliver, you can't be criticizing your grandmother's cooking until you're older, and then never to her face. But I promise you no more strawberry-potato pudding in your lunchbox."

"Okay, Mommy, okay." He let out a titter. "Now tickle Freddie," Oliver ordered about the dog that sat beside them, tail wagging, tongue lagging, looking from one to the other.

Obeying, Percy reached out and scratched behind the dog's forelegs. "Okay. Tickle, tickle, Freddie."

The dog panted, looking at her. She did it again.

"Just as I suspected. Freddie's not ticklish. Now hit the deck, young man, or you'll be late for school."

"Yes, ma'am."

Chapter Five

After hugging her son, Percy headed back to the kitchen. Sera was seated, while Mother portioned out the hot oatmeal from the pot into bowls as if it was thick glue, which Percy pretty much figured it to be by then. Their neighbor was nowhere to be seen.

"Where's Mrs. Goldberg, Mother?"

"She had to finish baking the bread for the store."

The Goldbergs ran a small mom and pop store on a nearby corner, temporarily managed by a cousin in Mr. Goldberg's absence.

"I'll drop by on my way out and check up on her."

Percy watched Sera pick up the small can of condensed milk and pour some on her cereal. Percy made a face.

"I don't know how you can drink that stuff undiluted, Sera."

Sera shrugged. "I like it."

It was Percy's turn to shrug. "If you say so. I'm going. I'll call you when I know what's what."

"Have some breakfast before you go, Persephone." Mother looked at the door. "Where's Oliver?"

Percy crossed to the table and grabbed two apples from the large fruit bowl. "Got no time. This'll do me. I'll grab a hotdog later. Oliver is walking the dog and then he'll be in for breakfast. From now on, Mother, ix-nay on the mashed potato and jelly sandwiches for the kid, okay?"

"Really, Persephone? I think they're delicious." Mother seemed surprised and puzzled. Percy kept a straight face.

"If everybody liked chocolate, what would happen to vanilla?" Percy paused. "Maybe I shouldn't have said that, given what's going on."

"Yeah, that was a little gauche," Sera said with a simper.

"New word for the day, Sera?"

Percy winked at her younger sister. Sera blushed then smiled shyly.

"I read it in Movie magazine. I think it means someone who's got no taste."

"Close, but no cigar." Percy turned back to her mother. "Mother, I told Oliver he should have a piece of fruit for dessert, so no more pudding or anything like that. How about giving him one of these apples? And a Spam sandwich. He likes those."

"He's the only one," Sera piped up. "I think Spam's disgusting."

"Says she who drinks armored cow straight from the can."

"I like condensed milk."

"There's more of that taste you've been talking about. And by the way, gauche means someone who is uncouth or vulgar."

"Sez you."

"Not just me. Webster, too."

"I don't even know the guy."

Percy opened her mouth for a retort, thought better of it, and took a bite of apple.

"I'm off to Brooklyn, Mother."

She crossed to a set of wall hooks, each holding a hat or scarf. Snatching at a dark brown fedora given to her by her father for Christmas, she plopped it on her head. Percy thought aloud, her mind racing.

"I think I've got enough gas. Glad Pop didn't take Ophelia on his latest job. I'd have to take two trains to get to the Brooklyn police station, otherwise." Ophelia was the family automobile, a black 1929 Dodge, and considered more of a pet than a car. "Speaking of Pop, he call yet? I've got to talk to him about the business." Percy glanced at her watch. "Naw, it's too early."

"Father phoned late last night." Mother smiled to herself, probably remembering the phone conversation.

Even though her parents called each other 'Mother' and 'Father', they were madly in love, almost like teenagers. You'd never know they had been married for forty-three years, the way they acted.

Pop's given name was Habakkuk - after a biblical prophet - and Mother's was Lamentation. With her willowy shape and unkempt long, white blonde hair, Percy felt Mother should have been named Dandelion. She often looked like she might blow away at any moment.

Steeped in family tradition or maybe along the lines of misery loves company, the couple saddled their three children with the names Adjudication, Persephone, and Serendipity. Every day the siblings thanked their lucky stars for the nicknames of Jude, Percy, and Sera.

Percy searched her mother's face. "Pop doing okay?"

Her voice didn't convey the constant anxiety living inside her, but Percy knew Mother felt the same way. Pop was sixty-five-years old and only recently recovered from a compound fracture of his leg, a leg almost lost as a result of the severity of multiple breaks and a bone infection.

"I hope they catch those German soldiers soon," Sera interjected before their mother could speak. She ran stubby fingers through bleached blond hair. "This weather has got to be hard on Pop's health, all that sitting around under a pier."

Percy gave a shake of her head as a warning signal to her sister that went unnoticed. Mother was worried enough without this conversation. Percy tried to turn it in another direction.

"I'm sure Pop's coping just fine, but it must be playing havoc with Atlantic City's businesses."

Oblivious, Sera made a face. "Pop's no kid and it's been snowing for days." She picked up a piece of toast. "Burnt, again. I can't even make decent toast, and this colored lard doesn't help."

"It's called margarine," said Percy. "It might be made of lard, though."

"I don't care what it's called, I miss butter." Sera looked up at her older sister. "I thought it was just rumor the krauts came ashore from a submarine, anyway."

Percy looked at her sister. "Maybe so, maybe not. But the government and the state of New Jersey have to make sure the enemy isn't rendezvousing nightly under the Boardwalk exchanging information gained during the day. Whether it's true or part of the hysteria of the times, we can't take any chances. I'm sure it will be over soon. I offered to go in his place, but they didn't think I could hide under the radar as well as a man." Percy shot a sideways glance at Mother, who remained uncharacteristically quiet.

Looking grim, Mother finally spoke. "The hours your father is working would be hard enough on a young person, but you don't say no to the government. It's our patriotic duty."

Percy reached out and laid a hand on her mother's arm. "Pop will be all right. He's got his warmest coat and he took his old army blanket to lay on the ground. You'll see."

Sera, now realizing how the discussion affected her mother, leapt up and came to her mother's other side. "Sure he will, Mother. Don't pay any attention to me. You know how I like to chin-wag. I've got to go and get ready for work."

She glanced in Percy's direction with a look of apology before escaping the kitchen. Percy watched the kitchen door swing closed then turned back to her mother with concern.

"You okay?"

Mother nodded and gave her elder daughter a half-smile. "Father and I had a nice, long talk last night." She looked happy for a moment but was overtaken by a distasteful thought. "The charges were four dollars and fifty-seven cents. Can you believe it, Persephone? Four dollars and fifty-seven cents. Four. Dollars. And --"

"And fifty-seven cents. Got it."

"I almost swooned when the operator told me at the end of the call. But Father needed to talk, poor soul. He's lonely, you know, on top of being tired."

"Sure. Morning, noon, and night hiding underneath a boardwalk can get anybody down, Mother." Percy hesitated before she spoke again. "How's his leg? Did he say?"

"No, but then he wouldn't. No matter how hard Father tries to pretend things are fine, I can tell he wants to come home."

"If he calls when I'm not here, tell him I need to talk to him sooner rather than later. You okay with taking messages again while I'm not here, right?"

Mother nodded with a smile, but Percy felt ill at ease about it. On top of everything else, Percy was still functioning as the Cole Brothers' secretary, as well as an investigator. The more she was out on cases, the more the job of answering phones, taking messages, and a dozen other things fell to Mother. The woman had enough to do running the household and taking care of her grandson in Percy's absence.

Something will have to be done about that, too.

The jangle of the foyer phone hurried Percy into the hallway. It was slightly before six am. Maybe it was Pop or something related to Howie's problem. Percy picked up the phone fast.

"Cole Brothers Investigations, Persephone Cole speaking," she said in a rush.

"Perce, it's me."

"Hey, Hutchers. Find out anything?"

Even though she and Detective Kenneth Hutchers 'stepped out' from time to time, she still addressed him by his surname. He, in turn, always called her by the one-syllable nickname of Perce, as if saying Persephone or even Percy was too much effort.

"According to the report, Goldberg was seen running away from the scene of the crime, covered in the murder weapon."

"What do you mean, 'covered in the murder weapon'?"

"Covered from head to toe in milk chocolate. The cops apprehended him hiding out in a phone booth half a block away."

"Who's the victim?"

"Carlotta Mendez, owner of Carlotta's Chocolates and Goldberg's boss. Came over from Spain with her family's secret recipe to start a chocolate business nine years ago. Single and in her forties. Helluva a way to die, drowning in a vat of chocolate."

"Oh, I don't know. Some would say there are worse ways of going. I thought she was found with a rope around her neck. Least, that's what O'Hara said on the phone."

"The autopsy isn't complete yet, but my pal over at the coroner's office says it looks like she died as early as midnight. Something about the condition of the skin. Also she might have chocolate in her lungs. It's in her mouth and throat. They don't know what the rope was about yet."

"None of this sounds right, Hutchers. There's more to this story."

"There is. Seems your pal, Goldberg, had a blow-up with Carlotta a few days ago when she demoted him from head chocolatier to assistant."

"Hmmm. That's interesting. Jude should've arrived at the station by now. He wants to get Howie arraigned and out of there."

Hutchers let out a chuckle. "Fat chance. Goldberg ain't going nowhere. They got him dead to rights."

"Hutchers, I know this man. He's Oliver's godfather. He didn't do this. I don't know who did, but it wasn't Howie. I need to talk to him, get the story straight."

"Well, I did what you asked. I told the cop doing desk duty to be on the lookout for Goldberg's wife, a tall redheaded, full-figured gal. That would be you."

"That's a better description than you've given of me before. The last time you described me as fat." Her voice took an unexpected turn toward the warm and familiar.

"I ain't never going to live that down, am I?" His voice, too, had warmth and humor, matching her tone. He cleared his throat then went back to business. "They'll let you into Goldberg's cell, probably for a good twenty minutes. That should get you something."

"Thanks, Hutchers. I appreciate it."

"Enough to marry me?" His tone was light but had a serious edge to it.

"Ah, you just want somebody to wash out your socks. Hire a maid." They both laughed. "I got to go, Hutchers. If you find out anything else --"

"You'll be the first I tell," he interrupted.

"Thanks." She hung up the phone.

Chapter Six

"Hey Goldberg, I got your wife here to see you."

The cop shouted out as he led Percy down the long line of holding cells. His words set off a series of catcalls and lewd sounds from cells holding individuals against their will or as prisoners of the state, depending on your point of view.

"Shut up, you miserable creeps or I'll call the guards down here and really give you what for."

He looked back at Percy and grinned. The men shut up and went back to sleeping, reading or pacing their cells, as before.

"Ain't this fun?" the guard winked at the woman trailing behind him.

No matter where Percy looked, everything was a battered shade of gray. Speckled with cracks and graffiti, walls, ceilings, and floor merged into one. Dozens of male prisoners, uniformed in similar gray, also blended into the tired and depressing surroundings.

Upon hearing the guard's voice, Howard Goldberg turned around with surprise and ran to the edge of his cell, grasping the bars with white-knuckled hands.

He, too, was wearing the same gray garb as the other prisoners. But both sleeves and cuffs had been rolled up, making him look like a kid dressing up in his father's clothes. Oversized scuffies, dirty and worn, clad his small feet.

Howie took after his mother in build, meaning short and plump. On a good day, maybe he could stretch his round, undefined body up to five-foot four.

His face was his saving grace. Not quite handsome, it was interesting, earnest, and caring. Within folds of fat and double chins, his intelligence and love of fellow man sparkled. He looked like one of the nicest people on the face of the earth. As far as Percy was concerned, he was.

The detective noticed one of his eyes had been blackened. An angry purple and red bruise had formed on his swollen, upper lid to below his eyebrow.

"Percy, Percy." Howie called her name then remained silent.

The jangling sounds of the keys caused them both to glance down at the lock. The guard seemed to have a hard time opening it. He fidgeted and fidgeted. Percy and Howie exchanged looks. The guard noticed the look and slowed down even more. Apparently, this was a game with him.

"Gee, do I turn the key to the left or to the right?" The guard's voice took on a taunting edge, as he drawled out the words. "Can't seem to remember."

"You do this fifty times a day," Percy remarked. "A smart man would've had it down by now. But I guess that ain't you."

"Anxious for a hug from the little man?" The guard turned with a wink to Howie, who stared back, unblinking.

Percy closed in on the guard a good four- or five-inches shorter than she, and grabbed one of the bars above his head with a taut hand. She leaned over him, looked down, and spoke in a low but threatening tone.

"Suppose I give *you* a hug, pal, and squeeze real, real hard? So hard, breathing's going to be on the tough side."

The guard froze, gaped at her then gulped. With a shaky hand, he turned the key and opened the door. Percy stepped inside the cell and heard the door close and lock behind her. She slowly turned around to face the guard on the other side of the bars, who backed away in silence.

"You got twenty minutes, lady." He finally uttered, waiting until he was half way down the corridor.

Percy turned back to a trembling Howie. He gave her a quick hug, his head landing somewhere in the middle of her chest. Then he pulled away and began to pace the length of the small cell. His entire body twitched with nervous energy.

"You look like you're going to jump out of your skin, Howie."

"Thank God, you're here, Percy. They think I killed Carlotta. They think I killed somebody! As if I could ever do anything like that."

"Calm down and tell me what happened. Let's see what we can do."

"How's momma taking this?"

"Your mother's holding up. She's made of strong stuff."

He didn't reply, but nodded his head. "Did you speak to Jude? He left a few minutes ago. I told him everything, everything. It's all so insane. I can't believe it."

"Yeah, I saw him. He was on his way to talk to a judge. Seems they want to make an example out of you. It's an election year."

"Oh my God, Percy." He threw himself down on the thin, uncovered mattress. The springs squeaked protesting his weight. "They're going to hang me. They're going to hang me." Face down, he sobbed into the stained ticking.

She crossed over and patted his back. "Don't give in, unless you did it." She paused for a moment. Her low, unemotional voice filled the space. "Tell me the truth. Did you kill that woman, Howie?"

He stopped sobbing and sat bolt upright, staring at her in horror.

"How could you even ask such a thing?" His voice held an incredulity she rarely heard from him."I could never do that to anyone."

She sat down beside him. "That's good to know. For a second there I wasn't so sure; you're acting so guilty. We'll get you out of this mess, but you got to straighten up, and work with Jude and me, okay?"

He didn't say anything, but swallowed hard then nodded.

"So tell me what happened."

He fought for control, wringing his pudgy hands, fingernails still rimmed with chocolate.

"I don't know. I found her. That's all."

"I need more."

"Sure, sure. When I got to work, the door was unlocked and the lights were on. I went in the back to find chocolate all over the floor, equipment, walls. Like somebody had a food fight. It was terrible. The closer I got to the kettle, the more spilt chocolate there was. Then I saw her legs sticking out of it. It was burbling with her in there. It was terrible," he repeated. His eyes got a far-away look. He winced.

"What time did you get to the factory?" She reached out a hand, covering the clenched ones in his lap, forcing the wringing movements to stop. "Focus, Howie."

Howie looked at his friend and managed a small smile.

"Sorry. Around three, it had to be. I've been working the early shift the last couple of days, ever since Carlotta gave her new boyfriend my job of overseeing things. Ronald Bogdanovitch." Before he went on, he made a face at the man's name.

"Ronald had her buffaloed, Percy, honest. I used to work from six in the morning to six at night. Twelve-hour days, six-days a week, help her run the place. But she changed it, just like that. Put me on the three to three in the afternoon heating and pouring the chocolate. Gave my job to Bogdanovitch, even though he doesn't know the first thing about it. Cut my salary, too. But it's not so much the money as the principle of the thing, you know? I was good at my job."

"Sounds tough. Tell me about this Carlotta. What was she like? Did she have any enemies?"

Howie pursed his lips together, moving them in and out. He did that when he didn't want to talk about something. Percy pushed.

"So you didn't like her."

"It wasn't so much that I didn't like her, Percy. She knew her chocolate. She just...she..." He broke off speaking and sat back on the bunk.

"Talk, man, we're running out of time."

He leaned forward again and looked to either side of him, making sure no one could hear him except Percy. "She used to come on to me. She was like that with all of the men, even the young ones, the ones who hardly spoke English. It was like she was..."

"Sex starved?"

"Yes." He looked down, embarrassed. "She was younger than she looked. In her early forties. I don't know exactly. But she was a dried-up, skinny, little thing with a great big nose--"

"So no Dorothy Lamour."

"No, and she wore this big black braid coiled around the top of her head. Made her look very matronly. But still, I think all she wanted was to be loved."

"She didn't know about you and Ralph, I guess."

Howie glanced up. Percy threw a gentle smile in his direction. "One old friend to another."

Howie smiled back then dropped his head again. "Nobody knows except you. Not even Mamma. Especially Mamma. She'd die. She always wanted me to marry you. Mothers." He shrugged, trying to regain his humor.

"How is Ralph?"

"He's over in France somewhere. He can't say. I got a letter from him yesterday."

"You still trying to join up?"

He paused then shook his head with finality. "No use. Rheumatic Fever from when I was a kid. Damaged my heart. My sad lot in life." He added the last part in barely a whisper.

"Let's get back to Carlotta, Howie. I hear you had a fight with her a few days ago."

"She fired two of the employees because Ronald told her to; Frank and Sissy. That wasn't right. Said they didn't need to spend money on any janitorial help; we could clean up after ourselves. Frank's just a kid, not even fourteen, helping to support his family. Sissy's trying to get a high school diploma. I know why he said to do it." Howie's voice got dark, accusing. "They're colored. That's the reason he wanted to let them go. The man's a bigot. He likes to talk down to people."

"Then you got demoted. That must have ticked you off."

"Sure, she demoted me, but I can get by. It wouldn't take her long to figure out she needed me, not just to run the place but to make the chocolate, especially now that she changed the formula. It's not as easy as it looks, especially the milk. If you don't mix it right and at the right time, it'll curdle or taste funny. Milk chocolate takes a delicate hand. It --"

"Let's shelve how you make the stuff, fascinating though it might be. The clock is ticking."

She tilted her head in the direction of the guard who was leaning against a wall. Howie glanced his way. The guard met his gaze and with a surly smile, tapped his watch.

"Howie, I'm going to ask you questions. Try to keep your answers short and sweet."

He nodded, with a chastised look on his face.

"You got anybody in mind as to who might have done her in?"

"Of course not. She came across mean sometimes, but I don't think she was. I think she was just..."

"Randy."

"Looking for happiness, Percy. Like everybody else."

Leave it to Howie to put the sweeter spin on things. Aloud Percy said, "Might have got her killed. This Ronald Bogdanovitch, his name sounds familiar. How long has he been around?"

"Two or three months. At first we were relieved. She left us alone, but after awhile she started turning everything over to him and things went bad, you know?"

"How so?"

"For one thing, we kept coming up short on supplies and when I complained about it, he said one of the 'dago's' was taking them. So disrespectful," Howie muttered.

"Any chance of that?"

"No. These are good people and they need the job. They wouldn't do anything to jeopardize it. Most of them can't even speak English well enough to work any place else, like Vinnie."

"This Vinnie, he a friend of yours?"

"Sort of. He's in a tight spot."

"Another one of your rescues?"

She grinned at him. He grinned back. For that moment they were merely two old friends.

"He's a good man, Percy. He's scared to death he'll lose the job and won't be able to get his wife's parents out of Italy. You know what's going on over there. I give him money from time to time to send to them."

The guard cleared his throat. They both glanced in his direction. He tapped his watch again and held three fingers up. Percy looked at Howie again.

"Why were you covered with chocolate when they found you?"

"I was trying to pull her out. I thought I could save her. Maybe she wasn't drowned or...cooked." He turned away with an appalled look on his face. "But she was too slippery. I kept losing my grip on her and the chocolate was hot, burning. Much hotter than it's supposed to be. I never turn the heat up that high. I almost fell in once, myself. I would have never gotten out without bad burns."

Percy was shocked. "Just how big are these pots of chocolate?"

"This one can hold a hundred and fifty gallons. We've got two more kettles, one at fifty gallons, the other at twenty-five. We do large batches at a single time. Saves time and money, but it's tricky. You can't leave it alone for two minutes. That's why I got put on the three a.m. shift to get the chocolate ready for the workers coming in the morning. Someone has to do it. She used to do it herself, but that was before she turned it over to me."

"So that might explain what she was doing there. Old habits. What's with such a big pot? Sounds like something from Hansel and Gretel."

"We just got the big copper pot, special order. Cost a fortune. Carlotta was talking to department stores, hoping they'd carry her chocolate, as well as the small shops she already sells to. It would have been a big deal. That's why she changed the formula."

"You mentioned that before. What does that mean, she changed the formula?"

"She wanted to give Hershey a run for its money in the tri-state area. She wanted to be ready for Valentine's Day. But chocolate's hard to come by with the war on. She had the idea of diluting the chocolate with ground up hazelnuts. I didn't approve, but --"

"So she was expanding. Interesting. Howie, the cops said when they found you, you were hiding in a phone booth a half a block away."

"I wasn't hiding." His voice rose in volume and pitch. He looked around and lowered it, leaning in again. "I wasn't hiding. I was trying to phone for help. When I couldn't get her out of the vat, I ran to the office. That's where the only telephone is. The door was locked. I didn't have a key. I ran outside looking for someone. There was no one else around, no stores open, nothing. So I went down the block to the phone booth."

"They say the phone had been ripped out of that booth months ago."

He gave her a wounded look and opened his arms wide to the world at large. "But I didn't know that. I'd just gotten there when a police car showed up."

"They give you that black eye?"

Ashamed, Howie nodded and looked down. "They said if I told anyone, they'd say I lost my balance and fell."

"Right into someone's fist, right?"

"They were trying to make me say I did it."

"But you didn't admit to killing her, did you?"

"Of course not." Howie sat taller with an indignant air. "Because I didn't."

"How do you suppose they got there so soon? I mean, three o'clock in the morning. Odd time to show up at a Brooklyn phone booth."

Howie shrugged then looked up at her, as it dawned on him. "Maybe somebody called them?"

"Maybe somebody did, Howie. Where are your clothes and shoes?"

"They took them for evidence."

Percy stood and stretched. She hadn't realized how hunched over she'd been sitting side by side on the bunk, asking Howie questions. Her back hurt from being in an awkward position.

"Are you going to help me, Percy?"

Howie sounded vulnerable and alone, much the same as he had decades ago when he'd found an injured dog too big for a small boy to carry. Percy came to her friend's rescue then as she would now. After they carried the dog home, Howie nursed it back to health and named it Butch. Butch became the Goldberg family dog until he passed away of old age.

Percy put one foot up on the bunk mattress and leaned in on her bent leg. "Howie, did you know you're the reason my son wants to become a veterinarian?"

He shook his head slowly, not quite seeing where this was going.

"You, Jude, and Pop, each one of you gives Oliver something he wouldn't have otherwise. Pop gives Oliver his wisdom and common-sense. Jude gives him lofty ideals and the joy of education, but you, Howie, you give Oliver his heart; his compassion for the world. You've helped my son find his way since the beginning when Leo the Louse took a powder. So you betcha I'm going to help you."

She moved to the cell door, just as the guard was approaching. Percy reached into her coat pocket, pulled out a book, and turned back.

"Almost forgot. Brought you Pearl Buck's *Dragon Seed* to help you while away the hours. Pretty good. If any of these lugs can read around here, give it to one of them when you're done."

She tossed him the book and he caught it in both hands. Percy gave Howie an encouraging smile.

"And try not to walk into anybody else's fist until I get you out of this."

Chapter Seven

Dear Diary,

It hasn't even been twenty-four hours, but as Shakespeare says, things proceed apace. After so much waiting and planning, it's finally time for part two. The groundwork has been laid. I've let nothing get by me, down to the last detail. Of course, if anyone gets in my way, they will regret it.

.

Chapter Eight

Dozens of porcelain platters held artfully arranged pieces of chocolate candy behind the large plate glass of the storefront window. The platters rested on miniature marble columns of varying heights lending a sober and neo-classic look to the sugary treats.

On the floor of the window display, candy dishes brimmed over with hand-decorated light and dark chocolate. Tiny pink birds and red flowers dotted the platters and dishes adding to the ethereal yet grand look. Percy couldn't tell if the birds and flowers were made of marzipan or ceramic. She'd have to pop one in her mouth to make sure.

To finish off the decor, silver bells hung from pink ribbons, twirling this way and that on miniscule currents of air. Atop the window, and painted in similar shades of red and pink, a banner read: *Carlotta's Chocolates, Wholesale and Retail.*

Percy had visited Howie and his friend, Ralph, at their apartment three blocks away on occasion. This was the first time she'd been to Howie's place of work in the two years he'd been employed there.

Pretty fancy schmancy place for a factory in Brooklyn, even one selling gourmet chocolates.

A 'closed' sign figured prominently on the plate glass door but when she turned the handle, it opened readily. Once inside, a strong smell of burnt chocolate assailed her nostrils. Nevertheless, Percy felt her mouth water.

Pavlov's dog, that's me. Wave chocolate under my nose, even if it's burned, and watch me drool.

She called out, "Anybody here? Hello?"

A small, swarthy, dark-haired man pushed aside a pink and red gingham curtain hanging in the doorway. Jaw and chin already wearing a five-o'clock stubble, he seemed out of place in this feminine setting. The man stepped into the room hesitantly and looked the tall woman up and down. Percy followed suit.

"You Vinnie?"

She offered a smile. He blinked rapidly before he answered.

"The shop, she is closed. There has been a dead. We no open now. You come back later." He spoke with a heavy Italian accent, stumbling over the words as if the English language was newer to him than the chocolate-stained apron tied around his waist.

"Yeah, I know about that. I'm a friend of Howie's, Howie Goldberg."

The blinking stopped and for a split second his face broke out into a smile, only to be replaced by a sad shake of his head. Then he reached behind him, pulled at the curtain, giving a quick glance to the back of the store. Vinnie dropped the cloth before going on in a whisper.

"Howie no do this terrible thing. I no care what *polizia* say. Howie good man. He good man." While following his words was difficult, Percy understood the underlying intent well enough. Here was an ally.

"I agree. Mind if I come in and talk to you a little about it?"

She stepped forward but paused as he stuck out his hand in the universal signal to stay back. He shook his head. Percy didn't move forward but stood her ground.

"He come, the boss. I no can talk now." Vinnie's voice was hoarse and urgent, fear coloring his words.

The delicate fabric was jerked aside. Vinnie, looking as though he had been physically struck, stepped away.

"I thought I heard voices out here. Who the hell are you?" The man speaking was tall, nearly Percy's height. High cheekbones and pale coloring showed a man probably of Slavic origin. Sharp blue eyes screwed up as he stared at Percy. She returned his stare with her own cool assessment.

This must be Ronald Bogdanovitch. Handsome but nasty. Wait a minute. He looks familiar.

She opened her mouth to speak, but the man continued with his tirade, turning to the shaking Vinnie.

"What the hell did you let her in for? Nobody's supposed to be here, you stupid Guinea."

"Vinnie didn't let me in."

Percy's tone was sharper and more emotional than she liked. She wouldn't let this man get under her skin, no matter how much she hated racial slurs. She forced a smile.

"The door was unlocked. I turned the handle and walked right in. In fact, Vinnie was just in the process of telling me to go, but --"

"So go, lady," Ronald ordered.

Percy studied him for a moment then shrugged. "Okay, I wanted to talk to you first, but I guess I'll have to go to the coppers and talk to them instead."

Ronald stepped forward, nearly colliding with Vinnie, who got out of the way just in time. "What about? Talk to the coppers about what? Who are you, lady?"

"My name is Persephone Cole and I'm a private investigator."

He looked at her and sneered. "Don't give me that. Since when are broads detectives?"

"Since now, buster. And if you don't like it, I can take my business elsewhere." Her voice was harsh, matching his tone. Then she smiled again. "Only I thought, all things being equal, you'd like to talk to me first. Might be worth your while, Bogdanovitch. Mine, too."

"How'd you know my name?"

"I get around."

He licked his lips as he thought, his face revealing indecision and distrust. It took him a moment or two, but he made up his mind.

"Okay, okay. Come on back to my office." He turned and pushed the curtain open again. "I'll give you five minutes, dick lady. No more." Before passing through, he stopped for a moment. "Lock that door, Vinnie, and if you know what's good for you, don't let nobody else in."

Percy followed but paused at Vinnie's side. Beads of perspiration covered his forehead.

"We'll talk later, Vinnie."

Vinnie's eyes started rapidly blinking again and Percy felt a pang of pity for the man. She touched him on the shoulder in a comradely way, but said no more.

As she trailed behind Ronald Bogdanovitch, she thought about what she would say to him when she got to his office. She was winging this and had to come up with something fast.

Chapter Nine

While following Bogdanovitch through the large industrial room, Percy gave it a quick once over. A twenty-foot or so high ceiling wore stark white water pipes and large ducts for heating. The same white paint came down the sides of the walls. Unimaginative, but clean looking. On the outside wall of the building, a row of high side-by-side glass-paned windows allowed what sunlight there was to fill the room.

Under the windows were white tin storage bins, some dented and missing paint here and there, but otherwise clean and orderly. The opposite wall was white-painted brick, floor to ceiling.

A large red and black sign reading *Hopson's Feed and Grain* bled through the white paint indicated that at one time, this was the outside wall of a building. Under *Hopson's Feed and Grain* was a row of metal cabinets, probably used by the help to store their uniforms and personal things.

This part was added on fairly recently. I wonder if Carlotta owned this building? I'll have to find out.

Percy followed Bogdanovitch through the rectangular room, and toward a back staircase that led up to the office. They passed machines and equipment similar to those used on war-time assembly lines, now still. One lengthy conveyer belt was laden with hundreds of pieces of fruit and nuts, visible under a transparent, thin sheet of gauze. Nearby, two long slabs of counter-high white marble gleamed rich and spotless, basking in the morning's sunrays.

Big bucks have been spent on this joint.

Out of the corner of her eye, she noticed a section near the end of the conveyer belt, containing a stainless steel industrial stove, copper pots and pans, and wooden spoons, all larger than life. Splattered, dried chocolate covered much of the stove and some utensils. Tiled flooring was interspersed with dark brown footprints going every which way. The scene added a sense of untidiness and confusion to an otherwise orderly room.

The errant chocolate was being washed up by a slender, young woman on her hands and knees wielding a scrub brush. As she heard footsteps nearby, the woman looked up. Percy paused and studied her, arrested by her beauty.

Here was one of the most exquisite, Madonna-like faces Percy had ever seen. Most likely Italian, any Renaissance painter would have killed for a model with such hauntingly perfect features. There was something tell-tale in her face, however, showing that despite the classic features, she was not much more than a child; certainly no older than fourteen or fifteen.

The girl sat on her haunches for a moment then stood, tall and rigid, not seeing Percy but watching Bogdanovitch. Hatred filled those beautiful and expressive brown eyes, so palpable Percy felt a jolt of shock. Then the girl turned her attention on the detective, features softening to a scared, guilty look. With a small hesitation, she returned to scrubbing the floor.

On silent feet, Vinnie came to the girl's side, dropped down, and reached into the sudsy bucket for a brush. He didn't look Percy's way at all. Neither one glanced at her again, but scrubbed with vigor. Percy's mind raced.

Jesus Christ, you'd think the son-of-a-bitch climbing the stairs was Mussolini or something. Maybe he's an American version. If he is, I'll fix his wagon.

The detective followed Bogdanovitch up the flight of stairs at the back of the factory. At the top of the staircase was a landing and a door. To the left, a large, rectangular glass window looked out over the work area below. Most likely Carlotta Mendez watched her employees at their jobs and wanted them to know it.

Filing this in her mind, Percy stepped into a small, office containing little more than two desks. Pale green walls were empty save a wall calendar behind one desk, and a framed but poor copy of Gainsborough's Blue Boy behind the other.

Bogdanovitch sat down at the desk with the calendar behind him and stared up at Percy, expectantly. She returned his stare, still standing in the doorway.

"Where is everybody? I understand you've got sixteen people working for you."

"We had to close today due to the fact that somebody just died." His answer was sarcastic and terse. "They come back to work Monday, docked for not working today, of course."

She closed the door, crossed the room, and stood in front of him. On his desk was an eight by ten picture frame, its back to Percy. She reached out and turned it around for a better view. Bogdanovitch smirked, but didn't try to stop her.

A studio photograph of a middle-aged, dark-haired woman with a hawk-like nose, small black eyes, and a smile that showed more gums than teeth stared back at the detective.

If this was Carlotta Mendez, and the braid coiled on top of her head like a sleeping snake left no doubt in Percy's mind it was, then Howie's description of the woman had been more than kind. This was a real bow-wow.

The man behind the desk seemed to read her mind. "She wasn't much to look at, but she had a strong personality."

"You like strong personalities, Bogdanovitch?"

He shrugged. "Depends."

"On how much money they got in the bank?"

He snickered while she removed her hat, long red hair tumbling down her shoulders and back. She shook it out in a brisk move. More comfortable, she threw her hat on top of his desk. He gave her a lopsided smile.

"You got red hair."

"Yup."

"I like women with red hair." He gave her a sultry, winning smile.

"Save it, pal. I ain't interested."

He shrugged then leaned back and put his legs up on the desk, crossing them at the ankles. "So now that you seen the lady in question, let's get down to business. What do you want? And this better be good."

Having formulated what she would say as she climbed the stairs, she put both hands on his desk and leaned in. "So the cops aren't so sure Howard Goldberg did your lady friend in."

A frown replaced the smile on his lips. "What are you talking about? They arrested him and everything."

"Yeah, but that don't mean it's over, Bogdanovitch. If you think they're seriously looking at Goldberg, think again. They got your number. They don't like you so much."

At those words he uncrossed his legs and sat up in the chair, remaining silent. A slight look of fear passed over his features, enough so that Percy knew she was on the right track.

"Sure. They know you were just after her money and this business, especially with your record. They know you're a small-time hood."

"Hey! Who you calling a small-time hood?"

"They also know you been schtupping that underage kid out there, forcing her to have sex with you."

"Did she say something to you? I told her to keep her trap shut. Nobody can prove it. Who told you that?"

"You, you lowlife, just now. And it's against New York State law. If I can figure it out, it's just a matter of time before the coppers do. They aren't as dumb as you'd like to think. They have a way of finding things out, Bogdanovitch. They got you pegged for an all-around louse. You got a record as long as my arm."

"That don't mean I killed Carlotta."

"Maybe not, but it's a good angle. Taking a cheap hood like you down would look good for law enforcement; better than some chocolate maker. And they got a few scores to settle with you. Like that bank robbery three years ago where a retired cop got paralyzed by a stray bullet."

All the color drained from Bogdanovitch's face.

"They couldn't prove nothing then and they can't pin this on me now."

"Maybe they can't, but maybe they can. Maybe I'll help them. Better you than Howard Goldberg. He's a friend of mine. I'm going to make sure he doesn't take the fall for this. I can be a very good friend."

Bogdanovitch got up and paced the room, a nervous twitch settling in his right shoulder. He rubbed it like it was an old wound then wheeled around on her.

"Why are you telling me this? What do you want?"

"If you didn't do it --"

"I didn't do it," he interrupted.

"Then open the doors of this fine establishment to me. Let me talk to the employees, nose around. I want to find out who did."

"It wasn't me."

"In that case, you've got nothing to worry about. I can make this investigation easier on you. Maybe make it go away."

"How can you do that? Who the hell are you, Wonder Woman? You're just some big broad in a man's suit." He sat back down in the swivel desk chair and swung back in her direction. "We're done here, lady. You don't know nothing. You're just on a fishing expedition. Get out."

Percy stood and picked up her hat. "Okay, have it your way. But you're going to regret it."

"How?" He let out a laugh more nervous than not.

"If I know coppers – and I do - they're not satisfied. They're going to come back and be all over this place, taking it apart piece by piece. Who knows what they're going to find when they get an *idée fixe*. That's French for a fixed idea in their thick skulls. You work with me, I work with you, we find out who did it, *tout de suite*. That's another French phrase. Means pretty damned quick."

"What are you, a frog?"

"I'm not French, but I know a few words in a lot of languages, 'cause I'm a pretty smart cookie. You don't play ball with me, I'm on my own and I've been known to stir things up until I find what I'm looking for. You ask around. See if it's not true."

"I don't want nobody in my business." He licked dry lips, eyes darting around the room.

"Too bad. We don't always get what we want. There's a dead woman lying in the morgue, who I bet doesn't want to be there."

Percy could read the indecisiveness on him like the cover of a book. She waited him out.

"I don't like this," he finally muttered. "Carlotta's murder changes everything. I got a couple of things going I don't need the cops looking into. I thought this murder thing was settled. The little guy did it and that was that."

"Nope. Too many holes. Why did he do it, Bogdanovitch? What's his motive? Getting demoted? Thin. Now you, maybe you're a scorned lover, or maybe you inherit this place."

He let out a laugh. "Not me, lady. Sure, I was working the angle but she died before I could pull it off. If it *was* me, I would have waited until she signed on the dotted line. Tell that to the coppers."

"Who inherits then?"

"She's got a cousin in Chicago. I'm just the manager."

"With a few perks that died with her."

"You ain't kidding. It would have been better for me if she stayed alive a few months longer. Her being dead puts the kibosh on a couple of things I got going."

"So you're just hired help like everybody else. You can be fired any time, like Frank and Sissy. I'd watch my back if I was you."

"What?"

"Even if the cops do leave you alone, her cousin might decide you're more trouble than you're worth. Think about it."

He did. "So how much do you want? What are you going to charge me if I hire you?"

"Not one red cent. All I want is access to the employees, their files, and your books --" She saw the look on his face and chuckled. "The legit ones, not the second set you been cooking for this place."

His eyes narrowed on her. "You *are* a smart broad."

"Bogdanovitch, I'm going to prove Howard Goldberg didn't do it. And believe me, whoever did is going down. That's a promise. If you're innocent, it can only work in your favor."

"Okay, lady whatever-your-name-is, you got a deal. But you stay out of my way."

"Persephone Cole, like I told you. Call me Miss Cole."

He waggled a finger in her face. "You got a week, Miss Cole. So do I."

"For what?"

He shrugged. "I've got to change a few things around, but let's just say whatever I'm in it for should be done by then. In a week I just might burn this place to the ground." He pointed a sharp finger at her. "You tell the coppers that, I'll deny it."

"Client privilege, buster, and furthermore, I don't care. But you tell the cops that, *I'll* deny it."

He threw her a nasty laugh then let out a sigh. "Let's just say, I don't need them on my back in the meantime. So do whatever you want around here, just don't be snooping into anything that ain't connected with the murder."

"Fair enough. Let's just put this in writing, so nobody questions my hanging around." She tore out a piece of paper from her notepad, scribbled on it, leaned forward, and laid it down in front of him. "All it says is, as the manager of Carlotta's Chocolates, you're giving me permission to be on the premises and ask questions of your employees. All nice and simple."

Bogdanovitch read the brief note, shrugged, picked up a pen and signed it. He shoved it back to her with a shake of his head. "You're one weird broad, you know that?"

"So where were *you* last night, Bogdanovitch?"

"A cool little blonde on the east side of Manhattan. A cigarette girl who can light my fire any time. Left her place this morning."

"She willing to say you were there?"

"She'd better. I set her up in that hotel. I drop by to see her three, four times a week."

"What's her name?"

"Helena Wilson. Dumb, but good in bed."

"Everybody's got their talents. Tell me about how you make the chocolate. You always mix gallons of chocolate at one time?"

"She said it saved time. I've only been doing this for a couple of months, so I don't know much, other than it's one big bore."

"Tell me about her process."

He shrugged, failing to see the reason, but being cooperative. "Sure. From what she told me, Carlotta took a bunch of cocoa beans she sent away for that come from different places, like South America. She blended them together, according to some kind of formula she had in a book. Then she added milk, sugar, oil, and other stuff. With the war on, the government's been commandeering a lot of chocolate."

"I hear."

"So lately she was mixing in crushed nuts to stretch it; I don't know what kind."

"Hazelnuts, probably. Another chocolatier is doing the same thing."

"She probably stole the idea from him. I wouldn't put it past her."

"Sounds like she wasn't a very nice person."

"She was a good business woman. She knew how to make a buck. Nothing wrong with that. But she had a lot of oddballs working for her. She even took in this Kraut who claims her grandfather was the one who invented the chocolate formula, and Carlotta's grandfather stole it from him. Gave the Kraut a job. Just like that. Something about keeping your enemies nearby."

"*Keep your friends close, but your enemies closer.*"

His eyebrows shot up. "Yeah. You know it, too."

"Sun Tzu, a 6th century Chinese general wrote that."

"Imagine. And people still paying attention."

"Back to the chocolate."

"Yeah. Right. The way it's set up, every day a large enough batch is made to coat the fillings on the assembly line. Then there has to be enough to pour into molds. With Valentine's Day coming, she bought bigger vats; planned on making enough chocolate at one time to fill any orders. The vendors were screaming for it; couldn't get enough. Don't understand it, myself. I'm into butterscotch ice cream."

"Be careful, Bogdanovitch. That's close to heresy; nothing's better than chocolate. What's all that on the conveyor belt downstairs?"

"The fillings are left out the night before, ready to be covered with chocolate when the crew gets in at six. I had to send them home today. They'll start again first thing Monday morning. The stuff will be a little stale, but who cares?"

"I'd like a list of their names, if you've got it close at hand."

"Sure." He snatched at a legal pad sitting on his desk and tossed it across to her. "Cops went over all this stuff earlier this morning. Nothing but a bunch of Guineas, Krauts, and other riff-raff working here."

"As opposed to the sterling characters you hang out with."

Bogdanovitch gave her a dirty look, but said nothing.

"Tell me about the formula." Percy picked up the sheet of paper and leaned in. "What's in it, specifically?"

"I have no idea, now that you bring it up. I looked over her shoulder once, but I couldn't read it. It was all in a foreign language."

"Spanish?"

He shrugged. "I guess. All I know is Carlotta keeps it...kept it... in a small book in her safe."

"The one behind Blue Boy?" Percy pointed to the cheap but large picture on the wall.

His eyebrows shot up. "You noticed that. Clever lady." He gave Percy an admiring glance then became serious again. "But I never got near the book. When she took it out, she kept it close to her all the time. She added the mixture herself every time a new batch was made. She never even trusted Goldberg with it. She treated it like it was gold."

"You mean you never went into that safe when she wasn't looking and took a peek, Spanish and all?" Percy shot him an incredulous look.

"I don't do safes. I know my limits. Besides, it wasn't worth the risk. I'm not after that."

"From what I understand, a good chocolatier's formula can be worth a great deal of money. If not that, what is it you're after?"

He sat up in his chair sharply, his right eye twitching. "None of your beeswax. Like I told you, you want to find out who killed Carlotta and clear Goldberg -- and me – you go right ahead, but keep your nose out of my business."

"Relax. Just curious. If you had nothing to do with Carlotta's death, you've got nothing to fear from me, pal. Leastways, not about the murder."

Unsatisfied, Bogdanovitch stood, kicked his chair away from him with one foot, glaring down at her. "I've changed my mind. I'm giving you two days, not a week. I don't know if you're as trustworthy as you claim."

"I never claimed to be trustworthy," Percy said, picking up the signed note and putting it in her breast pocket. She rose and reached for her fedora then moved to the door. "But if you didn't kill Carlotta, I'll see you're in the clear on it."

"You've got two days, lady, to find out. Now blow. I'm meeting someone and it's private. After that, I got plans."

Percy looked over her shoulder and gave him a half-smile. "Don't we all."

Chapter Ten

Percy descended the stairs just as Vinnie was pouring a bucket of chocolate-colored water down a deep, trough-style sink. The girl was nowhere in sight. The Italian man was fastidiously cleaning the bucket, deep in thought, as the detective approached.

"Where's the girl, Vinnie?"

Startled, he dropped the bucket in the sink, where it landed with an echoing clang.

"Sorry. I didn't mean to frighten you. You're a nervous little fellow, aren't you?"

Vinnie managed a wan smile, picked up the bucket, and began to clean it again.

"I'd like to talk to you for a moment, Vinnie." She laid a hand on his shoulder, which made him flinch. "It's all right. Your boss said I can speak to the employees."

Vinnie gave a frightened look in the direction of the office at the top of the stairs. "*Si, si,* but not for long. I have much work to do."

"What happened to the young lady who was here?"

"Ah! Teresa. She is my wife's -- how do you say -- nephew?"

"Niece."

"Niece. She go to school now. I look out for her."

You're not doing such a hot job, buster, but we'll talk about that later.

"Why don't you show me around the place, Vinnie? Tell me what's what. For instance, where is all the chocolate kept?"

"The cocoa beans are below, down the stairs."

"In a storage room?"

"*Si*. She grinds them there, mixes them, in the hiding."

"She kept the mixture a secret."

"*Si*. Is called formula. Very secret."

"So I'm learning. Who has a key to the storage room?"

"*Signorina* Carlotta and the man." Vinnie pointed to the upstairs office.

"Nobody else?"

Vinnie shook his head.

"Not even Howie?"

Vinnie shook his head again.

"There looks like there are two walk-in refrigerators." She pointed to one under the staircase and another smaller one at the end of the long wall tucked into a corner. "Why two?"

"Ah!" His eyes lit up and he gave her a smile then nodded to the smaller one. "That one is more cold. How you say, frozen?"

"Freezer."

"*Si*, freezer. My English not so good. Freezer is not so big like refrigerator, but you still walk inside. Sometimes the *signorina* used it for things to last long time. But the other one is every day, once ingredients are the ready."

"That's a pretty big word, 'ingredients'."

"I know the words for what we do, to make the chocolate prepar...prepar..." he stumbled over the word and paused, blinking.

"But not that one, huh? Preparations."

"*Gracie*. Preparations. The words, they fly in and out." He tapped his head with an apologetic smile.

"So it would seem."

Percy returned his smile then crossed to the refrigerator under the stairs. The appliance was covered in white paint save the small, round window in the door. She looked through the window.

"So the ingredients and fillings are kept in here?"

"*Si*. First, we dry the fruit. We cook the mint, caramel, other fillings. They are stored in here until they go into the chocolate. Sometimes they wait for weeks. Also the butter, milk, cocoa powder, everything is stored in here to keep the fresh, because you must buy when you can. I do this in Naples before the war." His face took on a happy look, lost in former memories.

"You were a chocolatier in Italy?"

He shook his head in self-deprecation, his face resuming its pained, unhappy look. "No, no. I no make the chocolate. I help my friend, Giuseppe, with his shop. I skin the nuts, make the fillings. Nobody makes the caramel like I do. Everybody, they say that," he added, with a burst of pride. His face became sad again. "Giuseppe, he die in the war. His shop, it was bombed. It is no more."

"How did you get here to America?"

"The *signorina* Carlotta, she know of Giuseppe and me when she was in Spain. She say she bring me, my family, to America. If I work the hard, then she sponsor *i genitori di mia moglie*...ah...mama, papa --"

"I get it. Your wife's parents," Percy offered.

"*Si, si*. You speak the *Italiano?* His voice was eager, almost childlike.

"Only enough to order dinner at Luigi's, but I know a spare word here or there.

"I make hardly the money to live, but for *la famiglia*, I would do anything." His face took on a dark look. "She no keep her promise."

"So Carlotta Mendez said she'd bring you and your family to the states first and your wife's parents later, if you helped her in the factory. At slave wages from what you're saying. Nice."

He nodded then swallowed hard. "She make the promise but always the delays. One thing then the other. It has been nearly two years and now she is dead. This is no good. And my wife, she is *delicata*. The war is hard."

"You ain't whistling Dixie, pal."

Percy crossed to the small freezer in the corner. It, too had a small round window, but this one was obscured by inside frost. On the outside was a metal hasp and lock, recently added by the looks of it. It shone brightly against the flat, white paint of the door. "This is kept locked, I see. What's in the freezer right now?"

Fear crossed Vinnie's face. "I do not know. We are not allowed in there. Before *Signor* Bogdanovitch come, the *signorina* she keep the things that can froze...ah...freeze to keep them good. But now I do not know."

Percy fidgeted with the lock deep in thought. "Interesting."

Vinnie took a few steps back and gestured for Percy to follow. "Come, come. We cannot be near it."

"He's got you running, hasn't he? A real Gestapo kind of a guy."

Vinnie looked up to the office at the top of the stairs. Percy's gaze followed his. Through the plate-glass window, the shadow of Bogdanovitch was seen pacing back and forth like a hand puppet against a backdrop. The steady murmur of his voice, no doubt on the telephone, wafted down the stairs.

"He is no good, no good," Vinnie said to himself, staring with narrowed eyes at the shadow. Percy watched his gathering sense of loathing, but said nothing aloud.

And I suspect you don't even know what he's doing to your wife's niece. Or do you?

"Okay." She patted the man on the shoulder. "Let's go to the front of the store."

Quick, long strides took her through the sixty-foot deep factory toward the small shop at the front of the building. Vinnie scurried to keep up then chugged around her, beating her to the pink and red curtain. He drew it aside for her to pass through.

Percy stood in the five-foot wide space between the wall and glass counter containing a display of chocolate candies. Behind the "L" shaped counter and to one side, was a small desk and two chairs.

The center of the desk held a stack of orders and receipts pierced through by a tall, metal spindle. The papers went half way up. The rest of the rapier-like tool stuck precariously into the air. She'd never allow anything that dangerous lying out, not with a small boy running around. Other than several manila files neatly piled in a corner, the rest of the surface was clean.

Vinnie hovered nearby, waiting like a working farm dog for her next command. Percy turned to him.

"Who mans the storefront?"

"Here the orders are checked and picked up. Two women, whose English is the good, sell the chocolate and talk to the peoples. Sometimes the neighborhood peoples stop by and buy the box of chocolates. But not many. *Signorina* Carlotta say it is the 'good will'."

Percy unfolded the list given to her by Bogdanovitch. "Who are the two women? Show me their names."

She lowered the paper for the small man to see. Vinnie pointed to two names.

"These are the ones. I cannot say the names easy. Although one of them, we call Shot-see." He separated the two syllables with care. "They are nice."

"Helga Appelman and Regina Mason. This Appelman, she the one they call Schatzi?" He nodded. "Anyone else on this list you want to give me the low-down on?" He stared at her perplexed. "Tell me about? You say these two women are nice. Who's not so nice on this list?"

"Ah! Here." He punched at a name on the list. "Alfred," he said, rolling the 'r' long and hard. "But he goes by Alf, like the sound of the bark from a dog." He shook a solemn head.

"A real crumb bum, huh?" She glanced down at the short Italian man and saw a puzzled look on his face. She clarified. "Another bad guy?"

"*Si, si*. This Alf, he is...mean. He hits into us on purpose, but says is accident. And he yells at Frank all the time for *niente*."

"That means 'nothing', right? And Frank would be the boy janitor."

"*Si*. A nice boy, but he is gone now." Vinnie thought for a moment. "He also does not know what he does."

"That would be Alf, not Frank."

"*Si, si,* Alf. He is to watch the chocolate on the belt, to make sure it covers the fillings, but he is not good at it."

"Anybody else who doesn't know what they're doing?"

Vinnie shook his head. "The others, they work hard."

"Good enough. Vinnie, I want you to keep what we're talking about here under your hat." He stared at her, non-comprehendingly. "That means between the two of us, okay? Nobody else."

He nodded somberly. "*Certamente*. You help my friend, Howie?"

"And anybody else I can, Vinnie. Looks like some folks around here are getting a raw deal. I'll be back Monday to talk to the workers."

"I leave now, too. The boss, he tells me to go away, as soon as place is clean."

"Well then, Vinnie, we'd both better do as the man says and blow. See you Monday."

Chapter Eleven

Dear Diary,

Now it's the waiting, although I have one or two things to finish up. Naturally, no one has any idea what is really going on, but everything is in place. If it wasn't for this damned war, I could go to Europe. But when I get what I came for, I will just disappear, as I have in the past.

Chapter Twelve

Percy hoofed it the three blocks to the apartment shared by Howie and his friend, Ralph. She had been there several times, when the Coles accompanied the Goldbergs for birthdays and holidays.

The food was always memorable. While Howie was mostly interested in chocolate, he could make a chopped chicken liver like nobody's business. His matzo ball soup was better than anything she'd had in the many delis on the lower east side. Mrs. Goldberg was no slouch in the cooking department, either, unlike Percy's mother.

The detective walked up the familiar flight of stairs but turned away from the front apartment belonging to the boys. She rapped on the door of the only other apartment on the floor, that of Howie's neighbor, Mrs. Latham. She heard the barking of a small dog on the other side of the door and wondered if someone was home. Luck was with Percy, and the door sprang open.

She looked into the youthful face of a woman with very sharp, hazel eyes and a ready smile. Mrs. Latham wiped her hands on a dishtowel and smiled up at Percy. The dog danced at the woman's feet, no longer barking.

"Hello, Mrs. Latham. I hope you remember me. I'm Percy --"

"Oh, yes. Of course, I remember you!"

The young woman's interruption was not one of rudeness, but rather eagerness, as if she wanted it to be clear she needed no reminder. She spoke with a slight southern accent, not overpowering, and quite pleasing to the ears.

"You're Howie's friend, Persephone Cole. Such an interesting name, Persephone." She beamed at the detective.

"My parents thought so, but please call me Percy."

"And you must call me Lola Mae. Come in, come in."

Percy stepped inside and Lola Mae closed the door. She turned back to Percy, words coming out in a rush.

"I think Howie and Ralph have such interesting parties, don't you? Ever since we moved in last year we've been invited to them." She took a quick breath and went on. "You have that sweet little boy, Oliver. So sweet. You are both well? And the rest of the family? Why don't you take off your coat and stay awhile? Would you like some coffee? I just made a fresh pot."

"Thanks."

Percy flashed the woman a winning smile, sloughed off her coat, and threw it over her arm. She followed Lola Mae and the dog through the large living room, past the dining room, and into a modern kitchen.

Even though this apartment was as the back of the building and supposedly more undesirable than the front, it was beautifully furnished, with a stunning view of a back garden, now snow-covered. Through a big kitchen window framed by crisp yellow curtains, an immense tree shimmered with icicled branches in the morning sun.

Percy looked around. The kitchen bedazzled the eye with all its modern conveniences, including an electric stove and wall oven. The refrigerator was twice the size of Mother's and gleamed with chrome and newness. Whatever Mr. Latham did, he was a success at it.

Percy noticed a book sitting on the kitchen table. She turned the book over to read the cover.

"I see you're reading Wilkie Collins' *The woman in White*. Good book."

"Howie loaned it to me."

"I gave him this book when I'd finished with it. Glad it's going around."

"When I'm done should I return it to you?"

"Naw. Give it to somebody else. That's what we do, pass them on. Always been that way."

"I'll have to give it to the library. I don't know many people." Lola Mae reached into a well-organized cabinet for two cups and saucers. "Bart's work takes him away so much and I'm not good at making friends. Except Howie. Milk and sugar?"

"Black."

Percy studied the younger woman in her early to mid-twenties, wearing no makeup. Thick, curly, light brown hair framed her face, stealing attention away from even, pretty features. Percy, while not one into the current heavily made up look, thought a touch of lipstick would do wonders for the girl's appearance.

"I remember now. You mentioned the first time I met you that your husband is away for stretches of time."

"Oh, yes. He's a traveling salesman, so most of the time it's just Poopsie and me, but sometimes I join him for a week or two wherever he is. I met him when I was in high school. He came to one of our gymnastic competitions. I wanted to be a professional gymnast, like Sonja Henie."

"I thought she was an ice skater."

"That, too, but I swear, she does everything. I'm her biggest fan." She looked lovingly down at the dog that stared up at her with a wagging tail. Attention now riveted on the dog, it sneezed with excitement. "But these days, I don't know what I'd do without Poopsie, my husband's gone so much."

Lola Mae removed a percolator from the back burner of the stove and poured coffee with a steady hand into the two cups.

"Ladies underwear, you know."

"Beg pardon?"

"Mr. Latham, my Bart. He sells ladies underwear to all the big department stores east of Chicago and as far down as Nashville." She looked around with a sigh. "He does very well, but I do get lonely. Biscuit? I make them from scratch."

Without waiting for an answer, Lola Mae turned back to the cabinet and grabbed two bread and butter plates. She picked up a wire basket on the counter draped in a red and white checkered cloth, and unwrapped the cloth to expose a dozen or so golden brown biscuits.

"That's where I met Bart, you know. Nashville. We've only been married two years. It's my first marriage but Bart's divorced. He's a little older but very steady. Strawberry jam? I make it myself. Howie loves my strawberry jam. I give him some every Christmas. Or I should say, Chanukah. He's Jewish, you know." She held out the basket to Percy.

"I know. Thanks."

Percy reached for two still warm biscuits and put them on the plate. The apples she had for breakfast were long gone and she was hungry.

She relaxed a little. There would be no trouble getting any information from the eager-to-chat younger woman. That is, if she had anything good to offer besides homemade biscuits. Lola Mae sat down at the small green Formica table and turned to her with an eager smile.

Percy broke open a biscuit and slathered it with jam, while giving Lola Mae a capsulated version of Howie's predicament. After she'd finished, pausing only to allow a few ohs and ahs from the woman, she got to the reason for her visit.

"So the long and short of it is, can you give me any information that might help Howie about last night? Did you see him, talk to him? Anything you can remember at all?"

"Well, I didn't talk to him, but I did see him through the peep-hole of the door leaving early this morning, Poopsie and I." She turned to the dog. "Didn't we, Poopsie?" The dog wiggled and barked at her feet. "Ever since he started leaving for work in the middle of the night --"

"That would be close to three a.m., right?"

"That's right. Anyway, Poopsie starts barking the minute he hears Howie's door open and close and then his footsteps down the stairs. We're not used to it, you see. He used to leave for work right before six a.m. I get up around then, so sometimes I'd take Poopsie and we'd walk Howie to his job. It's only three or four blocks away, so it's a nice walk for a little dog."

"So Poopsie barked this morning?" The woman nodded. "That would be sometime near three a.m. This is important, because the victim might have died around midnight. You're saying, you heard a noise in the hallway, got out of bed, and looked through the peep-hole where you saw Howie leaving for work?"

"Oh, yes. I don't know why he's been working different hours lately. I mean, he's been leaving for work at six since I've been here and all of a sudden --"

"Would you be willing to tell the cops that?" Percy interrupted Mrs. Latham, who stared at Percy in confusion. "Tell them that you saw Howie leave his apartment at around three o'clock this morning? Can you be specific with the time?"

"It was two-fifty-five exactly. I looked at the clock and almost didn't get up. I thought it might be Howie but I wanted to make sure. I saw the back of him just as was going down the stairs. You think I might help clear Howie? How exciting!" Her hazel eyes sparkled and she broke out in an amiable grin.

"I don't know," Percy answered, thinking out loud. "They might say he tiptoed out earlier, killed her, and then snuck back, only to make a racket leaving at his usual time, so he could have you for an alibi."

"You couldn't sneak around with Poopsie." Lola Mae's tone was firm. She gave her small dog an adoring look. "Poopsie hears every little noise. And barks at everything. He likes to patrol the hallways."

"He thinks of this building as his, huh?" Percy smiled at the woman. "You be sure to tell the cops that when they question you, which should be sometime today. They're looking to hang this on Howie, so you need to be sure to mention Poopsie's superior hearing."

Percy winked at her then stood, feeling the interview was over and she should get on with the day.

"Thanks for the grub. I've never had southern biscuits before. They're delicious. Lots of butter, right?" The woman nodded. "I love butter," Percy said mostly to herself.

"Oh, I'm so glad. I use all my rationing coupons for butter and cream." An earnest, eager to please face looked up at the detective. "Percy, should I mention to the police about the woman who came here and tried to get into his apartment the other day?"

Percy sat back down. "What woman? When was this?"

"Oh, let's see. Maybe last Friday? No, it was Thursday." Percy waited while Lola Mae sorted out her thoughts. "Yes, it was Thursday, around ten-thirty in the morning. Poopsie started barking at something in the hallway and I went to the door and looked through the peep-hole, like I always do."

"Go on," Percy encouraged.

"And there was this woman, a little younger than me, well-dressed in sort of a green-gray coat with a fur collar, and a matching hat. Very stylish. She had blue-black hair." She turned to Percy. "The same color as your son's hair. You don't often see people with blue-black hair and pale skin. Is that what they call black Irish? I've never known what black Irish really means, do you? Mr. O'Hara down the street --"

"What was she doing, this woman?"

"I'm sorry. Sometimes I tend to prattle on. Mr. Latham is always telling me to get to the point." Her tone was self-deprecating but charming.

"Don't worry about it. This might be important, Lola Mae, so don't leave anything out. Prattle on, but let's stick to the woman." Percy grinned slightly.

Thrilled, the woman leaned forward in concentration, Poopsie sitting enraptured at her feet. "Well at first, she knocked softly on Howie's door. So softly, I don't know how anybody who was inside could hear; if anybody was inside. But Ralph – that's his roommate – is fighting the war overseas and anybody who knows Howie knows he's at work at a ten-thirty in the morning."

The woman got caught up in the story, much as people do when gathered around a campfire late at night telling scary ghost stories. "Then she looked around and leaned her ear into the door. You know, the way you would if you wanted to hear if anybody was inside. Then she tried the doorknob to see if it the door was unlocked. You know, to see if it would open."

Mrs. Latham paused and looked at Percy expectantly. Percy picked up her cue.

"But it didn't."

"No, it was locked."

"Anything else?"

"Oh, yes."

"Then go on."

Mrs. Latham assumed her campfire posture again.

"When it didn't open, she began jiggling the knob, trying to force it, you know? Poopsie started to growl and then he barked like crazy. Lord, how he barked. I think it frightened her. I opened my door to see if I could be of some help, but by the time I got the door all the way open, she was running down the stairs. I heard the downstairs door slam shut about a moment later."

"Is that it?"

"Yes." Somewhat deflated, Lola Mae stopped speaking and shrugged. "Now that I say it out loud, I guess it wasn't that important."

"You never know. It could be." Percy patted the woman encouragingly on the shoulder. "Did you tell Howie about his visitor?"

"I left him a note. It said 'A young lady came by today about ten-thirty to see you'." Lola Mae turned and looked at Percy. "Should I have told him she tried to get into the apartment?"

"A little late for that, but the police should know."

"Oh, I'll surely tell them. Funny about that, though. I mean, she didn't look like a thief or anything. She had a gentile, ladylike appearance about her. That's why I opened the door to see if I could help her."

"Would you recognize the woman if you saw her again?"

"Oh, yes. You don't see many people with that blue-black hair. Except, like I say, your son. Does his father have blue-black hair?"

Percy didn't answer but stood. "Well, thank you, Lola Mae, for your time. You be sure to tell the police everything you told me." Percy headed for the front door.

"Oh, I will, I will." Lola Mae followed, preening with earnestness. "We're so glad to be of help, aren't we, Poopsie?" She glanced down at the dog at her heels that sneezed again.

"What kind of a dog is that?" Percy tried to keep up her end of the conversation as she made her way to the front door.

"A Pomeranian. They look just like little foxes, don't they?"

"They do."

Lola Mae began to prattle again. "Howie's such a wonderful neighbor. Every week he gives me chocolate croissants that melt in your mouth. He even taught me how to make them, but mine never come out as well as his. As my mama would say, he has the gift; he surely does."

Percy turned around as she got to the front door and extended her hand for a handshake.

"Thank you again, Lola Mae, for speaking with me. You be sure to tell the cops exactly what you told me. And thanks for the biscuits and jam."

The woman took Percy's hand in hers and instead of shaking it, gave it a light squeeze.

"Now don't you be a stranger, Percy Cole. You drop by and see Poopsie and me anytime you want. We're usually here. And bring that darling little boy with you. He's such a charmer."

Percy's smile was genuine. "I will, Lola Mae. And thank you again."

Chapter Thirteen

Dear Diary,

The waiting is hard, but I have endured much harder things. Soon stupid people will 'discover' what I want them to know. It's all going exactly as planned.

Chapter Fourteen

Percy stopped at Henry's Drugs, a small neighborhood pharmacy and luncheonette well kept up. The building had been recently painted black and white giving it a crisp look. The upper half was mostly plate glass windows, filled with advertising posters, emblems, and a myriad of products from Carter's Little Liver Pills to corsets for the discerning woman.

Dominating signs read 'Rx' 'Luncheonette' and 'Prescriptions' but the largest, a symbol of a mortar and pestle, hung over the door. That meant a pharmacist was on duty at all times.

Many drugstores offered meals as well as the complete soda fountain. But what pulled Percy in, besides the sign in one of the windows advertising meatloaf sandwiches for fifteen cents - price including a soda - was another symbol, a black telephone receiver, indicating a public payphone.

Percy licked her lips in anticipation of an early lunch after her phone calls. The thought of a meatloaf sandwich made her stomach growl. The two biscuits had only served to whet her appetite.

After all, I'm a growing girl. And growing wider every day.

She went to the phone booth at the corner of the store, stepped inside, and dug out some nickels from her pocket. Her first call was to Jude, thankfully in his office.

After repeating word for word the conversation she'd had with Lola Mae Latham, her brother hung up with the words, "I'm calling the police station right away with this new development. Good work, Percy. Catch you later."

With a yearning glance at the sandwich counter, she grappled for the bag of Pistachios in her pocket, fed another nickel into the slot, and dialed home. Mother answered on the fifth ring.

"Hello, Mother. How are things on the home front?" She felt around in the small bag for a nut. Popping one in her mouth, she thought about how unsatisfying they were when you wanted a meatloaf sandwich.

"Persephone dear, I'm so glad you phoned."

Her mother's voice sounded relieved, yet anxious.

"Father called here about thirty-minutes ago and I told him about poor Howie's situation and that you and Adjudication were taking the matter in hand. Then I told him you needed to talk to him as soon as possible. Something to do with the office. He left a number for you to call. I have it right here. Did I do right, dear? I shouldn't have kept him on the phone, should I have? Oh, no. It's way too expensive. We just paid four dollars and fifty-seven cents last night for a long-distance call. Besides, how would you have gotten through if I was still on the phone with Father? Silly me."

"You did right, Mother." Percy smiled on her end. "Before you give me the number, did Oliver get off to school all right?"

"Oh, yes, and I did just as you asked in his lunchbox, a spam sandwich and an apple. I threw in some marshmallow-covered cauliflower as a little surprise for dessert. I'm saving you some. They're delicious."

"I'll bet." Percy's tone was serious, despite the roll of her eyes. "So Pop's waiting for me to call him?"

"Yes, he said the Firehouse across the street will go and get him when you call. Firemen are so nice, aren't they?"

"They're the good guys, Mother. No doubt about it."

She hung up, opened the door of the phone booth, and asked the nearby white-smocked pharmacist – probably Henry - for change for a dollar bill. While the stooped-over, man counted out nickels and dimes with a smile, she thought about how she would phrase what she wanted to say to Pop about the changes in the office.

Percy wasn't sure how much she should tell him. She'd already sounded out Fred Rendell Sr., father of Oliver's best friend, Freddie, about doing the legwork for the agency. The conversation took place before Howie's arrest, when she was already carrying the office's workload by herself. She didn't want this to continue, not with an eight-year old boy to think about.

Besides, she liked Fred Rendell. Rendell was an intelligent, quiet man who'd recently lost a hand in the war effort and was home on honorable discharge. Lately, she'd noticed a deepening depression in him. Percy figured it wasn't just the lack of anything to fill up his days. The family had to be struggling to pay the bills, what with just his wife's part-time secretarial job.

Grappling with bills was something Percy knew only too well. When Pop was in the hospital having his bad leg operated on, she'd played a lot of *eeny, meeny, miny, moe* with who got paid and when. Times were tough enough for able-bodied souls. There weren't many jobs for a man with only a left hand.

But Pop, although amiable and fair, was a proud man. He'd only recently got used to the idea of having a detective for a daughter. He might balk at her taking the lead on where Cole Brothers' Detective Agency went. In fact, she'd put money on it.

Nonetheless, Percy took a deep breath, lifted the receiver from the cradle, and recited, "If it were done when 'tis done, then 'twere well it were done quickly."

Chapter Fifteen

She put her third nickel into the slot and dialed 'zero'. The coin jingled through the box and came out the return slot. She waited while the phone rang. When the operator came on the line, she gave her the number Mother had dictated.

At the prodding of the operator's voice in her ear, she deposited sixty-five cents for the first three minutes. Ten cents for each following minute, she was told. After chatting briefly with the fireman on duty who said he'd run and get Pop, Percy was left to ponder again on what to say to her father. She was rarely a person left tongue-tied, but her father had a way of doing that to her at times.

These are the ties that bind.

It was a long wait and just as she began to wonder if she'd have to deposit more money, she heard Pop's out of breath reply.

"Hello, hello?" He sounded like he'd run all the way.

"Hey, Pop. How you doing?"

"Persephone, my dear girl. It's good to hear your voice. Just give me a moment to catch my breath. I ran nearly a block to get here."

"I thought Mother said the fire station was across the street, Pop."

"Well, that's what I told your mother. I didn't want her to worry. But that's all right. It keeps a man in condition." He let out a chuckle and Percy joined in. "What is it you need, daughter of mine?"

"Pop, Mother told you about Howie being arrested for murder and how both Jude and I are working to free him."

"Yes, indeed. When I return I'll join in the fight."

"When will that be?"

"To be honest, at least a few more days. Maybe a week. I'm hoping to be home for Valentine's Day. You know how much Mother looks forward to me buying her a box of candy, a corsage, and taking her out dancing."

"It's been a tradition for as long as I can remember, even if you took her two-stepping in the kitchen."

"And once her corsage was one of the neighbor's Geraniums," Pop said then lowered his voice to a whisper. "Speaking of flowers, it's looking like some of the young men working at a florist shop nearby might be who we're after. None of them speak with a German accent, but some people are fluent in more than one language. Your Uncle Gilleathain was one. He spoke French, German, and Spanish like a native. At least, that's what they tell me. It all sounded like gobbledygook to me."

Percy let out a laugh. "I miss you, Pop. And I still miss Uncle Gil," she added softly.

"You and me, darling. You and me. But there's no stopping Parkinson's Disease when it gets its way with you. Maybe someday they'll be a cure." Pop cleared this throat. "But this is costing money. What's on your mind?"

As if on cue, the operator's dulcet tones interrupted them.

"Please deposit another ten cents for one minute, please."

Percy dropped in five dimes and listened to the musical tinkling of each one fall into place.

"I put in another fifty cents, Pop, so we can talk without getting cut off." She took a deep breath. "Pop, with you tied up on the government job in New Jersey --"

"It's good pay, Persephone," he interrupted. "And it's our civic duty."

"I know, Pop, and I agree. But even before this thing with Howie, I've been trying to juggle the Kilgallen job and the Sheppard robbery. You know how Mr. Sheppard is pushing to get his paintings back and is convinced that after they were stolen, they've been palmed off on one of the uptown galleries. I've been walking my feet off on that one, because time is of the essence, but I've narrowed it down. And Mrs. Kilgallen is pushing me for proof of her husband's infidelities, but it's all very low-keyed. She doesn't want a divorce, just to know."

"You still following him around?"

"Like a shadow when I can, but there's only so many hours in a day."

"There's no substitute for legwork. I wish I was there --
"

"But you're not, Pop." Percy interrupted, keeping her voice pleasant but firm. "And we have to deal with what we got. So I've been thinking."

"Shoot."

"We need to bring somebody in freelance to do the bulk of the running around for us. Not the noodle part, just the footwork. And I think I've found somebody." Percy went on in a rush. "Fred Rendell, little Freddie's father. Rendell's been discharged from the army and looks like he's going crazy for lack of something to do."

"That so?" His voice was as noncommittal as hers had been with her mother's idea of marshmallow-covered cauliflower.

"We wouldn't even have to pay him until each job was finalized, when we got paid."

"You don't say."

"If you agree, he'll be on a trial basis for a month or until the Sheppard and Kilgallen jobs are completed. This way, I can devote myself totally to Howie."

"Sounds like you've got it worked out. I'm thinking you've already spoken to the man."

Percy hesitated and decided to be honest. "I have, Pop. Yesterday, even before Howie was arrested. We're getting bigger. I've already been putting in ten-twelve hour days, with you gone. If you agree, The Cole Brothers' Detective Agency has got itself a freelance employee. At least, for a while. What do you say, Pop?"

"How does he feel about taking his orders from a woman?"

"You mean, until you get back?"

"I mean, in general. You're in charge now. It's time I passed the torch, so to speak. That doesn't mean I'm going anywhere but I think it's time for the next generation to hold the reins. I'll still give you the benefit of my knowledge; just try to keep me from it."

He let out a loud laugh, but Percy was silent for a moment, trying to absorb this development. Less than a year before he was dead-set against her being more than the office secretary. She swallowed hard.

"You're sure?"

"Never surer. I've been doing some thinking, too, freezing under that damned boardwalk hour after hour. And we're changing the name From Cole Brothers' to Cole Detective Agency. Gilleathain would have wanted that. He saw the promise in you years ago. It took me a bit longer. So how does Rendell feel about taking orders from you?"

"We talked about it yesterday, Pop. He seems okay with it. Sylvia says he's not your average, run-of-the-mill man."

"You mean like your hard-headed father?"

Percy laughed. "Didn't say that, Pop."

"Didn't have to." Her father went on. "I don't think we should pay Rendell more than ten bucks a day, being as our going rate is fifteen. And he's on his own with small expenses, like bus fare, things like that. What do you think?"

"Perfect." She grinned into the phone. "He starts today."

"How's it going with Howard? You going to be able to spring him?"

"I hope so, Pop. Listen to this." She told him quickly about Ronald Bogdanovitch, Carlotta's Chocolates, and the latest development from Howie's neighbor, Lola Mae Latham.

"What made you go to see Howard's neighbor?"

"Instinct, Pop. A gut feeling."

"That's what separates the greats from the not-so-greats. Now it's up to Adjudication to get the district attorney to see reason."

"He's got his work cut out for him. Jude tells me the D.A. wants to make an example of this case."

Percy heard the click-click of the payphone, indicating time was running out. She looked in her other hand and saw one more dime and a nickel. She put in the dime and waited for the high-pitched clinking to stop.

"Running out of coins, Pop. We got one more minute. Anything else to say?"

"Yes, if you can, take Mother out to a movie or something, Persephone. She's lonely. I can hear it in her voice."

"She says the same thing about you, Pop." Percy smiled into the phone. *The original Romeo and Juliet, without the death scene. That's my parents.*

"Well, it's almost over." Pop let out a husky sigh. "I should be home in a few more days."

"According to Bogdanovitch, I only got two days to find out all I can at the chocolate factory. Then supposedly he kicks me off the premises."

"You watch your back with that one. He's small time, but he's got a bad rep. Maybe you should carry a little protection, at least for a while." He was referring to the German Mauser her Uncle Gil had brought back from WWI and gave her on her sixteenth birthday.

"Will do. I always keep it locked in Ophelia's glove compartment, along the lines of 'you never know'."

"Amen to that. Kiss Oliver for me, will you? I miss my grandson."

"He misses you, too, Pop. Got to go. There's a meatloaf sandwich with my name on it at the counter. Probably loaded with fillers, but it smells good."

"No doubt better than Mother's. Remember the time she put a bag of uncooked lima beans into a pound of ground beef, thinking to stretch it? It came out hard as a brick."

"Didn't we use it as a doorstop for years after, Pop?"

Poking fun at Mother's 'creative' recipes was a long-time family tradition. They were careful not to tease Mother directly, though. She took her homemaking skills very seriously.

"Signing off now, Pop. Love you."

"Love you more."

Chapter Sixteen

"Good afternoon, Miss Cole."

The thin, baritone voice interrupted Percy's thinking. She swiveled around in the hard chair she'd been occupying. Fred Rendell stood in the doorway against the backdrop of the pink and red curtain.

"Come on in, Rendell. I dragged this chair over to where the killer copper kettle was. Some things are bothering me and I wanted to mull them over on the spot. Glad you could get here so fast."

"It's been an hour, ma'am."

Surprised, Percy checked her watch then looked up at the sound of the man's leather shoes crossing the cement floor. She studied the slender, compact man, wisps of fine dark hair not covered by his black felt hat fluttering as he walked. No more than thirty, Rendell had been in the infantry and still retained the toned body of a man who until recently had been crawling on his belly to get the job done.

He wore grey slacks with a thick, dark green cardigan sweater. The day having turned warmer, his worn, brown leather jacket was thrown over his left shoulder, clasped by his one good hand. Hanging out of the other side of the long-sleeve sweater was his wooden hand, sheathed in a black leather glove. She'd seen the piece of teak wood cut in the shape of a hand at rest, hard and unyielding. He called it a prosthesis. She called it a damn shame.

"Haul that stool over here and sit." Percy pointed to a lone white stool sitting against the wall next to the storage bins.

With a quick stride, he went to the far wall, threw his jacket over the top of the stool, picked it up with his one hand, and carried it nearer to her. Rendell removed his jacket from the top and hitched himself up on the stool, easy and lithe. He still wore his hat, but pushed it further off his forehead. She watched his movements with sharp eyes.

"You left-handed or right-handed?"

"I was right-handed. I'm left-handed now."

He shot her a smile, simple and direct. No self-pity dwelled in his eyes that Percy could see. He took those eyes off her and looked around.

"So this is the place. When they're not killing people, they make chocolate here." He gave off a small laugh.

"They do." She reached inside her breast pocket and took out a small notebook and pen. After she flipped it open and found the right page, she looked at Rendell. "You bring a notebook like I asked?"

He nodded, reached into his left trouser pocket, and pulled out a small spiral book found at any stationary shop.

"Can you write with that left hand?"

"Nobody but me can read it, but I write well enough."

Percy cracked a smile. "After we talk, take my notebook over to that counter and copy this top page and the two after that. These are my notes about the two cases you'll be working on. Don't make contact with anyone, and don't let anyone know you're tailing him. Think you can do that?"

He nodded before saying, "Part of my job in the army was a tracker."

"So Sylvia mentioned. Your wife also says you're lucky to be alive. They still don't know why that landmine didn't take off more of your body than just your hand."

"My buddy took the brunt of it. He stepped right on it. They never found much of him." He changed the subject. "So what happened here? Sylvia didn't know."

"Dead body partially dumped into a giant chocolate vat. The vat's gone now, but it was right there."

Percy nodded her head toward a squatting, stainless steel gas stove with a huge single burner. Two arms came up from the floor on either side the stove, and curved toward each other.

At the end of each arm was a steel clamp. Behind the stove was a rudimentary pulley system coming from the ceiling. To one side, the long and narrow conveyer belt made out of a rubberized canvas rested, silent and still.

"Wouldn't the vat have to be pretty big? I mean, to hold a body?" Rendell raised an eyebrow.

"A hundred and fifty gallons. Not big enough to cover the entire body, but big enough."

"And the vat normally holds chocolate? How do they control that much chocolate as of a day?"

"I haven't seen the vat, myself. The police have it. But the way it's been explained to me, these clamps are on a swivel and locking mechanism and attached to the pulley. When the chocolate is ready, a funnel is fastened to the vat and it's raised off the fire. The vat is swiveled over the conveyer belt. It's angled and locked in place. The chocolate feeds into the funnel, and comes out onto whatever is moving along on the conveyer belt. When they need more chocolate or it needs to be rewarmed, they make adjustments. That was part of Howie's job, to control that."

"But why would someone put a woman into a vat of chocolate? It seems like a messy thing to do, ma'am."

"Especially as she was strangled by a rope beforehand, yes."

"You'd get chocolate everywhere, especially on you."

"And that is exactly what happened to Howie. Chocolate everywhere. Very damning."

"But you don't think he did it?"

Percy shook her head and gave her new employee a faint smile before saying, "No, and I'm going to prove he didn't. You'll be on your own for the most part on these two other jobs, but you need to report everything back to me. If you've thought about it and you're going to have a problem taking orders from a woman, tell me now."

It was his turn to shake his head. "I was raised by my mother, grandmother, and three older sisters. Women telling me what to do is old hat to me." He let out a small laugh at some past memory. "Nobody was quicker than granny, although Sylvia's pretty close."

He looked her square in the eyes. Percy nodded.

"Good. As long as we're clear on that."

"Yes ma'am. Crystal."

"You have two cases; one urgent, one not so much. The urgent one involves three stolen paintings, missing for nearly two days. They belong to a collector, a man who owns an up and coming modeling agency. His older, society wife is subsidizing his business while it's getting off the ground. She's also the one who forked over the dough for the paintings. The wife's in California right now but our client doesn't want her to find out the paintings are gone, especially as we now think members of his family might be responsible. It was an inside job, no forced entry. They knew right where they were going. In and out in less than five minutes."

Rendell whistled. "That's a pretty sticky situation."

"By the time cases get to us, they're usually covered with glue. Mr. Sheppard's wife could return from California any time. We haven't got long. I've narrowed it down to three suspects, all his siblings. One of the brothers owns a gallery uptown on 74th Street. Two others work in a gallery on 68th Street and Lexington Avenue. He doesn't necessarily want them to be caught and punished; too much publicity. But he does want the paintings found and returned."

"What's the second case?"

"A cheating husband. Not such a tight time-frame on that one, so we'll put it on the back burner for now. Back to the art."

She gestured with a nod toward the edge of the counter against the wall.

"I left photographs of the missing paintings on the counter over there. They were used for insurance purposes, so they're pretty grainy. But they'll give you an idea. In my notebook are the dimensions of the paintings and the brothers' names, with a bit of their history. I'm going to stress again we don't have a lot of time. It might already be too late. The paintings have been missing for almost forty-eight hours. They could be crated and heading for parts unknown, but maybe not. This is Friday. If it was me, I'd do what I needed to do over the weekend. Less prying eyes."

She reached into her pocket, pulled out a small badge, and chucked it on his lap.

"You'll need to see where each gallery stores their paintings, not just the ones on display. I find saying you're with the gas company gets you in almost anywhere. Hang that from your shirt pocket. If somebody challenges you on it, make an excuse and leave. You see anyone when you came in?"

"Yes, some Italian guy. He was heading out. That's what I should be doing, after I copy your notes."

Pocketing the badge, he stood, moving toward her. Percy turned over her notebook and watched him go the marble counter to transfer information and to examine the photographs she'd left there. After a moment, his head snapped around. Rendell's face was covered with an amazed expression.

"One of these looks like a Picasso."

"You know your art, Mr. Rendell."

Neither said more. Rendell turned back to the counter and scribbled furiously. Percy let her mind return to where it had been. She came back to the same place repeatedly.

Sixty-four dollar question: why put a woman into a vat of chocolate, especially when she's got a rope around her neck that probably choked the life out of her? Answer: Maybe if you were making a point, there'd be no better way. Okay, second question: She was a little woman, but even if she weighed less than a hundred pounds, it's still a lot of dead weight to haul around. That says it's more likely a man. Of course, I could do it, but then I've got the strength. Comes with being bigger than your average male.

"I'm leaving now, Miss Cole. Anything else?"

Percy looked up into the solemn brown eyes of Rendell. "Yeah, write anything and everything down. And keep a list of all your expenses. Some of them we might reimburse you for. Don't count on it, but you never know."

"Then I'll wish you good day, ma'am." He touched his hat in a gesture of respect. He gave her a quick grin and nod then turned on his heels to leave. Percy watched the back of him.

He's eager to start and asks good questions. I like that.

Chapter Seventeen

Percy rose and crossed to the set of lockers running down one wall of the room. Twenty in all, sixteen had names printed on tape in the upper right hand corner of the door. Out of the sixteen, four had locks on them, cheap and easy to open. The twelve lockers without a security device were first, starting at the one nearest the door. Percy flipped open the handles of each and did a quick check. They revealed nothing out of the ordinary or of importance.

Inexpensive smocks, obviously provided for by the factory, and hairnets hung in each one, with the occasional addition of a piece of soap or pair of shoes. Each smock was thread-bare but clean. The hairnets were in much worse shape, holey and ripped.

Maybe they have to pay for the hairnets themselves.

Percy pushed her hat forward on her head, reached back, and removed a hairpin from near her pony tail. After flattening the pin, she inserted it in the first lock of the four secured lockers. Within ten seconds, the lock released itself and she opened the door of the locker.

Several boxes of chocolate were inside a wrinkled paper bag tucked into a corner of the floor. On a top shelf, three wads of crumpled paper had been tossed. She grabbed one and smoothed it out. A deposit slip to a nearby bank read for fifty-dollars in the account of Alfred Ziglar. With a hasty hand, she picked up the other two. They, too, were for fifty dollars.

"Hey! What do you think you're doing? Get out of my locker, fella!"

Percy turned to see a short, wiry man around her age hurry toward her.

"Why, you ain't nothing but a broad!"

His shock was amusing to Percy as he raced across the floor to her. She looked at him with a smile.

"I'm a detective broad. You must be Alfred Ziglar."

Instead of answering, he snatched at her hand containing the deposit slips. Percy pulled back and held them higher than his reach.

"Not so fast, Alf. That's what they call you, right? Alf?"

"What's it to you? You give me those back before I call the cops." He gestured toward the deposit slip then glared at her menacingly.

"Go ahead, call the cops. Or you could just answer some questions."

"You got no right to be here. I could have you arrested."

"I got every right. Ask your boss, Bogdanovitch. You could say I'm working for him. You know what happened here last night?"

"Sure, I know. The owner got iced by that Jew boy."

"Watch your mouth, Alf. Or somebody might have to wash it out with soap for you."

"Says you." He sneered at her. "Give me back my property. You ain't got no right--"

"What's with the monthly deposits for fifty bucks? Seems like a lot of money for an ex-con like you."

"How do you know I'm a--"

"You got the same pair of shoes they give every jailbird coming out of the pen who doesn't have any of his own. Besides, you smell like one."

"Why you --" He made a lunge for her.

Percy sidestepped, as he came toward her. She reached out and using his momentum, threw him against the door of the locker. Percy held the gasping man at arm's length and stared down at him.

"You know, I don't like you, Alf. So don't give me any reason to knock you around any more than I have to. I'm going to ask you again, what's with the deposit slips?"

Alf struggled to be free, but Percy held him with a tight hand at his throat. Arm taut, she leaned against his neck with her body weight, which was considerable.

"You being a bad boy and stealing somebody else's money?"

"I ain't stealing nothing." Red faced, he fought to get the words out, despite her hand clamped around his throat. "That money's mine." He pushed hard against her hand. She pushed back.

"That means you're putting the squeeze on somebody. No other way a scumbag like you would have that kind of dough three times in a row and all at the beginning of each month."

Thrashing about, the man broke free. Percy grabbed the front collar of his shirt, spun him around in a circle, knocking him against the locker again. A button ripped from his shirt in the scuffle, and skittered across the floor with a clicking sound. This time she picked him up by his neck, and raised him to her eye level. He stared at her terrified, as he felt his feet being lifted off the ground.

"You're starting to make me mad, Alf. Now I want to know where you got this money and until you tell me, you're going to be 'hanging' around, so to speak."

"I got it from the owner, Carlotta. I got it from her." His voice was hardly more than a squeak but understandable.

'A shakedown? For what?" He tried to look away. Percy banged his head against the tin of the door. "Talk, Alf, before I put you inside your locker, roll it down the front stairs, and all the way back to jail."

"It's for something she done. Something she done way back. She don't want nobody to know. But I knows, see? Let me down. Let me down."

She allowed him to slide down the locker door to the floor. "What didn't she want anyone to know?"

Safely on the ground, some of his bravado returned. "I ain't telling you."

"But she's dead now, Alf." Percy's voice took on a reasonable tone. "What difference can it make?"

"Somebody else cares, so I ain't telling you."

Alf gave Percy a sudden, hard shove, throwing her off-balance. He made a break for the door, leather shoes thudding against the hard concrete.

Percy's initial reaction was to follow but she stopped herself. She brushed off her hands, spied the button lying in the middle of the room, and strode over to it. Deep in thought, she bent down to pick it up.

Alf, Alf, Alf, what were you blackmailing Carlotta for? And did she threaten to turn you in? And did you decide to silence her in a macabre sort of way? I need to find out why you were doing time. Maybe you like to repeat yourself.

Pocketing the button, she opened and searched the three remaining lockers, found nothing, and relocked them.

It was too much to hope for. So whoever killed Carlotta wore his own clothes or took the stained smock with him. Maybe by now they threw the clothes away. Did the cops searched nearby trash cans? Probably not. Next on my agenda.

She looked up at the small office at the top of the stairs. The lights were on, yet no one came out to see what all the racket was about at the lockers. Who was up there? Percy strode across the floor and up the stairs toward the office.

The door was unlocked and she pushed it open to see the room was empty, despite the blazing lights. Not only that, the door to Carlotta's safe, a safe Bogdanovitch claimed was impenetrable, was wide open, Blue Boy lying on its side against Carlotta's desk.

Somebody knew the combination or was a better safe-cracker than Bogdanovitch claimed to be.

Flinging her hat on the desk, Percy hurried over and looked inside the safe. Empty. Her attention was drawn down to the floor. A Spanish passport and two legal-size documents were splayed out to the side, as if thrown from impatient hands. Without touching them, the detective squatted down for a better look. Besides the passport, one looked like a will, the other a deed. No book with a formula. Percy grabbed a pencil from the top of the desk, flipped the passport open, and began turning the pages.

Born December fifteenth, 1901. That made her forty-two. Younger than anyone thought, but that's the way of the world for bow-wows.

She pressed open the page showing entry into the United States and found something surprising.

She came to the U.S. in 1918 from Barcelona. Seventeen years old. Pretty young. I wonder if she came alone.

Percy strained to read the small print further down the page.

Spent six months here. Hmmm. Interesting. Didn't come back again until 1937, when she stayed.

Using the pencil, Percy closed the passport and pushed it to where it had been on the floor. She flipped over the first document, blue covered. It was, indeed, a will, and left much of what Carlotta owned -- including the formula for her chocolate -- to her next of kin, with the exception of the chocolate factory, itself. Surprisingly, she'd left the business et al to Howard Goldberg.

Holy Cow! This includes ownership of the building.

Considering the fight Carlotta had with Howie, plus the demotion, this surprised Percy.

Obviously, she's hadn't changed her will yet, if she intended to. But crap, whether she intended to or not, this adds a bigger motive for poor Howie. The cops are going to love this.

She'd been wrong about the other document. It wasn't a deed but a formal list of financial holdings. They were considerable. She scribbled the names of the businesses in her notebook and stuffed it in her breast pocket.

Well, well. Apparently, Carlotta Mendez was as much of a whiz at making money as she was at making chocolate. This doesn't look good for Howie. Not good at all. He had a double motive, means, and opportunity. No one's going to buy a dog's hearing over that.

A footfall at the bottom of the stairs brought Percy back to the here and now. Defter than seemingly her size would allow, she sprang up, snatched her hat from the desk, and dashed behind the partially opened door.

Chapter Eighteen

Through the crack, she watched the cop with whom she sometimes kept company or shared a case, pass by. She pushed the door open and stepped out from behind it.

"Hey, Hutchers. How they hanging?"

The man who matched Percy in height and dedication to his job, wheeled around with a startled look on his face. "Jeez Louise, you scared me half to death! What are you doing hiding behind the door?"

"I thought you might be Bogdanovitch. If so, I wanted to be ready. Not your nicest guy. What are you doing here? Don't you have a job in midtown Manhattan?"

"Day off. Worked two weekends in a row. Even coppers get a break now and again. I called your office, spoke to your mother, and she told me you were here. I thought I'd run down just to make sure you didn't get into any trouble." He did a double-take at the open safe and the papers on the floor. "Looks like I'm a little late."

She crossed a little closer and smiled. "I found it like that."

"Did you, now?"

"Cross my heart." She waved the pencil under his nose. "Of course, I pushed a few things around, had a little look-see."

"And what did you see?"

"I saw the sea," she half-sang, with a wink.

"Perce, this ain't no time for Fred Astaire songs." His voice was gruff. "You shouldn't be fooling around with evidence. You sure you didn't bust that safe open?"

"Hutchers! You do me wrong." Percy feigned insult. "I would never bust open somebody's safe. Not my style."

"That's true. You're more likely to bust open somebody's head."

Percy shrugged. "I was about to call the cops --"

"Sure you were," Hutchers interrupted.

"Eventually."

She tossed her hat on top of the desk again. "I found the door unlocked, the lights on, and the safe wide-open, with not a sign of Bogdanovitch anywhere. Carlotta's passport, her will, and a list of properties lying there for the reading. No lie. Hutchers, this doesn't smell right."

"Nothing ever smells right to you including me, but I like you, anyway." He gave her a lopsided smile. "You going to call the cops, report a possible burglary?"

"Eventually," they both said in unison.

"In that case, put your hat back on, I'll take you to a late lunch --"

"It's nearly three," Percy interrupted.

"Early dinner then. And I'll tell you what I know so far on this case. We can pretend we never been in here."

"Sounds aces, but I've got some thinking to do." She moved behind the desk and sat down, removing the bag of Pistachios from her pocket, tossing it on the desk. "Lock that door, take a load off, and have a Pistachio. Once I'm done thinking, we can hash this out."

Hutchers let out a guffaw, returned to the door and closed it. After a moment's thought, he threw the lock. Back at the desk, he took off his hat, and tossed it next to hers. He sat, putting crossed legs up on a corner of the desk to watch Percy think.

For a full fifteen-minutes they sat in silence. Percy sat. Hutchers watched. She came out of it, almost as if waking up. She turned to the man across from her with a smile.

"There's a lot more to this case than meets the eye. First off, this was not your standard robbery. They left the passport, which is worth big bucks on the black market, and there's a couple of other things that don't jive, either. I haven't figured them out yet, but at least I know what they are."

Hutchers reached for a handful of Pistachios and broke one open with his thumbnail.

"When you get through straining your brain, we should call Brooklyn's Finest. They're not going to like being left out of this."

"A little nervous about it, pal?"

Percy grinned at him. He took his feet off the desk and leaned forward, about to say something.

"Just kidding, Hutchers. Relax. I'll call right now. By the time they get here, we can finish our little talk."

She picked up the phone and dialed zero. "What's the name of the guy in charge of this case, anyway?"

"Lieutenant Griffin." Hutchers leaned back in the chair and returned his feet to the desktop. "Not the brightest bulb in the bunch, but thorough."

"Good to know."

After she gave the information to the precinct, and hung up the phone, she turned back to Hutchers.

"They'll be here in less than ten minutes, so let's talk fast. In the will on the floor, Carlotta leaves the formula for the chocolate and all her financial holdings to her next of kin. The chocolate business and this building goes to Howie Goldberg."

Hutchers let out a soft whistle. "That don't look so good for your friend."

"No, it doesn't and I got to fix this."

"If you can't, he's going to fry in the chair for sure once the D.A. sees that will."

"The way I figure it, whoever opened that safe was in a hurry. They rifled through the papers, dumped what they weren't looking for, and took what they wanted. I think I know what that was."

"Yeah?"

"Yeah. A formula for chocolate. She kept it in the safe. Bogdanovitch told me."

"Who the hell would take a recipe for chocolate?"

"Almost anyone in the chocolate game, that's who. Interesting how Carlotta set it up, too. She was one smart cookie; not fair but smart. She may have left the business to Howie, but she left the chocolate formula to her next of kin."

"Meaning what?"

"One's no good without the other on the surface of it, but it might have been a clever maneuver."

"How so?"

"It keeps the real wealth in the family but gets an outsider to work his butt off for you, especially if the outsider has to lease or pay the family for the chocolate formula. There's might even be a clause in the will - one I didn't get a chance to read -- about Howie not being able to sell the business without giving the Mendez family the right of first refusal. Speaking of family, she left everything else to her next of kin, and it's quite a bagful."

"According to Griffin, that would be the cousin in Chicago. But if you're thinking he did it, unless he sprouted wings, it ain't possible." Hutchers dumped a handful of shells into a nearby ashtray. "His name is Paulo Mendez, and the gentleman in question was at his father-in-law's birthday party last night until eleven-thirty. At least, that's what his wife and fifteen other guests say."

"Why, Hutchers, I'm impressed."

"Don't be. Griffin did it. I told you he was thorough. Dumb but thorough. Chicago checked it out and called Griffin back with the news. I had coffee with him a little while ago. He couldn't talk enough about the case. Happy as a clam it's his."

"Do tell."

"Here's a news flash. Seems he also got a phone call from one of Goldberg's neighbors. Said she and her dog heard Goldberg going down the stairs around three a.m. this morning."

"Oh?"

"Said she had a visit from this nice lady detective, who jarred her memory about it."

"No kidding."

He gave her a knowing look. "Gee, I wonder who that might have been."

"Yeah, there's so many lady detectives, Hutchers."

"It was the 'nice' that threw me."

"I must be losing my touch if she thought I was nice. That sway Griffin or not?"

"Not really." Hutchers scratched his nose. "Griffin doesn't think much of it. There's a million ways Goldberg could have left and not been heard. He could have gone down the fire escape for one thing, done the deed, and returned the same way. He only lives on the second floor. But for my money, it convinces *me* of Goldberg's innocence. That and the fact you say so."

"Glad to hear it. I could use all the help I can get. Got anything else?"

"The coroner says Carlotta Mendez was probably strangled with the rope until she was unconscious and then tossed head first into the chocolate. That would account for the chocolate in her lungs."

Percy thought for a moment. "A desecration of her body."

"If that means they turned the heat up on the stove to cook her until she was dead, I would say yes."

They locked eyes, her clear green ones searching his dark brown. "I don't like crimes of passion or vendettas, Hutchers. Things get out of control."

"And dangerous. Never forget that."

"You bet. Anything else? Griffin should be here any minute."

"They're on the lookout for Bogdanovitch. Have been all morning. They'd like to land something on him. They owe him."

"I figured that would happen. Long shadows."

"You wouldn't happen to know where he is."

"Nope. Last time I saw him was around eight o'clock this morning. He's got a girlfriend over on the east side who might know. But I'll save that little tidbit for Griffin. You know, throw him a bone."

Both heard the sound of multiple footsteps on the stairs.

"Sounds like a herd of elephants, so it must be the cops, Hutchers." She reached for the bag of nuts and crammed what was left in her breast pocket. "Get your feet off the desk. We don't want to look too comfortable here. And you'd better unlock the door."

Chapter Nineteen

Hutchers opened the door to the office just as Lieutenant Griffin stepped up on the landing. When he saw the fellow officer he'd shared coffee with not an hour before, he froze in place.

"Ken Hutchers? What are you doing here?" Griffin moved forward and crossed the threshold.

"Just passing through. Not my party," Hutchers said. He stepped aside to let the men enter. Griffin was followed in by two policemen in uniform.

"And who the hell are you?" Griffin scowled at Percy.

Percy rose slowly. "I'm the model citizen who called to tell you of the possible break-in."

Lieutenant Griffin stomped across the room and glared at Percy. "That ain't telling me who you are."

"My name is Persephone Cole and --"

"I heard about you."

Griffin's tone was accusatory. He turned to face Hutchers, who was standing neutral in the corner, hat in his hand, arms at his side. The lieutenant pivoted back to Percy.

"You're that gal dick. The one who's too big for everything, including her britches."

He spoke as he crossed to the desk and practically spat out the last two words. Unruffled, Percy gave him a big smile.

"Aw, now why do you want to go saying insulting stuff for? We can all be pals here. After all, I didn't say anything about your taste in ties and I could say plenty."

"I should arrest you for breaking and entering." He leaned in threateningly.

Hutchers rolled his eyes. "Save it, Griffin. Scare tactics don't work on her."

"No, they don't." Percy stood tall and looked down at the slightly shorter man. "For the record, I got permission from the manager to be here. You know him, guy named Bogdanovitch."

"Bogdanovitch! He a pal of yours? You know where that S.O.B. is? We got a couple of questions for him."

"Not a clue and he's no pal of mine."

"That still don't explain what you're doing here."

"I'm investigating the murder of Carlotta Mendez."

"We got the man who did it. I think *you* broke into that safe."

He turned and pointed in the direction of the safe. Percy shook her head, and sat down.

"Use your brain, Griffin, if you got one. If I did this, would I be calling you to come and arrest me? And Howard Goldberg didn't kill her."

"Oh, no?" His voice was challenging. "That's not what the D.A. says."

"Since when does anybody listen to the D.A., even a flatfoot? It would be a first." Percy let out a chuckle.

"Isn't he the one who issued a public apology for mishandling state funds?" Hutchers threw the comment in with a grin. "That's what I read in the Times, anyway."

"That would be the guy, Hutchers." Percy grinned back.

"Never mind, you two." Losing the argument, Lieutenant Griffin turned away and moved toward the safe. "What's this on the floor?"

Percy looked in the direction. "Looks like papers to me."

"You do that?"

"We've been all through that. I'm the model citizen --"

"Yeah, yeah."

He waved a dismissive hand at Percy and crouched down. He turned to one of the policeman standing at the door.

"Go get a kit out of the squad car and check this place for fingerprints."

The angular officer left at a clipped speed, nearly bumping into the door on his way out. Griffin watched him then looked at Percy.

"Mind if we have a set from you? Just to be sure."

"Hers are already on file." Hutchers interjected.

"Yeah, you got to do that in order to get a P.I. license." Percy smiled in the squatting man's direction.

Griffin grunted, took out a pen, and pushed the papers on the floor around. He went on.

"I don't think you got any jurisdiction in Brooklyn. Your license is for Manhattan, isn't it? Might have to run you in on general principles."

Hutchers looked away and whistled to himself softly. Still smiling, Percy shook her head slowly.

"License is good for the five boroughs, Griffin. You should know that." Percy stood, picked up her fedora, and plopped it on her head. "And as much as I love listening to you blow hot air, I got other things doing. See you around."

She moved from behind the desk and started for the door, turning back midway.

"By the way, if you're looking for Bogdanovitch, you might check out his girlfriend, Helena Wilson. He mentioned she lives on the east side of Manhattan. You inspect the nearby trash cans?"

The change in subject threw Griffin. He stood up, looked at her, and stuttered.

"Trash cans? What the hell for?"

"For a smock or something that's covered with chocolate our killer might have been wearing. Something he threw away after he killed Carlotta Mendez."

Griffin snickered and squatted down again. "No point in doing that. We got our man."

"That's what I thought." Percy walked to the door, stopping by Hutchers, with a whispered question. "You coming?"

"Where we going?" He whispered back, one eyebrow arched.

They both stepped onto the landing and started down the stairs, side by side.

"I thought we'd look into some trash around here, say within a five-block radius."

"Oh, gee." Hutchers set his hat on his head, pulling down on the brim. "Just what I want to be doing on my day off, routing through Brooklyn's garbage."

Chapter Twenty

Dear Diary,

I need to be careful. That woman detective is snooping around. I didn't count on her. I gave the cops what I want them to know, but I don't want her finding out anything else.

Chapter Twenty-one

Percy tried the front door of her family's apartment and sure enough, the door was unlocked. A huge sigh escaped her, one of frustration and fatigue. She shook her head and glanced at her watch. Five-fifteen. It felt like a much longer day.

She went to the gold-gilded telephone table in the foyer, the one she'd been trying to unsuccessfully get rid of for years. Unfortunately, Mother treated it as if it were her fourth child. Making a disgruntled face, Percy dropped a brown paper bag on it and true to form, it wobbled ever so slightly at the disturbance.

"Hello? Anybody here?" She called out to a silent apartment. "And how many times have Pop and I said to keep the front door locked? Anybody can walk right in here."

A split-second later, the swinging door to the kitchen at the end of the hall pushed open. Mother stood in the doorway with a big smile on her face.

Percy walked toward her. "I know that smile. You wear that when you have to tell me something you know I'm not going to like."

Percy halted and faced her mother. She looked down at her mother's slender five-foot seven-inch frame covered by another one of her meticulously made, hand-sewn dresses, this one in a small paisley print.

"Let's have it."

Mother gestured for Percy to follow her inside the kitchen, the door swinging closed behind them.

"Now I don't want you to worry, Persephone, but --"

"Something's happened to Oliver!"

"Oliver's fine, dear, but there was a slight problem at school. He's in his room doing homework and --"

Persephone swallowed hard with relief. "What happened?"

"I'm not completely sure, Persephone, but the school called earlier and said Oliver had gotten into a fight with an older boy right after school in the school yard."

"Oliver? In a fight? He's usually such an easy going kid. I'm surprised."

"Well, I couldn't get much out of him, even with offering him more marshmallowed cauliflowers. But I put some mercurochrome on his cheek. The cut isn't too bad."

"The cut?"

With a quick intake of breath, Percy wheeled around, and slammed at the kitchen door. It swung open wide and she hurried through. Once she arrived at the closed door of her son's bedroom, though, she paused.

Okay, don't panic. There's sure to be some reasonable explanation for this. Give the kid a chance to explain himself.

Percy tapped on the door, and waited for the youthful voice to say come in. None forthcoming, she pushed open the door and saw her son lying on the bed on his stomach, coloring in his book.

Legs bent at the knees and crossed at the ankles, they bounced up and down, as if with some secret rhythm in his head. A small, superficial cut on his right cheek was decorated in the pinkish orange of mercurochrome. Other than that, he seemed fine.

"Hi, sweetie."

Oliver looked up and gave her a wan smile. "Are you here to yell at me?"

"I don't know. Am I?"

Oliver put his legs down and swung around on the small bed, coming to an upright position. "It wasn't my fault.

He said bad things about Uncle Howie and when I told him to stop, he pushed me."

Percy sat on the bed beside her son and brushed a lock of coal-black hair out of his face. "And who was this?"

"Benny Culpepper. He's always picking on us little guys."

"Is he?"

"But this time I didn't let him. He said his father told him that Uncle Howie was a killer and was going to hang by his neck until he was dead! Then he pushed me." Tear spurted from dark brown eyes and Oliver swiped at them.

"And then what did you do?"

"I pushed him back! He's always stealing our lunch or pulling us off the slide when he wants to go on it. Just 'cause he's bigger than us."

"A bully, huh?"

Oliver didn't reply but shrugged. After a moment, he nodded.

"He took ten cents from Freddie the other day. I didn't see it, but Freddie told me on the way home."

"What happened after you pushed him back?"

"He hit me in the face. So I jumped on him and knocked him to the ground. Then Miss Dennis ran over and grabbed both of us and took us to the principal's office."

"I see."

"Miss Dennis said I shouldn't have hit him back even if he did hit me first."

"That's easier said than done, Oliver. Sometimes you have to fight back. While I don't think you should ever start anything --"

"Oh, no ma'am," Oliver interrupted, a sincere look on his face.

"Sometimes you have to be the one to finish it. That's the way of the world."

"Yes, ma'am."

She pulled her son onto her lap, resting her chin on the top of his head. "Life isn't always fair, Oliver, and you're going to come across people like Benny Culpepper now and then. Sometimes you got to let things go; sometimes you got to fight back. You'll see as you go along. When you feel you have to stick up for yourself, do it. I'll back you all the way."

Oliver thought long and hard. "What if I don't know what to do?"

"It's been my experience, when you don't know what to do, it's best to do nothing. It usually keeps 'til you decide."

"Okay, Mommy. The principal called in Benny's mom and dad. He's in big trouble. I was told to give you this letter."

The small boy got up and went to his desk, strewn with school books, comic books, and his favorite super-hero action figure, Buck Rogers, won at a local fair. He picked up a small sealed envelope and handed it to his mother. Percy opened it up, unfolded the slim paper inside, and read from the neat handwriting.

"It says here, *Until today, Oliver has always been a good boy who gets along well with his teachers and fellow students.*"

Percy read the rest of the note in silence then turned to her son. "The principal's going to let it go this time, but he hopes nothing like this happens again. I hope not, too, Oliver."

"Yes, ma'am." Oliver looked away, guiltily. After a moment, he muttered in a voice almost too soft to be heard. But his mother heard the words.

"Benny said I didn't have a father."

Even though Percy's heart clutched in her chest, she kept her voice calm and even.

"That's silly. Everyone's got a father."

"Then where is he, Mommy?" Oliver's innocent face looked up into hers, covered with confusion and hurt. "Did he die in the war?" He gulped after he said the last words.

Jeesh, he could have, for all I know. I've always been so glad he was gone, I didn't think about where he was. Aloud she said, "I don't know, Oliver. I haven't heard from him since before you were born."

Thoughts jumbled around in Percy's head as the realization sunk in. How much to tell her son? How much to burden him with?

"Didn't he know about me, Mommy?"

Yes, he did, Oliver. That's why he went away. "Maybe not."

"Wouldn't he come back if he did?"

Probably not, the louse. "I don't know where he is, son."

"But you could find him, couldn't you? Maybe he doesn't know how to find us."

It's never been a secret where we are. If he wanted to see you, he knows where to look.

"After all, Mommy, you're the world's greatest detective."

"I don't think I'm the world's greatest detective --"

"Yes, you are. That's what grandmother says. She says you can find anybody, anywhere."

I'll have to talk to her about this. "She's exaggerating, Oliver. You know mothers always think the best of their children. Like I do of you."

"Couldn't you at least try to find him, Mommy? Couldn't you?"

She studied her son's face, so earnest, so sweet, so innocent.

Just what I need, another case to solve. And this one looking for Leo the Louse. "Of course, I could."

Chapter Twenty-two

"All straightened out, dear?" Mother was standing at the sink scrubbing carrots. "I thought I'd make a ginger-carrot soup for supper. I found a recipe in a magazine at the grocery store."

"That actually sounds...good, Mother. I'm shocked."

"Shocked I'd find a good recipe? Why, Persephone!"

Percy did some fast thinking. "No, Mother. Sorry. That didn't come out right. I'm shocked about something else." She sat down hard on one of the chairs at the rectangular table before she continued.

"Oliver wants me to find his father."

"Good." Mother started humming one of her tuneless ditties, as she scrubbed another carrot.

"Good? How can you say that? You know why Leo left."

"That was eight years ago, Persephone." Mother came to the table and sat across from her daughter, carrying three dripping carrots, a paring knife, and a chopping board. "Maybe he's changed. There had to be some good in Leo or else you never would have married him in the first place."

"Maybe. Oh, I don't know. Remember, he signed all legal rights for Oliver over to me when he left. Jude made sure of that."

"I never thought that was quite right." Mother began to chop the carrots on the board in slow, rhythmic cuts, seemingly concentrating on the job at hand. "Your child is your child. Nothing you sign is going to change that."

"What are you talking about?" Percy's voice was low and challenging, even though her face drained of color and her mouth twitched with strain. "He went so far as to let me change Oliver's surname to my maiden name. That doesn't sound like a man who wants to have a son."

"You were testing him, Persephone. We all knew that." Mother looked down at her chopping board. "You would have given anything if he'd refused to sign."

Percy picked up cut pieces of carrot, stacking them in careful rows, also looking down. "What if he comes back into Oliver's life only to leave again? He's good at that."

She leaned forward, now staring at the older woman. Mother stopped chopping and stared back at her daughter.

"Then Oliver will know. You can't shield him from something like this forever. Leonard is his father and Oliver has the right to see what's what."

"He's only eight years old, Mother."

"I know. So young."

Mother gathered the sliced carrots and piled them onto the cutting board. Putting down the knife, she laid a soft hand on top of her daughter's.

"Persephone, I've learned some things raising my three children. You can only protect them so much. You try to raise them right, you try to be there for them, but sometimes they have to learn things are the way they are."

"Oliver and I were just discussing that about a bully at his school."

"What did you tell him?"

"Life isn't always the way we want it."

"And there you are."

Mother rose carrying the cutting board and vegetables to a large pot on the stove. She slipped in the chopped carrots.

"The recipe calls for chicken stock but I was thinking some sauerkraut juice would give it a little personality."

Both women were silent for a span, lost in their own separate thoughts.

"Okay." Percy rose with determination. "One Leo the Louse coming up. I'll start with his mother."

"Oh, yes, that sad woman."

"I never found her sad, Mother. I always found her to be a bitter, selfish bitch."

"Self-absorbed people tend to be so very bitter most of the time, don't they? And that's sad."

"You're a wise woman, Mother." *A lousy cook but a wise woman.*

Percy headed for the hallway. "I put a bag on the telephone table in the foyer, Mother," she threw over her shoulder. "Let it be until I get back."

"Where are you off to, Persephone dear?"

"Our local library. I should be back in an hour. And come lock the door behind me."

Chapter Twenty-three

"Good evening, Mrs. Cobb. I'm looking for the telephone numbers and addresses of residents in Grand Rapids, Michigan and can't find them. Have they been moved?"

Percy kept her voice barely loud enough for the librarian to hear. Mrs. Cobb was a thin-faced woman with dyed black hair, wearing large turquoise earrings. Painted red lips smiled at Percy.

"Hello, Persephone." Mrs. Cobb lowered her voice before going on. "I haven't seen you here for quite a while. I was beginning to think you didn't like us anymore. How often have I heard you say a detective's best friend was the library?"

"Where time and eyestrain usually get you results. Unfortunately, I've been busy, and haven't had much time to come here."

"Well, welcome back. As to the information you require, yes, all the telephone books have been moved to the QQ shelves near the back of references. We've had to make room for a small recruiting center. Of course, with the war and all, we don't have as many books as we normally do. Probably the latest phone book we have is 1941."

"That'll have to do."

"Yes, we all must do our part for the war effort. I can't tell you when we've had a new "Women's Illustrated" magazine in here. It must be six-months." Mrs. Cobb picked up a stack of books to set in order and flashed Percy a big smile. "Be sure to give your family my best."

"You bet." Percy returned her smile and moved away to the reference section.

Percy crossed the faintly lit library, smelling of musty books and wood wax. Her boots clicked against the dark oak floor, as she entered the section of the library she hadn't been in for several months.

Ceiling high rows of books filled with every known subject just waited for someone to browse through them. But no one else was there except her.

Sometimes I think my best friend in the world is Ben Franklin. If he hadn't invented the public library, I don't know what I'd do.

Thirty-minutes later she dialed a number from one of the payphones in the lobby of the library. A tired voice answered on the fifth ring.

"Hello?"

"Mrs. Donovan? This is Percy Cole." There was still air then Percy heard the escape of breath on the other end of the line.

"What do you want?" The voice was now harsh and high pitched.

"I need to speak to Leo. Do you have a phone number or an address where I could reach him?"

"You broke his heart." The woman began to sob. "You threw him away and you broke his heart."

"He left when he found out I was pregnant with Oliver. I --"

"You're a wicked, wicked girl."

"Mrs. Donovan, he even signed papers giving up custody of --"

"You killed him," the woman interrupted. "You killed him, sure as if you drove a stake through his heart." Her faint Irish lilt made the words all the more chilling.

"Killed? You mean Leo's dead?"

"These three years now. Drank himself to ruin because of you. Drove his car right into a tree. You did that. You!"

"Where did this happen, Mrs. Donovan? Where was --"

But the line went dead. Percy stood for a long time holding the receiver. Then she hung up, pivoted, and went back into the library.

* * * *

"Hutchers? It's Percy."

"What's wrong?"

Percy had never called Hutchers at home. He was grateful. Since the divorce, his children hardly ever visited him, but she knew he liked knowing there would never be a question of another woman telephoning him at home, except their mother.

"You don't sound so good, Perce."

"Just tired. I was at the library until it closed a few minutes ago. Checking a lot of things. I'm home now."

"Your voice is hardly more than a whisper. What's up?"

"Listen, Ken, you need to do me a favor."

"'Ken'? You never called me Ken in your life."

"Well, I'm calling you that now."

"Okay, okay. Don't get testy. What do you need?"

"I want you to look up anything you can on a Leonard Donovan, born 1907 in Grand Rapids, Michigan. There's a time issue here, and I know you can get the information faster than I can. I'm told he died in a car accident three years ago."

"Who says he did?"

"His mother."

"She should know."

"Maybe. But before I tell Oliver his father is dead, I want to know for sure."

"Oliver's father?"

"Yeah."

The line went silent for a moment. Hutchers let out a long breath.

"Sure. Leonard Donovan, 1907, Grand Rapids, Michigan. I'll get right on it tomorrow morning." He paused. "You going to be okay, Perce?"

"That's the plan. You hear anything more about the case?"

"I know Bogdanovitch ain't showed up yet and they put out an APB on him. I heard it on the squawk box about an hour ago."

"Don't you ever take a night off?" Her voice changed, becoming less constricted and friendlier.

"I took a night off once in 1937. Didn't know what to do with myself."

They both laughed softly.

"Thanks for doing this, Hutchers."

"Aw, forget it."

"No. I can't forget this. Thank you."

"I'll get on it first thing tomorrow morning."

"And mum's the word."

Percy wrapped her hand around the cradle and pushed down, ending the call. Deep in thought, she clutched the phone for a moment, resting the heavy receiver on her shoulder, fingers still depressing the disconnect button.

Chapter Twenty-four

How long she sat, she couldn't be sure. The sound of the ringing phone startled Percy, bringing her back to the present. She looked at her watch. Ten minutes after eight. She'd hung up on Hutchers only minutes before. Did he think of something? Did he find out anything so soon?

She didn't answer with the usual business patter but muttered a stark, "Hello?"

"Miss Cole, it's Fred Rendell." His voice had an urgent quality to it.

"What is it?"

"I found the paintings. Livingston Art Gallery. They weren't in the backroom of the gallery, with the rest of the art. They were stuffed in the boiler room."

"You're sure?"

"Yes ma'am, stashed behind shelving, naked as a jaybird in their frames. Shame, expensive artwork like that in a boiler room."

"I'm sure that's only temporary housing, at best. What made you think to look there?"

"They were acting pretty squirrely when I was looking for the gas leak, didn't let me go anywhere on my own. I unlocked the back door off the alley when they weren't looking, waited 'til they closed, and snuck back in. Found the art not ten minutes ago."

"Smart thinking. Where are you now?"

"Across the street in a phone booth, but I got a good view of the alley. A truck pulled in when I was dialing you.

Two men went inside, only the gallery's been closed for over an hour. I don't know if they're there to take the paintings --"

"Good chance they are. Paintings don't do so well in dry, hot places. These people know that. Odds are they're moving them tonight, probably right now."

"Yes, ma'am. That crossed my mind."

"Rendell, go get the license plate number of the truck. And if you can, let the air out of one of the back tires. But don't let them see you. I'll be there in twenty minutes. I'll flash my lights twice. Look for me."

Percy depressed the disconnect button again. She thought for a moment, picked up a card, and dialed a number written on it.

"Let me speak to Mr. Sheppard." She listened for a moment. "Gone where?" She listened again. "The Opera? I'm sure he has box seats in the Golden Horseshoe. Anybody who's anybody does. I want you to call the Metropolitan Opera House and have this message sent to him in his box on the double, it's urgent. Got a pencil? No? I'll wait." She paused. "Got one now? Good. Here's the message: Meet me outside at intermission. I need to see you. Pablo might be with me. Signed, Percy Cole. Read it back to me." She listened again. "Good. Now call the Met and see he gets the message right away. There's five bucks in it for you. Thanks."

* * * *

Percy parked about thirty yards away from the back of the Livingston Art Gallery. She had a good view of the back door of the gallery, as it was lit by a streetlight. She signaled twice with her lights then got out of the car.

Out of the darkness, Rendell ambled toward her, his lit cigarette announcing his arrival.

"That was fast, Miss Cole. You made it in about fifteen."

"I had the lights. What's going on?"

"Nothing yet. I did go back about five minutes ago, chanced it, and opened the back door. I heard hammering, so I skedaddled."

"Good. Let's go."

Followed by Rendell, she crossed the empty street on an angle heading for the backside of the gallery.

"For our purposes, it's a good thing this section of the city is filled with nine to five businesses." She withdrew the German Mauser her uncle gave her from her coat pocket. "It's pretty deserted now."

"You think you're going to need that?" Rendell's voice was filled with surprise, rather than fear.

"Never know. These paintings are worth plenty."

"Freezing out here."

Rendell blew on his hand and wrapped his wool scarf tighter around his neck. They stood in the shadows, half protected from the blustery weather, and about thirty yards away from the dark paneled truck.

"Wonder what they're doing in there all this time, ma'am?"

"I would say they're still crating up the paintings for a nice long trip, but the paintings aren't going as far as they think they are. I see you let the air out of both back tires."

"Yes, ma'am. If anything's worth doing, it's worth doing well."

"You bet."

The gallery door to the alley opened forcing Percy and Rendell to back up into the recesses of the night. A horsey head attached to a skinny neck popped out of the doorway and looked both ways. The blue-white lighting of the street lamp took all the coloring out of his face. The rest of the man's body emerged, struggling with a large, but narrow rectangular crate.

He was followed by another man of a similar build carrying a smaller crate. As they huffed to the back of the truck, the first man noticed the flat tire on his side.

"What the hell?" He set the crate down, leaning it against the truck.

"What is it, Tom?" The other man also leaned his burden against the truck.

"A flat tire." The first man hit the side of the truck in frustration. "Of all the damned luck!"

Percy stepped from the shadows, aiming the Mauser at them.

"Your luck's run out, gentlemen."

Both men wheeled around as one and gaped at her.

"Just stay where you are, don't make a move, and nobody'll get hurt."

"What the --" the man named Tom said. He made a gesture of a move toward her.

"Don't do it, Tom," Percy warned. "I'll shoot you as sure as I'm standing here."

Tom froze in place, his face registering perplexity and anger. The man standing behind Tom leaned into him. "I told you it wouldn't work. I told you we couldn't get away with --"

"Shut up, Bill." Tom turned back to Percy. His face now wore a smug look.

"You can't prove nothing, lady. You don't know what we got in those crates. You better get out of here before I --"

"We got paintings in those crates, Tom," said Bill with a confused air. "We did it together, remember?"

"I told you to shut up, didn't I?" Tom turned on his brother, who cowered back in fear.

"Gentlemen, gentlemen," said Percy in a loud voice. "I must insist you clam up or I'm going to be forced to start shooting, just for a little peace and quiet." Both men turned back to her and stared, saying nothing. "That's better. Now here's what's going to happen. You two are going to sit down on the ground, take off your shoes and trousers, and hand them over."

"What?" Tom blustered. "I'm not going to do that, you fat old crow. I'll--"

"I'm afraid you are. Or I'm going to haul your scraggy butts off to the nearest police station for grand theft. Should be about twenty years for that. Now sit."

She gestured with the gun to the ground. Both men lowered themselves to the ground and began to take off their shoes.

"Meanwhile, Rendell, go get the third painting from inside. Should be fairly close by."

Rendell crossed behind Percy and entered the back door.

"That's the Renoir. Be careful with it," hollered Tom.

"I'm sure you packed it well," said Percy.

"It's freezing out here, lady. You going to leave us in nothing but our skivvies?" Bill's voice rose to a plaintive wail.

"I am. But if I were you, Tom, Bill, after we leave, I would get in the truck and turn the heater on. Or drive the truck back home with the two flat tires. It'll take you awhile, but you'll get there. Those aren't bad options, considering the third is jail time."

"Wait a minute," said Tom. "You're not turning us in; you're stealing the paintings for yourself?"

"Something like that." Percy heard a noise coming from inside the doorway. "How you doing, Rendell?"

"Got it," said Rendell, crossing the threshold with a narrow crate in his hands. "This is heavy, though. Weighs a good fifty pounds."

"Must be hard to carry with only one hand, pervert." Tom's voice matched the sneer on his face. By this time both men had removed their shoes and were pulling off their trousers.

Without saying a word, Rendell set the crate down, leaned it against the side of the building and went to stand in front of the man sitting on the ground. With his left hand, he slapped Tom across the face so hard, the man fell backwards against the cold cement.

"But that one hand still works pretty good," Rendell said. He turned away and once again heaved the crate to his chest then crossed the street to Percy's car.

"Okay, you two," said Percy, "throw your trousers to land at my feet." They tossed their pants to the ground in front of her. "Now roll over and lie down on your tummies, like good little boys."

Both men rolled over on their stomachs. Percy reached down with one hand and pulled the belts out of both sets of trousers.

"I'll get you for this, bitch," said Tom.

"Don't rile her, Tom," said Bill.

"Yeah, don't rile me, Tom," said Percy with a laugh. "I might take your socks."

Rendell returned from the car. He stood watching the scene before him with a smile on his face. Percy thrust her gun into Rendell's hand.

"Here, you hold this while I truss them up like last year's Thanksgiving turkey. If they move, shoot them. I want to get out of here. I'm getting cold."

"Yes ma'am. Shoot them if they move; got it. It'll be my pleasure," said Rendell, aiming the gun at the two men lying on the ground.

"Gentlemen," said Percy to Tom and Bill. "Kindly put your hands together behind your backs." When they didn't move, her voice took on a harder edge. "Do it!"

They obeyed and she put a foot on Tom's back, wrapped one of the belts around his hands and pulled tight.

"Now you, Bill." She did the same thing then stepped back.

"The way I see it, you should be free of those belts in about fifteen minutes. You'll be good and cold, but consider it penance for trying to steal from your brother."

"How'd you know--" asked Tom. Then he stopped himself.

"There isn't much I don't know. So you think about that the next time you consider a life of crime. Mama's watching you."

She looked over at Rendell who was enjoying this as much as she was. She winked at him with a smile and gestured for the gun. He winked back as he handed it over.

"You get the Picasso, I'll get the Matisse," she said to Rendell.

She turned to Tom. "And the word pervert does not mean a handicapped person, you moron."

She huffed the crate to her bosom and walked to her car. Rendell followed with his heavy load.

"Rendell, I'm surrounded by people who never crack open a Webster Dictionary. It's enough to make a grown woman cry."

"Yes ma'am," he said with a laugh.

With a little work, they slid the crates into the backseat of Ophelia.

"Nothing like a big old roomy car, Rendell."

"Where to now?"

"Next stop, the Metropolitan Opera House."

Chapter Twenty-five

After a night with very little sleep, Percy rose early, kissed her sleeping son good-bye, wrote a reminder note for Mother about no more mashed potato and grape jelly sandwiches for Oliver, and left.

She drove to a service station near Orchard Street and paid the outrageous sum of seventeen cents a gallon. After spending one of her hard-earned dollars gassing up, she headed for Brooklyn.

Saturday's traffic was slight and she arrived in the neighborhood sooner than she expected, at exactly seven-thirty. Behind the factory was an empty lot that seemed to belong to no one. Percy pulled in.

Comprised of gravel, dirt, and frozen weeds, it was a good place for her to keep her car nearby but out of the way of prying eyes. When she wanted people to know she was there, she'd tell them.

After parking next to the battered chain link fence, she got out of the car and went around to the front of the store. She withdrew a set of keys she'd lifted from Bogdanovitch's desk the day before, the opportunity presenting itself during her chat with Hutchers.

Percy opened the front door and turned around to see if she was being watched. She'd be the first to tell anyone, a good dose of paranoia never hurt any detective.

Once inside, she locked the door and moved behind the glass counter. Her hand struck at the light switch, as she pushed aside the red and pink curtain and looked into the large room, empty and mute.

Percy felt uncharacteristically on edge. Something didn't feel right, but she couldn't put her finger on what that was.

She dropped the curtain, sat down, and set the brown paper bag she'd brought with her on the desk. At odds with herself, she picked up the spindle of papers, avoiding the needle sharp point. Twirling it in her hand for a moment, she watched the papers flutter in the wake.

A quick look through the orders showed nothing out of the ordinary. They were standard, written on a form with the amount, date of delivery, and who took the order. Either the name Schatzi or Regina signed off on each one.

Percy stood. The feeling of uneasiness continued to wash over her. She wasn't sure if it was the news she'd learned about Leo the Louse or something else. While she wasn't one who believed in the supernatural, she knew sometimes things registered in the subconscious that didn't come to the surface right away.

She pushed back the saucy red and pink curtain again, closed her eyes, and visualized how everything had looked in the large room the morning before, down to what was in the lockers. When she had labeled things in her mind, she opened her eyes and stepped into the large production room, surveying each corner thoroughly. Then she saw it.

Hurrying across the floor toward the freezer, off-limits to anyone save Bogdanovitch, she pulled at the padlock resting underneath the hasp, a little lower than it would have been had it been snapped into place. The movement caused the lock to swing from side to side. Removing it with nervous fingers and freeing the hasp from the strike plate, she flung the door open wide.

A blast of frigid air struck her in the face. Percy looked down at the frozen body of Ronald Bogdanovitch, hands bloodied from beating on the inside of the freezer door.

Chapter Twenty-six

Dear Diary,

I had no choice but to do what I did. The man was becoming a liability. I'm not worried, though. Let's see what the cops and Percy Cole's next move will be. As Sherlock Holmes would say, 'The game's afoot.'

Chapter Twenty-seven

After nearly three hours of sitting, Percy moved around in the hard, wood chair looking for a way to get more comfortable. She knew it wasn't possible. That's why the cops chose these chairs, an extra inducement to confessing.

After she found Bogdanovitch, she'd gone to his office and called the cops, who arrived minutes later. Shortly after, Lieutenant Griffin hauled her down to the police station for a lot of sitting in his empty office.

Now Lieutenant Griffin returned and stared at her, his eyes almost slits in his head. He leaned forward at his desk, a desk far too messy for Percy's taste. The more organized her desk, the more organized her mind, but everybody worked differently. 'To each his own', said Mrs. O'Leary, before she kissed the cow.

"So you're saying this was no accident, somebody killed him?"

"Yes, Bogdanovitch was killed by the same person who killed Carlotta. And it couldn't have been Goldberg. You got him locked up, remember?"

The lieutenant looked at her, working his mouth, as if he had something to say, but didn't quite know what that was. Spittle gathered in the corners, and finally he spoke.

"Ah, you're crazy. He accidentally locked himself in the freezer, for cripes sakes. Case closed."

Saliva sprayed on the desk and on Percy's resting hand. Percy looked down at her hand.

"I hope you don't have anything. This is how people spread germs."

"You got more worries than me having cooties, lady. If you think somebody locked him in the freezer, maybe it was you. And maybe you came back to make sure it did its job. You wouldn't be the first killer reporting a body that turned out to be the one who done him in. If you don't level with me, I'm going to lose my temper and send you to the big house for life."

Percy sat back in her chair, stretched, and stared at him with a smile on her face. "Do they actually call prison the 'big house' or did you get that from a James Cagney movie?"

"You're going to be laughing out of the other side of your face when I get done with you." He leaned in again. "So why'd you say he's been done in?"

"For the tenth time, before I could open the door to the freezer, I had to take off the lock and pull back the hinged part of the hasp that was closed over the slot. For those of you that are slow learners – no names - there's no way he could have done that himself from inside the freezer." She thought for a moment. "The lock looked closed to the naked eye. Somebody did that on purpose. You got to admit, that's interesting."

"What's interesting about it?"

"Why not lock it for real? Why the ruse? I get the feeling someone's playing with me; like I'm being tested on my observation skills."

Piercing eyes met his watery ones. The expression on her face invited him to think about or comment on what she'd said. He blinked several times before he spoke, but changed the subject.

"How'd you get into the building? You broke in, didn't you?"

"Like I said before, I used the keys Bogdanovitch gave me. Here they are." She jingled the keys in the man's face then returned them to her pocket. "And I showed you the written agreement between him and me."

"Well, it looks like his handwriting but it's a damned fool thing to do."

"Maybe, but I had every right to be there. I called you as soon as I found him, like the law-abiding citizen I am. And I also gave you that paper bag with the chocolate-covered smock in it I found yesterday in a garbage can not a half a block from the factory."

"So?"

"So what do you need, Griffin, a brick wall to fall on you? The smock wouldn't even fit Goldberg's big toe. A thinner person wore it. The killer."

"Sez you."

Percy shook her head in disbelief. "It's a round robin we're having here and I'll pass on the next round. So where's this cousin? The one inheriting everything? Show up yet?"

"On a train from Chicago. Should be here by Monday morning, if the snow don't stall everything."

"Oh, yeah? What's been going on out there while I've been stuck in here for the past three hours?"

"It's snowing." He made a sneer, upturning one side of his mouth.

"You look funny when you do that. Well, I got to go build me a snowman." She stood, reached for her coat, and picked up her hat.

"You ain't going nowhere until I say so."

"Either arrest me for something or get out of my way."

They stood in a face-off when the door burst open and an older, balding officer, dressed in a too-tight uniform, hurried into the room. He thrust a note in the Lt.'s hand.

Lieutenant Griffin read the note through carefully and looked up at Percy. "Well, you got friends in high places."

"Do I? News to me."

"This Jude Cole is your brother, right?"

Percy shrugged noncommittally.

"Well, he seems to have a few pals in the D.A.'s office. You're free to go. For now. But I'll be seeing you."

"In all the old familiar places?"

"What's that?" He gave her a puzzled look.

"It's the second stanza of the song, "I'll Be Seeing You." Written by Sammy Fain and Irving Kahal. 1938. Going to be one of the war's most popular songs, you mark my words."

"I never heard of it."

"You never heard of a lot of things, you lummox. Doesn't mean they don't exist."

In frustration, he turned his back on her and shouted over his shoulder, "Ah, get out of here."

Percy let out a laugh. "On my way."

She hummed a few bars of "I'll Be Seeing You," as she pushed open the door and exited the police station.

Chapter Twenty-eight

In the three plus hours she had been inside the Ninetieth Precinct, a heavy snow steadily fell and continued. She crossed the street, the crunch of her boots in the snow being the only sound she could hear. She loved the fact that soft, falling snow had a way of deadening sounds in an urban setting.

If she closed her eyes, she could feel as if she was in the country again, the two-weeks in the winter of '33 she'd spent on her honeymoon. Snowbound in the Catskills. It had been lovely.

Percy was surprised at her train of thought. She hadn't reflected on her time with Leo the Louse in years. Whatever feelings she'd had about that time, her love for him, she'd learned to squelch years before.

With annoyance, Percy pulled herself together and passed the freestanding telephone booth, even though she was sure it was working. Being directly across from a police station made the odds in her favor. But three-hours was a long time to be away from the job, so she trudged the six-blocks back to the chocolate factory.

On the way she contemplated the site. Now the building was totally hers, but what would it be like on Monday? Would sharing it with the employees going about the business of chocolate making impede her investigation?

When she arrived, she looked more like a giant snowman than a woman. Percy shook the snow from her body, stamped her boots, and reached for the door.

Climbing the stairs to the office, she studied the seemingly peaceful scene below her, where two people had died in less than forty-eight hours. After the fiasco with the lock, she was worried she'd overlooked something else.

For now, searching Bogdanovitch and Carlotta's desks for the employee files and reading them was paramount. She should have a lot of peace and quiet, what with both users dead. But first, some phone calls.

After two short rings, her mother answered the phone. "Cole Brothers Detective Agency, Mrs. Cole speaking."

Not said in the most professional tone, Percy thought, but certainly better than she'd come to expect. Mother tended to stammer and stutter, uncomfortable with using the 'new fangled' telephone most of the time.

"It's me, Mother. How's everything there? How's Oliver doing?"

"Oh, Persephone! I'm so glad you called. Oliver is just fine, playing in the backyard with Freddie and the dog. But the phone has been ringing off the hook for you. Now where did I put that list? Just a minute."

Before Percy could reply, she heard the clunk of the phone hitting the desk and shuffling of paper. She waited patiently. Finally, Mother returned.

"Are you still there, dear?"

"I'm here, Mother."

"All right. Let me marshal my thoughts. First of all, a man named Mr. Sheppard called twice. The first time he just left his phone number. Then the second time he called, he said to tell you, and I'm reading this from my notes, dear..."

Mother broke off and cleared her throat before reading.

"*All is well. Pablo and friends are back on wall, and a check is in the mail with an extra fifty to show appreciation.*"

Mother went on. "Now just who is this Pablo? The name sounds Spanish. I hope it means something to you, Persephone. It doesn't to me. I don't know any Spanish people unless you count the cook at the corner restaurant, who puts too many hot peppers in the red sauce."

"Sheppard is indicating he's happy with the job we did. Instead of two hundred for the job, we're getting two-fifty. I'll call him later today with my thanks and a reminder he owes his butler a nickel-note."

"He owes his butler five dollars! What a generous man Mr. Sheppard is."

"He doesn't have much to say about it," Percy said with a laugh. "What else?"

"That nice Mr. Rendell, you know, Freddie's father, called. He said he was just checking in, and on his way to the hotel."

"When?"

"When what, dear?"

"How long ago did he call?"

"About a half an hour ago. I remember, because I was just opening a can of pineapples when the phone rang. Such a lovely shade of yellow, Persephone. So bright! And all the way from Hawaii. Although I don't know how they keep it fresh in the can for such a long trip. Sailing over all that water."

"It's a heating and storing process, Mother, similar to you putting up your marmalade jam."

"I haven't done that for years, dear. We can never get enough oranges now." She clucked her tongue. "This war, this war," she lamented.

"Yeah, it's tough. Go on."

"Your beau called."

"Mother, if you mean Hutchers, he is not my beau. What did he want?"

"He said to call him as soon as possible. He says it's urgent. He even gave me a number for you to call right away."

"Why didn't you say so?"

"Well, I just did, Persephone."

"I mean, why didn't you start with...never mind. What's the number?"

"Oh, dear. I ran out of room on this paper. I must have written it down somewhere else. Just a minute, dear. I'll find it."

The sound of more shuffling could be heard on the other end of the line. Percy tried to stay calm.

"Here it is, dear. GRamercy 3-6711 or is it 6911? Oh, dear. I can't make it out. Well, it's one or the other."

"Got both of them, Mother. Thanks. Is that it?"

"Yes, other than Goldbergs' wanting to know how things are going. They say they don't want to bother you, but hope Howard will be home soon. How is that going, dear?"

"I'm working on it."

"You can't be more specific, Persephone dear?"

"Not really."

"Oh, dear."

"I'll drop by the Goldbergs' place when I get home and talk to them, if it's not too late. Best I can do, Mother. I have to go now, make a few calls."

"All right, dear. Pineapple cabbage for dinner tonight. Just want to whet your appetite."

"Can't wait." Percy smiled into the phone despite herself. "By the way, when Rendell calls back, give him this number, Mother. NIghtingale 9-3939. Write that down, okay?"

"NIghtingale 9-3939." Mother's voice was obliging, if not slow.

"That would be NI. Why don't you read it back to me?"

"NI 9-3939. It's in Brooklyn. Right, dear?"

"It is. Thanks, Mother." Percy disconnected and tried the first number of the two given to her for Hutchers. He answered right away.

"Detective Hutchers, here."

"It's Percy."

"Yeah," he said. "Hold on." He shouted to someone nearby. "Phil, I'm going to take this call in the back room. Hang this up for me when I get there."

Percy waited until she heard an extension pick up, the murmur of voices, and another disconnect. Any feelings of fatigue or cold Percy had moments before were now gone in her anxiety over what urgent information Hutchers wanted to share.

"There, now we got no prying ears to worry about," Hutchers said.

"What's up?"

"I've been looking into this accident that killed your ex-husband, Perce."

"Call him Oliver's father."

"Sure, sure. Anyway, the more I been digging, the fishier the whole thing looks."

"Like what?"

"Like how much do you know about the accident?"

"Nothing. Heard about it yesterday."

"Okay, so September seventeenth, 1939, Leonard Donovan wraps himself around a tree. The car bursts into flames and he's burned to a crisp. Supposedly."

"Why supposedly?"

"You hear about dental records?"

"Sure. Used mostly in Europe and recently by the Army."

"They're starting to use them more and more in police cases here. Especially, where there's no identification they can find. It was Donovan's car. It was a man about his age and build. But when they tried to do a dental match, it didn't."

"Go on."

"Then his mother said he was in a skiing accident a year before, had some oral surgery done, and it wasn't going to match. But she couldn't remember the name of the dentist or where he was. He was on vacation, she said."

"They think she was lying?"

"Could be. That's what the attending officer's notes say."

"Was Leo in some kind of trouble?"

"Not that they know of, but he could have been a draft dodger. He'd been contacted three times to appear at a draft station and never did. I didn't tell you the most damning part yet."

"Shoot."

"Two weeks later, somebody used his driver's license to rent a car turned in over the Canadian border. You have to admit, that looks suspicious."

"Did they reopen the case?"

"Naw. They didn't find any of this out; I did. I just put it together today. This whole thing is another casualty of the war effort. We've got fifty-three percent of our men fighting overseas. I'd be there myself if it wasn't for my asthma. We can't do all the cross-checking we'd like to."

"His wallet could have been thrown from the car, found by somebody else who used his driver's license to rent a car to get to Canada."

"True enough. Or Donovan could have killed someone, put the body in the car, and staged the whole thing to get out of serving. Men have been known to do that."

"Hutchers, Leo the Louse was just that, but the man I knew would never kill somebody and put them in a burning car."

"Maybe. Maybe not."

"You need to resurrect this, Hutchers?"

"Might have to. Murder is murder."

"Fair enough. Give me a couple of days before you do anything. Then it's up to you."

"Fair enough. It waited this long. It can wait two more days."

Percy hung up the phone and put her head down on the cold, hard wood of the desk. Oliver's father a murderer. She did not want it go that way.

Rising, she crossed to the one window in the office with a view overlooking the parking lot. The other side of the icy glass showed an almost idyllic scene, not at all what was out there in reality.

The falling snow had blanketed the city's streets, sidewalks, trash cans, fireplugs, and vehicles in a velvety white. Everything that normally had ready identification now looked like the hills and vales of a wintry wonderland. On a personal note, somewhere in those lumps was Ophelia, buried under drifts of snow.

Sitting back down at the desk, Percy redialed her friend at the police station. He answered on the first ring. Without any preamble, she said,

"Hutchers, check out dentists in the Catskills. It was one of his favorite places to go."

There was a pause. "Okay, will do."

"Thanks." She hung up.

Chapter Twenty-nine

Dear Diary,

I don't trust this Percy Cole. She's got brains, but I've set it up where she'll never figure it out. Nonetheless, I'll watch her. If necessary, I'll do more than watch. She won't stand in the way of what is rightfully mine.

Chapter Thirty

Spread out papers, manila envelopes, and account books littered the tops of both desks. Percy had learned some interesting things about Carlotta as a person and employer.

Her weak spot was a good looking man. Occasionally, she bowed down to someone with a superior knowledge of chocolate, such as Howie. But other than that, she was pretty hard-nosed, with high, unforgiving standards, for which she paid her staff as little as possible.

Consequently, there were constant turnovers for all but a few positions. Most that held on were recent immigrants, those who felt lucky to have any job at all, even one working for a tyrant.

Regarding the employees, the two working the front desk were of interest. In particular, they made more money than the others. Not much, but more. Was it their English skills or something else?

Regina Mason had no references or previous employers. In her file, Carlotta noted she didn't like Regina, yet gave the girl a job, anyway. Also, the mention of Regina being adopted, the word underlined, struck Percy as an odd thing to add to an employee's file.

The other was the girl nicknamed Schatzi, who lived in the Bronx. A far piece to travel, especially for a job that paid better than the others, but only so-so. Was this the woman Bogdanovitch said Carlotta hired to keep close?

I'll get to her later.

She dialed a phone number. Percy was about to hang up, when an out of breath, young female voice answered.

"Hello?"

"You got a Regina Mason there?"

"Just a minute." The voice bellowed, as if she were out at a ballpark screaming for a hotdog. "Ginny! Somebody wants to talk to you. And stop getting so many calls here. I'm not your answering service."

The sound of a receiver being dropped on its cord and thudding against a wall several times led Percy to believe she'd called a rooming house with one payphone in a hallway for boarders.

A tremulous voice said, "Hello?"

"Miss Mason, this is Persephone Cole, private investigator. I've been hired by Mr. Bogdanovitch to do some investigating into Carlotta Mendez's death."

Percy heard a sharp intake of breath. She had no intention of mentioning Bogdanovitch's recent demise. It wouldn't be in the papers until the following day. And if the employees thought he was alive, Percy had more leverage.

"Miss Mason, you still there?"

"Yeah, yeah. What do you want?"

"I'd like a few minutes of your time. Just a few questions. You live about three blocks from the factory, right?"

"So what? It's Saturday and it's snowing."

"So we can do this either here in the office or down at headquarters. Your call."

It was a bluff, a big one, but they often panned out for Percy. She felt the woman's hesitation on the other end of the line. She pushed.

"Fifteen minutes of your time, Miss Mason, and then you're free. The front door's open. Just come on in."

"All right, all right. I was going out to buy some cigs, anyway. I can be there in about ten minutes."

Percy hung up and made two other fast calls, one right after the other. Then she rose and crossed the room to a two-burner hotplate, newish and rather spiffy. On one of the shelves above, she found some ground coffee, cups, and a coffee pot. She went to a small sink in the corner, ran some water, and put on a pot of coffee.

The phone rang. She snatched at it, leaning over the desk.

"Yes?"

"Miss Cole, Fred Rendell here. I'm in the apartment."

"Have any trouble getting in?"

"No ma'am. It cost me a fiver for the bellboy uniform, but it fits well enough. Took the master keys for this floor from one of the hooks in the laundry room."

"Find anything?"

"No clothes hanging, nothing in the drawers. Place is clean as a whistle, except for a few dirty dishes in the sink, and a little trash in the can in the bathroom. I don't think the maid's been in yet."

"What's been left, specifically? Go look and then describe every item to me. Don't leave anything out."

"Yes ma'am." He set the receiver down and was gone for the better part of a minute. "Okay, in the sink are two cups and saucers, looks like they were filled with tea. On the counter is a teapot and a bowl."

"Tea in the pot?"

"Yes ma'am. Not much, though, and none too fresh. Getting a film on top."

"So it looks like Helena Wilson has been gone for a day or two."

"Yes ma'am."

"What was in the bowl?"

"Nothing but a little water."

"Lipstick on one of the cups?"

"Yes ma'am."

"What color?"

"Ah...red?"

"You're there, Rendell. You should know. Is it red lipstick on the cup?"

"Yes ma'am."

"What shade of red?"

"Shade? I thought red was red."

"This is no time to be a man, Rendell. Be a detective. Red comes in a lot of shades, orange, pink, purple. Which is it?"

"Purple, I would say. A purplish red. And a lot of it, too."

"What about the trash can?" She heard sounds of movement and a hollow swishing sound.

"Not much. Just some face tissues at the bottom. Two of them."

"Any lipstick on the tissue?"

"Yes ma'am. Purple red. And a few strands of long, blonde hair, almost white."

"Same color as Jean Harlow?"

"The actress? Yes."

"Very good. Is there a desk?

"Yes ma'am."

"There should be hotel stationary in one of the drawers. Find an envelope; put the strands of hair in it and one of the tissues with lipstick stains. Save them for me. Then you'd better high tail it out of there, Rendell. Go on home before the snow catches you. And put whatever you spent on this expedition on the tab."

Chapter Thirty-one

"Hello? Anybody here?"

Percy heard the woman's voice call into the vacuum of the empty room below, echoing off the high ceiling. She stepped out of the office and onto the landing.

"Up here Miss Mason."

Percy waved and went back into the office. She poured herself a cup of coffee, strong and hot, and took an appreciative sip. By that time, the door to the office opened. She turned to see a young woman in her early twenties, thick dark hair pulled back in a chignon. Attractive, almost foreign looking, the woman stared at her in open defiance.

"Want some coffee?" Percy gestured with her own cup.

"No. What do you want?"

Percy shrugged. "Suit yourself. Pretty good beans, especially with what you can get these days. Sit down."

She gestured with the cup again to one of the empty chairs. Even though Percy had found most of the information she'd wanted in Carlotta's desk, she was sitting at Bogdanovitch's. Gave off the edge of power.

Regina Mason flounced over to the chair much the way her sister, Sera, did when she was forced to do something against her will. They were roughly the same age, and Percy wasn't put off by this type of behavior from the youngsters of today.

Regina Mason threw herself into the chair, leaned to the side, and crossed one leg over the other, bouncing her top leg in a steady rhythm. Snow dripped from the bottom of the rubber boot onto the floor.

Percy sat down and studied the younger woman who grew more uncomfortable under her gaze. Finally, the girl spoke.

"I haven't got all day. What do you want?"

"I want to know about your relationship with Carlotta Mendez."

"I worked for her. So what?"

"So it says here in Carlotta's notes that you were the daughter of a friend of hers."

"Yeah, that's right. They known each other since before I was born. So what?"

"And where was that?"

"Right here. New York. So what?"

"We're going to move along a lot faster if you stop saying 'so what?' after each answer. You're adopted, right?"

"Yeah. So..." Regina began to say, 'so what', thought better of it, and kept her mouth shut. "Lots of people are. It's not a crime," she added after a moment.

"True enough. What's your mother's maiden name?"

Regina turned and looked at Percy. "I'm not going to tell you. I'm not going to tell you anything more. And what are you going to do about it?"

A smug look crept across the girl's face. Percy shot up from her seat, slamming the nearly empty coffee cup on the desk.

"Listen here, Regina Mason. You are within a hair's breadth of being arrested for her murder. Some of the things Carlotta wrote about you in her files could be interpreted as a motive on your part."

Percy's exaggeration of the facts had the desired effect. The smirk gone, Regina sat upright, uncrossed her legs and stared at Percy, mouth wide open with astonishment.

"What are you talking about? That little guy, Howie, did it. The chocolate maker. It says so in all the papers."

"Don't believe everything you read in the papers. Besides, new evidence has come to light. You."

Percy came to the front of the desk, sat down on the edge, and leaned over the girl who shrank back. Percy crossed her arms over her chest and went on.

"Carlotta Mendez didn't like you, didn't trust you, and yet she hired you. That's not what most employers do. I want to know why."

"She knew my mother," Regina mumbled.

"So you said. But that doesn't explain why she gave you this job."

"I got into some trouble back home."

"Where's back home?"

"Rochester. Upstate."

"What kind of trouble?"

"I got...I got arrested for stealing something. I went to jail for six-months. They took my kid away. She's with my mother. I can't have her again until I can prove I can take care of her. So Carlotta gave me this job, 'cause Mom told her to. They're friends. Nobody else would."

"That's a pretty good friend. How did they meet?"

"They knew each other from when they were young. They met here in Manhattan. Mom did something for Carlotta, I don't know what, and Mom said she owed her. So when I needed help, she called Carlotta and asked her to give me this job. It stinks but it's better than nothing."

"What was your mother's maiden name?"

"Clancy. Iris Clancy. So what?"

"You like Carlotta? I know she didn't like you, but did you like her?"

Regina shrugged and looked away. "She was all right. She worked me hard, but she was fair most of the time."

She looked at Percy, eyebrows set low over her eyes. And Percy knew in that instant the girl was lying or leaving something important out.

"Interesting shade of lipstick. What's the name of it?"

My...my lipstick?" Clearly thrown, Regina stuttered when she answered. "I don't know. Blood Orchid, I think. Do you like it?"

"Nah, it's too purple for me. I like mine more orange, but that color looks good on you."

Exasperated, Regina Mason looked Percy directly in the eye. "What's the matter with you, lady?"

Percy uncrossed her arms and leaned in, breathing in the girl's face.

"Never mind what's the matter with me. You're the one on the hot seat. What kind of information did you or your mother use to make Carlotta Mendez give you a job?"

"Who says we used anything? You got a lot of nerve saying things like that. You got a lot of nerve."

"If you don't want me digging around in Rochester, you're going to tell me."

"You leave me alone! And don't you dare bother my mother in Rochester. She's had enough!" She leapt out the chair, and ran out of the room, slamming the door behind her.

Percy stared at the closed door. *"Enough of what, Ginny? What has your mother had enough of?"*

* * * *

There was a knock at the door.

"Come on in, Alf."

"Somebody called and said they got something for me?"

The man started talking before the door was fully opened. When he saw Percy sitting behind the desk, he froze.

"You! Why I oughta --" Alf was torn between fleeing and facing the woman he had come to dislike so intensely.

"Take it easy. Like I say, come on in. Take a load off, and I'll give you those bank statements back."

He stood his ground. "What do you mean, you'll give them back?"

"One good turn deserves another. Sit down." She gestured to a chair. "I'll even give you a good cup of coffee. One you won't see down at the local eatery."

Alf crossed the threshold, wary and on his guard. Halfway inside, he stopped.

"What you mean one good turn deserves another? What have I got you want? You can't have no money. I got plans --"

"Easy, Alf. I don't want your money. What I want is information. Now use your brains for once, come in, and sit down."

Alf obeyed and slowly sank down on the chair vacated not fifteen minutes earlier by Regina Mason. Percy got up, picked up a moderately clean cup, blew out the dust, and poured coffee into it.

"There's no milk. Got some sugar, but you look like a man who likes his coffee straight."

With a smile she set the steaming coffee in front of Alf. He stared at her, confusion clouding his face. He wrapped his hands around the cup, picked it up, snow dripping from his battered hat onto the already wet floor.

He took a deep, needy drink, never moving his eyes from the woman. Looking like he might bolt at any unwarranted move, Percy sat down again in a decided collegial manner.

"Relax, Alf, relax. Have a pistachio."

She pulled the small bag out of the hip pocket of her trousers, and tossed it over to his side of the desk. He eyed it narrowly, but continued drinking the coffee. Percy took another sip of her own coffee.

"Here's how I see it. You had no cause to kill Carlotta Mendez. She was your meal ticket; the golden goose. You were set to make a lot of money from her as long as she was alive."

He lowered the cup with shaking hands. "That's right. I had no cause to do her in."

"And you have a good deal going with Bogdanovitch on the side, selling black-market food and booze that's been stashed around here. Stuff that 'falls off the trucks' as they say. Nice piece of change selling them to la-dee-da restaurants on the Upper East Side."

His lower lip quivered. He was becoming nervous.

"Yeah, maybe. I don't get the bulk of it. I'm just the go-fer."

"Don't worry. What you and Bogdanovitch do is between the two of you. Just to show you what a nice gal I am, I'm going to overlook the two dozen lobsters in the freezer. They're yours for the taking."

She took the three deposit slips out of her pocket and waved them in front of him.

"Here's what I want, Alf. What you had on Carlotta. That's all you have to tell me. Then I give you back these slips, you take the crustaceans, and nobody's the wiser."

"I...I..." He stuttered, licked dry lips then was silent.

"I'll even throw in the cartons of Chianti hidden under the staircase. But that's as far as I'm going. Otherwise, you keep sitting on this, and I'll turn everything over to the cops. And it's back to the pen for you."

"I...I..."

"Come on, Alf. I'm giving you a good deal. Take it. Don't be a dope. What did you have on Carlotta Mendez?"

After a long hesitation, the words came tumbling out. "She had a kid. She had a bastard baby back when she was young. She didn't want nobody to know, but I found the birth certificate in the safe one day when I was --" He stopped talking and looked at her.

"Riffling through, looking for something valuable? I know you were a safecracker in your heyday. I thought it was likely you broke into Little Boy Blue."

"Yeah, well," he said with pride. "There ain't no safe I can't get into if I got enough time." He leaned forward, now completely relaxed, even boastful. "I been in there a couple of times when no one was around."

"You in there last night, early this morning?" He looked guilty, thrown off guard. "I can see the answer's yes. I didn't see any birth certificate when I went through things on the floor or in the safe."

"She was dead. What was she going to do with it?"

"Whereas you saw a chance of possibly making a little more dough. Why didn't you take it before? You knew about it for at least three months." He mumbled something. "What? Speak up."

"She caught me the first time, when I was reading it. She threatened to call the cops. I told her if she did, I'd blab it to the world. So we made a deal. I give her the certificate back, she gives me fifty bucks a month, and I keep my trap shut."

"Did you tell Bogdanovitch any of this?"

"Naw. I told him I couldn't get in the safe; it was too tough for me. I didn't want him to know. I had my deal with him on the side, like I did with her. Why should I split with him?

"Smart thinking."

"When I seen that certificate, especially with her pretending to be so sanctimonious and everything, I knew the gravy train had come to town." He looked at Percy's reaction to his words. "You surprised I found her uppity?"

"No, surprised you know what sanctimonious means."

"I heard it on that radio show, *Inner Sanctum*. You can learn a lot of stuff from the radio, if you just listen."

"That's Edward R. Murrow's point of view."

"He's that game show host, right?"

"Newsman. But go on, Alf."

More relaxed, he set down his empty coffee cup and acted as if Percy and he were trading secrets.

"You know she went to mass every morning? Every morning," he repeated. "Her with a bastard kid." He laughed, coughed, and shook his head. "Takes all kinds."

"Do you know if it was a girl or a boy?"

"A girl baby. Five pounds, eleven ounces."

"You've got a sharp memory."

"I should. I got the goods right here since I took it." He leaned over on one hip and slapped the elevated hip with his hand. Then he realized the implication of what he said. He shrank into the chair. "I gotta go. You give me the deposit slips like you promised and I'll be on my way."

Percy glared at him. "Not before you give me the birth certificate." She smiled. "After all, it's not going to do you any good, what with Carlotta being dead."

"Yeah, but there's the kid. Maybe I could..." He stumbled over his words, not sure of what his next step might be or if he should confess to it.

"You know who the kid is, Alf, other than her name? Do you know where she is? If she's still alive?"

He shook his head and looked bewildered, as if he hadn't thought it through.

"How are you going to find any of that out? Could take a lot of digging. Now the cops, they're good at digging. But if they find that certificate on you, they're going to think you had more to do with Carlotta's death than you did. You and I know you didn't, but cops are dumber." She sat back and gave him a knowing smile.

Trembling in the hard back chair, Alf sat for a moment, staring hard at the large woman behind the desk. Then he reached into his pocket and drew out a shabby leather wallet. He opened it, still staring at Percy. Almost as if hypnotized, He removed a small, square folded paper made thin by time.

He handed the certificate to Percy, who leaned forward and took it solemnly, also without taking her eyes off him. She handed him the three deposit slips. Then she winked at him.

"Now, don't it feel good to do the smart thing, Alf?"

"You mean what you say about the lobster and hooch, lady?"

"I always mean what I say, Alf."*Even when I don't.*

"You ain't going to tell the cops?"

She shook her head.

"You won't tell Bogdanovitch, neither?"

"Like he's no longer among the living, Alf."

"Good. Cause he won't like me holding out on him if he knew. He's got some mean friends."

Not any more, pal.

* * * *

"Thanks for coming, Vinnie. Sorry to get you out in this weather."

"No, no is the trouble. I live the close. And my wife, she needs *latte,* milk, for baby. I go out now because soon too hard to walk."

"The snow. Right. I didn't know you had a baby. How old?"

"*Il bambino di sei mesi,*" he said happily. Then Vinnie looked for the words in English. "Ahh...."

"Your son is six-months old?"

"*Si, si. Giuseppe.*" He looked at Percy expectantly.

She cleared her throat. This was harder than the others. She liked this man, felt sorry for him.

"You named him for your friend back in Italy. Nice. How old is your wife's niece?"

"She is the *quindici anni*...ah...fifteen years."

"She's very beautiful, your niece. That must sometimes cause some problems."

"Si, si." Vinnie's face took on a sad, haunted look. "That is not always the good. Sometimes..." His voice broke off and he looked away.

"Sometimes unscrupulous men take advantage of such a beautiful young girl. " Vinnie nodded but did not look at her. "Like Bogdanovitch."

Vinnie nodded again and wiped at eyes suddenly filled with tears. He fought back the emotions, but sat very still, with his head down. He let out a sob then covered it with a half cough.

"Why don't you tell me about it, Vinnie? When did you find out what he did to her?"

"Maria, she is my *moglie*... ah... my wife. Yesterday, she come to me when I am home from the work. She is sad. She has the heart ... how do you say...breaking?"

"Heart broken."

"*Si*. She say Teresa not go to school, but cry all the day. Then Maria tell me she see Teresa cry many nights for long time now, but never say why. But now Carlotta, she is dead, and Teresa scared. She think he, Bogdanovitch, do this terrible thing to Signora Carlotta. Maybe he kill her, too." He looked at Percy pleadingly. "So she tell us what he do to her. She never tell before because she has the shame."

"What he did to her was wrong, punishable by law in this state."

Vinnie nodded, twisting in the chair. Anger bubbled within him until he could sit no longer. He leapt up and began to pace the room.

"He spoil her life. This...child. He spoil her for her life. What good man want her now for wife? She is no longer a *vergine*. Her life is ruined."

"You found this out yesterday *after* Carlotta was murdered?"

"*Si!* When I find out, I want to kill this man. I kill him with my hands." He looked down at strong hands, tense and claw like. "So I come back here. I no care about the job. I rather sleep in the street than work for this man. He dishonor *la famiglia*."

"So you wanted to confront Bogdanovitch." He didn't answer but nodded. "And did you?"

Vinnie shook his head.

"He no here. I wait but then can no longer. I go home to the shame."

"I see. Your niece, Teresa, she a good girl?"

"She was. No longer."

"Not good in that way. I mean, as a person. Is she a good person?"

He nodded sadly. "She is dolce, sweet. Always. With *il bebe*, always the smile." He shook his head. "But the shame."

"I'm going to give you a piece of unsolicited advice, something I rarely do. Don't let Bogdanovitch destroy your life and that of your niece's any more than he already has. Being a good person is better than being a virgin. Virginity is just one night. Goodness is forever."

Vinnie stared at her in disbelief or astonishment, Percy couldn't tell which. She lost patience with him.

"Go on, get out of here, Vinnie. I got some thinking to do. And if any of the employees ask Monday, it's business as usual until further notice."

Chapter Thirty-two

Dear Diary,

The Cole woman is still sniffing around. I don't like this. She's smarter than I thought. Not as smart as me, but she might be troublesome. Maybe I need to deal with her. My plans are my plans and I will not let her ruin them.

Chapter Thirty-three

The three flights up the stairs were murder. Percy was already tired from trudging through deep snow drifts and fighting the wind from the subway station to the apartment building. Her thick boots were wet through, especially at the toes. She was cold, tired, hungry, and sad. She couldn't shake the heaviness of what Oliver might have to face in the near future.

She let out a sigh, shook the melting snow from her coat and hat, and tried the front door expecting it to be, once again, unlocked. This time she couldn't push it open and was pleasantly surprised. Maybe Mother actually listened to her elder daughter and locked the door.

Pulling out her keys, Percy could hear the muted strains of the radio playing Glenn Miller's *Don't Sit Under the Apple Tree with Anyone Else But Me* and looked at her watch. Seven-thirty. She visualized the events that usually take place right before this time.

Dinner would be over and Oliver in bed. Mother, having cleaned the kitchen, would be listening to the radio, waiting for one or both of her daughters to come home. The thought gave her a warm rush. After she unlocked the door, she pushed it open on silent, well-oiled hinges.

Percy shook the last of the wet snow off her coat before entering and hung it up on the coat rack just inside. She sloughed off her boots and crept on sodden socks down the hallway to her son's bedroom door.

A grin covered her face when she saw the bed holding her sleeping son, who smiled and twitched in his dreamland state. Even the dog lying stretched out beside him, seemed to be smiling and twitching in the same dream.

Crossing the room on tiptoe, she reached out a hand and smoothed the hair back from his face. His coal black hair reminded her in that instant of Leo, which caused her to frown. Was Leo the Louse also Leo the Murderer?

Oliver stirred under the soft touch of his mother's hand.

"Hi, Mommy." His voice was merely a whisper, softer than a breeze. Percy felt a lump come to her throat. The dog stirred at his side, tail thumping in a slow, sleepy rhythm.

"You go back to sleep, Oliver. I'll see you in the morning. I love you."

"Love you, too, Mommy." His voice was groggy, almost unintelligible, but one a mother understands.

In that moment, Percy wanted to lie down between son and dog for the rest of her life, cuddling between the two warm bodies. Instead, she kissed her son on the forehead and gave the dog a soft pat on the head.

On the other side of the door, her pragmatic nature came back, along with a smile.

Persephone Cole, here and now, you are one lucky woman. Stop looking for trouble that may never land on you.

Still hearing the radio from the parlor, Percy went to her bedroom, ripped off her wet socks, and put on the warm slippers given to her by Sera for Christmas. She ignored the hems of her still wet trousers, left her room, and crossed to the parlor.

"It's me, Mother," Percy said, before giving the door a gentle shove open. At seeing the couple sitting together on the sofa, Percy interrupted herself in happy surprise. "I – Pop! How…When did you get here?"

His favored leg was propped up on the coffee table. Both arms were wrapped around his wife, who in turn, was snuggled into him. A contented look covered both their faces.

Utter bliss these two, Percy thought. *Utter bliss.*

The couple disentangled themselves as Percy laughed. "Well, I hope I interrupted something."

"Now, Persephone, you keep a respectful tongue in your head," her father said severely, but with a wink. "Mother and I have been waiting for you to get home. You look all done in."

With one arm still around Mother, he extended the other, beckoning to his daughter. Percy came over to his side and sat down.

"Welcome home, Pop, but what happened? Is the job over? Did you catch the spies? And how did you get here? In case you haven't noticed, there's a blizzard going on in the tri-state area."

"Up to the Great Lakes, too. Don't want to be out in this weather if you can help it."

Mother rose before Pop could say more, and looked down at them both. "I'll let you two talk, while I go in and heat up your supper, Persephone. Have you been in to see Oliver?"

Percy nodded.

"I was sure you would have. Such a good boy. In the morning, you'll have to let him show you the three snowmen he and little Freddie made in the courtyard, if they aren't buried under six feet of snow by then. Serendipity helped the boys dress them, by using all our spare hats and scarves."

"I thought Sera had a date tonight, Mother."

"The young man cancelled it. Robert. You remember him. Such a nice boy. Home on leave. Said he had to go to the Bronx to help dig his parents out of the snow. But she had a fine time with the boys. I watched them out the window while I was cooking supper."

Percy was only half listening, but when Mother stopped talking, the silence brought Percy back. She looked over at her mother, as if seeing her for the first time.

"I want to thank you, Mother, for all you do for the family, and for my son and me. I know I don't say it often enough."

"Amen to that, daughter." Pop reached out and took his wife's hand in his and pulled her toward him. "We're all blessed with this fine woman I married forty-something years ago."

"Ah, go on," Mother said, braking free and shaking the compliments off with a wave of her hand. "I'm leaving before you two become as maudlin as a Lillian Gish movie."

With a laugh, she left the parlor for the kitchen. They watched her as she closed the door and listened to the pad of her feet down the hall. Finally, Percy turned to her father.

"So what happened, Pop? I didn't think I'd see you until next week at the earliest."

Pop's face sobered. The light-hearted banter was replaced by a sense of gravity.

"It came to a head around eleven this morning. About twenty officers surrounded the florist shop, bullhorns blaring, demanding the three men inside give themselves up. Two of them were killed trying to shoot their way out. The third, a lad of seventeen, was found in back, shot by his own hand rather than be arrested. It was a sad thing."

Pop was silent, lost in his thoughts. Percy took his hand.

"Sounds like a bad day. I've had one myself. Not to play Can You Top This, but I found Bogdanovitch's body this morning in the freezer at the chocolate factory."

"Good Lord. You okay?"

"Sure."

"That the man who was the new manager, who took the job away from our Howard?"

"Yeah. Cops think his death was accidental, locked himself in."

"But not you."

She shook her head. "The same person who killed Carlotta turned Bogdanovitch into a frozen popsicle. Too bad I couldn't see him through the window before I opened the hasp that was closed over the lock. Sort of shot myself in the foot with that one. Messed with the evidence."

"These things happen, Persephone."

She shook the mood away. "Never mind, Pop. You still didn't tell me how you made it home in this blizzard."

"Pete Hopper, he was my direct boss, wanted to get back to New York for his wife's birthday tomorrow. He's never one to let the elements get the better of him. He hired himself a snow clearing truck - what do they call them things?"

Percy shook her head, thrown for the moment.

Pop went on, "It's got a shovel on the front end that just plows through the snow like it isn't even there."

"A snowplow?"

"That's it! A snowplow. It's the big words that get me, Persephone."

They both laughed at his joke, more so than they normally would have. For a moment the tension lifted.

"It's good to have you back, Pop."

"It's good to be here. Anyway, Pete invited the two of us who live in Manhattan to jump in and ride back with him. We had fifteen minutes to get all our gear together before he left. We were ready in ten. It was a slippery six-hour ride, but by God, we got here." Pop gave out a loud laugh then looked at his daughter for a moment. "You stop off at the Goldbergs before you come up?"

"I did, Pop. Told them what I know, which isn't much. They seem to be doing okay."

"They got their faith. Did Adjudication tell you he's heard there'll be a five-thousand dollar bail set for Howard Monday morning?"

Percy raised her eyebrows. "No, I haven't talked to him today. Been kind of busy falling over dead bodies."

"The Goldbergs don't have most of the bail money. They might scrape together a thousand. Of course, Howie has something set by. And the neighbors are offering a few dollars here and there. Good people all, but..." He broke off and stroked his daughter's hand with his.

"But things are tight, Pop."

"The depression still holds a lot of folks in its grip. I thought we'd offer the eight-hundred we got squirreled away, but you're a part of that, so you need to give me your okay."

"Sure, Pop. We'll get it back. Howie's not going to skip bail."

"That's what Adjudication says. He's going to take a loan out on his house for whatever comes up missing."

Percy smiled. "It looks like the Goldbergs not only got their faith, they got us."

"They'd do the same for us in a heartbeat."

Percy nodded, absentmindedly. Pop studied her.

"Something else is troubling you, Persephone. What is it?"

Percy sat upright.

"It's Leo, Pop."

"Mother mentioned Oliver asked about his father. It's to be expected, Persephone. You couldn't put it off forever."

"I know. But like a lot of things, it's taken an unexpected turn."

While she explained the latest events, her father rested his head on the back of the sofa, eyes staring up at the ceiling.

"So if I'm understanding this, either Oliver's father is dead these three years, or he may have put someone else behind the driver's seat of a burning car and left the country to avoid the draft. Bad scenarios, both."

"If there's a better scenario, I'd like to know what it is. Even if he didn't kill anybody, and his wallet was stolen, where is he? I should never have looked into it. When Mrs. Donovan told me Leo died three years before, I should have just let it go at that."

"Well, first of all, that's not your nature. You check things out. You don't believe hearsay. You were brought up better. Besides, if I remember rightly, Kathleen Donovan is an emotional sort woman, apt to blame others for faults that should be laid at her son's feet. That's why he never grew up enough to assume the responsibility of a wife and family."

"Maybe so, Pop. But I'm left with how much to tell Oliver when the time comes."

"You tell him what he needs to know and we'll all be there for him."

"Yeah, Pop, you're right." Percy let out a long, deep sigh. "While we're laying it all out there, Leo and I were never divorced. I kept meaning to, I just never did."

"I know. Adjudication told me tonight he offered to file for you back then and you said no. Mother and I thought you took care of it before you moved back home. Maybe you thought Leo'd come back to you?"

She shook her head. "It was the money, Pop. It would have cost me twenty-five hard-earned bucks to divorce Leo, even with Jude's help."

"And you were hurt and angry."

Percy closed her eyes and thought for a moment, ready to protest. Memoires swirled in.

"I figured let Leo spend the money; after all, he's the one who left. And then life went on and I kept putting it out of my mind. What I don't understand is why I didn't get notified when the accident happened. I was still legally his wife."

"Hmmm. That's a good question, Persephone. Bears looking into. I see a trip for me down to the Hall of Records first thing Monday morning."

"Still got your beer drinking buddy working there?"

"Avery? Yes. But our visits to the beer gardens are less and less."

"Pop, while you're there could you look into a few other things?"

"If that's what you want. Won't that be stepping on Fred Rendell's toes, though? How's he doing, by the way?"

"Better than most, Pop. But for as good as Rendell is turning out to be, he still needs more training. If you could run a few checks, it would help me out. I need to be at the chocolate factory first thing Monday morning. The cousin inheriting the place should roll in from Chicago and the workers will be returning."

"Course I will, Persephone. With my bum leg, sitting in a warm office looking up facts and figures sounds like heaven. What do you want me to do?"

Percy pulled out a sheet of paper from a pocket. Neat writing went down almost to the bottom of the page. She handed it to her father. Pop let out a whistle.

"Quite a list."

"They're in order of importance, so do what you can. Here's the first thing though, Pop." Percy reached inside her jacket's breast pocket, and pulled out the small, folded paper.

"This is a birth certificate. The baby girl was named Marianna and she was born at St. Vincent's Hospital on the Upper East Side. Maybe there's information about orphanages or religious orders that took in the unwanted babies. Maybe the mid-wife remembers something."

Pop nodded.

"Thanks."

"But for tomorrow, Persephone, you're going to rest and visit with your family and your son. No working on Sunday. Them's the rules."

Percy chuckled. "I remember no matter how hard you worked, you always took Sunday off for us kids."

"You bet, Persephone. I always knew what was important." He lifted his game leg from the coffee table with care, and stood up on it with a slight wince. "Now come on to the kitchen. Mother has a surprise for you."

"She already told me. Pineapple and sauerkraut. Not looking forward to that."

"Well, don't tell her I told you, but she deliberately didn't mention the ham she managed to get with her rationing coupons. She wanted to surprise the family."

"Ham? You don't mean Spam, do you?"

"I mean ham."

"There's a ham in the house?"

"Enough for a week, if we're careful."

"Well, if I didn't know how lucky I was before, I know it now."

Chapter Thirty-four

Even though it was not quite seven am, Vinnie was almost finished clearing snow from the front of the store. The sharp sounds of his shovel striking and scraping snow off the cement had a steady rhythm to it. Other than that, silence. The usual sounds of traffic or humanity going about its business were nowhere to be heard. The city hadn't had time to dig itself out yet.

Huffing and puffing, face red from exertion, Vinnie looked up with a slight smile at the approach of two people. Percy, Fred Rendell at her side, stopped in the cleared section of the sidewalk. All three people were bundled up in the cold, their breaths rising warm against the frigid air.

"Almost looks like Brooklyn's in lock down, doesn't it?" Percy smiled from one man to the other. Each nodded in agreement, even though she was sure Vinnie had no idea what 'lock down' meant.

The snow stopped falling only a few hours earlier, burying the city under six feet of snow. Then the temperature plummeted to the low teens and held there.

Percy looked up, blinking at the burning sharpness of the air. Above was a clear sky that often follows a bad winter storm. Fluffy snow had already turned to hard ice.

Somewhere underneath all that ice Ophelia lay buried in the adjacent parking lot. Percy might be riding the subways for several days until she could dig the car out.

"Vinnie, this is my business associate, Fred Rendell. You're to give him the same cooperation you give me."

Percy smiled winningly at Vinnie, whose face turned even redder.

"Rendell, this is Vinnie. He's been helping me out around here."

Both men nodded again, this time to one another.

"The cousin here yet, Vinnie?"

"No, *signora*. But this on door."

He pulled out a telegram addressed to Ronald Bogdanovitch from the pocket of his worn woolen coat and handed it to Percy. Without hesitation, she ripped it open and read with greedy eyes. She then turned to Vinnie, who had continued his shoveling.

"Apparently Paulo Mendez is snowbound in Cleveland and won't be coming in until sometime tonight, at the earliest," Percy said to both men. She shoved the telegram into a pocket and moved to the front door. "Until then, I'm in charge. Let's go inside, Vinnie. You can finish that later. I wonder how many employees will make it in today?"

"We didn't have any trouble getting here by subway from Manhattan, ma'am," offered Rendell.

"Most of these people don't travel far, do they, Vinnie?"

"No, *signora*. They live the near. Except for Shot-see." Vinnie said, as he propped the shovel against the outside wall.

"Yeah. Helga Appelman," Percy said. "I noticed she comes in from Queens. Got to be a full hour away by subway."

Vinnie nodded and dutifully stood behind Percy as she unlocked the door. She stepped inside followed by the two men.

"Brrr," said Rendell. "It's almost as cold in here as it is out there."

"Sure is," said Percy. She turned to Vinnie. "Let's get some heat going. You know where the furnace is?"

"*Si, si*. But *Signora* Carlotta no like the heat turned on until business open."

"She's not with us, anymore, and chances are Mr. Bogdanovitch won't be dropping by, either." *Unless we hold a séance.* Aloud she said, "So I'm in charge, assisted by Mr. Rendell. Go stoke the boiler or whatever it is you have to do."

Vinnie nodded, turned and headed for the boiler room at the back of the building.

Percy and Rendell trailed behind as far as the workroom. There Vinnie's niece, Teresa, was counting and moving about pieces of candy on the conveyor belt designated to be covered with chocolate. She looked up and offered Percy and Rendell a radiant, but shy smile then returned to work. They mounted the stairs to the office.

"You know what occurs to me, Rendell?" Percy closed the door to the office and crossed to Bogdanovitch's desk.

He shook his head. "No ma'am."

"It occurs to me that nearly anyone knowing anything about the chocolate business is either in jail or dead. I wonder how much Vinnie knows? He used to work in a chocolate store back in Italy." She turned and yelled down.

"Hey, Vinnie."

Seconds later, Vinnie ran up the cellar stairs and looked up, expectantly. Percy looked down.

"Come up here, will you?"

He nodded and ran up the stairs two at a time.

Percy waited on the small platform outside the office.

"So what's Teresa doing down there?"

"I ask her to move the candy on the belt. It stick when in one place too long. That no good."

"And then what?"

"When workers come, we start the moving machine --"

"The what?"

"The candy, she is coated with chocolate and put in the boxes."

"Where's the chocolate to pour on the candy? I thought there wasn't any."

"No, always is some - how you say - extra. Howie always make the extra and is stored."

"I see."

"*Si*. In refrigerator. Each day. But not for tomorrow. No more since..." He broke off speaking and shrugged.

"And that's different from making chocolate. You're just heating it up?"

"*Si*."

"You know how to heat the chocolate up?"

"Is simple. This I do many times," Vinnie said eagerly. "The flame, she is low and..."

"Let me cut you off at the pass, Vinnie. Go get cracking. Heat up the building, heat up the chocolate. Howie should be back this afternoon and maybe he can make a new batch. Meanwhile, the workers can start the assembly line and this place can stay in business. Your niece going off to school soon?"

"*Si, si*. She leave soon. She good girl, like you say." He blushed at his admission.

"Glad to hear it. Go on now, get to work."

Percy turned to Rendell once Vinnie closed the door on his way out.

"Rendell, I'm leaving you in charge. Under no circumstances tell anyone Bogdanovitch has met his maker. Tell them he's sick or something."

He nodded. She went on.

"Take this list. I want you to tick off the workers who come in. I also want the approximate age of each female worker. Don't worry about the men. You're to keep everyone here until I get back. Tell them they're getting paid, even if they do nothing but stand around. Pop will probably call with a few answers for me. Get a phone number of where I can reach him. I'll call you from Queens to see who doesn't show besides Helga Appelman."

"You know she won't be here, ma'am?"

"If what I suspect is true, she's about to head off for greener pastures with a little blue book, but hopefully delayed by the storm."

Rendell raised an eyebrow at Percy, but she said no more.

* * * *

Aside from an elderly woman and three sailors, Percy had been on the train by herself. She exited the subway at Queens Plaza and labored up the slippery, ice-covered steps to street level.

Not much of winter's wrath had been cleared yet, but then it was only eight-thirty Monday morning. School had been cancelled and many businesses remained closed, encouraged by a mayor who wanted the public to stay home until the city got back on its feet. Now the sole person on a residential Queens street, the detective stood and surveyed the white mess quickly graying under the inherent dirt of the city.

Percy's attention was drawn to a lone, clanking truck traveling precariously on black ice down the street. Going no faster than five-miles an hour, it suddenly slid almost in slow motion, side-swiping a snow-covered car. With a muted crunch, the truck came to a halt, intertwined with car, snow, and ice.

After watching the accident and the cursing truck driver for a moment, Percy moved to cross the street. Patches of ice and clumps of frozen snow hampered her footing. In order to make any headway, she had to push through piled-up snow in the gutter, the lowest two-feet high.

With great care, she stepped into the slick street. Along both sides, buried cars made the road look more like a toboggan run. Once across, Percy struggled over another heap of guttered snow and onto the sidewalk.

After two attempts, she found the six-story building, address obscured behind years of dirt and the storm's rage. On the nearby sidewalk and stoop, the snow was still pristine and clear of footprints. No one had left or entered the building since the night before. Percy was relieved.

She climbed the two floors to the apartment, and knocked on the door with authority. According to Appelman's file, the girl was born in 1920 and raised in Belgium. But records have been known to be falsified and she could be an American playing a part. Like Pop had said, some people are good at accents.

If Helga Appelman aka Schatzi, was genuinely from Belgium, everything Percy had read about the culture meant the people were used to oppressive authority. Percy was counting on it.

The door opened a crack and a young woman with dishwater blond hair and a washed out complexion leaned her face into the narrow space.

"Ya?" Even on the one word, the woman had a heavy German accent.

"You Helga Appelman, better known as Schatzi? My name is Persephone Cole and I'm a private detective."

"What is it you want? Go away. Go away."

She started to close the door in Percy's face. Percy gave it a good shove. The girl was thrown off balance, and pushed backward. Percy strode inside, tall and authoritative.

"First of all, get yourself a chain so nobody can do that again. And second, I'm not going away until you and I talk."

"What about? I call the police if you do not go."

"Save that threat for someone who doesn't know you stole a book containing a chocolate formula worth big bucks. I want it back."

Schatzi reacted as if she'd been struck. She wheeled around and headed for a small kitchen at the other end of the square bedsitter. Percy, taking large strides, was by her side in a flash.

But not fast enough. The girl turned brandishing a potato peeler, its small metal blade reflecting the sun from the only window in the pathetic one-room apartment.

"You really don't have the hang of this, do you?"

Percy reached out, grabbed the girl's wrist, and twisted it. The peeler fell to the linoleum floor with a clink.

"To get away with that, honey, you need to come at a person with at least a butcher knife. Of course, in that case, I would have had to shoot you."

The girl grabbed her wrist and burst into tears.

"Ow! You hurt me. You hurt me."

"You were going to peel me like a potato. Now let's talk. Chocolate. Formula. Theft."

Schatzi covered her face with her hands. She leaned her shaking body on the claw-foot tub standing against the back wall of the kitchen, its top covered with cracked wood. Her voice was child-like and plaintive.

"I am no thief. They steal from me. She steal from me. Don't hurt me, please."

Percy studied Schatzi and decided to try a different tact. She wrapped a strong arm around the sobbing girl, and guided her to the small kitchen table near the lone window.

"Come on, kid. I'm not going to hurt you. Come on. It's going to be all right. You sit down, you tell me what I want to know, and it's going to be fine."

Sobs wracking her youthful body, the girl slid down into a chair. Percy sat in the chair opposite the small table and let her be. When the sobbing subsided, Percy's voice was gentle.

"You want some coffee? Something stronger, if you got it?"

The girl shook her head and looked up. Tears still streaming down her face, she muttered in her native tongue.

"Schatzi, I don't speak German, so let's conduct this conversation in English. You speak English, right?"

"I speak English because I must not speak German here in America. People will think I am not Belgian, but a Nazi!"

Her attitude changed, becoming more belligerent. She slapped at tears on her face and sat up straight in the chair. Percy smiled encouragingly.

"I can believe that. A lot of Americans don't know the difference between Germany and Belgium. It's all the same to them. But I do. Your English is pretty good."

"Ya, I study. I also speak Spanish. Italian, too, but the French, not so good."

"You're an educated gal. Good for you. But let's talk about your family's stolen chocolate formula."

"How you know that? But is true. It is ours."

"Carlotta kept pretty good notes. According to her, your grandfather created the formula for the chocolate she was getting rich on, not her own grandfather."

Schatzi leaned forward, self righteousness filling her being from head to toe. "Her family make the money that should be ours. Then she change the formula six-months ago."

"The hazelnut concoction to stretch it out? All due to the war."

"Fa! So there is a war. That is no reason." The girl's face was covered with a sense of outrage. "She is bad, bad, but she is also *trottel*."

"What's that?"

"What is the word in English?" Schatzi sought inside herself for a moment. "Moron. Ya, moron. You steal it and then you do it wrong? But until recently she is not so moron."

"Moronic."

Percy's correction of the girl's English was automatic, as she would have with her son. Despite everything, she'd taken a liking to the Belgian girl and smiled at her. Schatzi smiled back and shrugged.

"Moronic," she repeated shyly.

"Seems to me it bothers you more that she altered the formula than she stole it."

Schatzi's vigor returned. "Ya. What she stole was good. The chocolate my family make."

"How'd it get stolen?"

"Thirty-years ago Carlotta Mendez' *lehrling,* ah, grandpapa apprenticed for my grandpapa in Belgium. He steal the formula and start chocolate shop in Spain. Then Carlotta come here to America with it. He was bad man. She is bad woman. The family, they are bad, bad, bad. "

"So if your grandfather developed this high and mighty formula, how come your family didn't have a copy of it?"

"My grandpapa was *dumm.*"

"Dumb?"

"Ya."

"You seem to have something against everybody, sister."

"My grandpapa was *dumm* not to leave a written copy before he die."

"When was that?"

"Five years he is dead now. But because it was stolen all those years ago, he would not tell us or write down the formula. Always is in his head. He say never again on paper."

"Once burned, twice shy." Schatzi gave Percy a puzzled look. "Go on."

"Fa! Chocolatiers always keep the secret formulas to themselves; it is worth much money. But when grandpapa die in the night, as do many old people, we have nothing."

"So then what?"

"I know the story and the chocolate. I come to America a year ago. I taste the chocolate I ate all my life at home. I go to Carlotta in Brooklyn. I tell her I want the formula, to have back what is rightfully ours." Schatzi jutted out her chin like a rebellious five-year old.

"I'll bet that went over big."

"She say no. But she offer me job, which I take, because I know how to do this work and I want to be near my chocolate. It is my life, my family's life. I take the job even though I am working for a thief. I should be the one in the office, with all the money."

"How did you wind up with the formula? You kill her for it?"

Schatzi looked stunned. "*Nein, nein.* I hear she is dead, drowned in the chocolate, the bad chocolate, the fake chocolate. I know the book with my family's formula, the real chocolate, is in the safe. I go there in the night. I know that man, Bogdanovitch, is there, the leech."

"Letch. But you could say he was a leech, too."

"Ya. I know he will be there. I dress pretty. Put flowers in my hair, wear the last of my perfume. I know what he does to women, what he likes to do. I know if I do what he wants he may give me the formula. It means nothing to him and everything to me. I would be the hot."

"You planned to seduce him."

"I seduce him, ya."

"Said the fly to the spider. What happened?"

"He was not there."

"While you were being hot, he was freezing. What happened when you got to the office?"

"The safe, it is open. Lots of things on the floor. And the blue book, the formula, was lying there, like God had saved it for me."

"Oh, yeah, let's bring God into this. Then what?"

"That is all." She shrugged. "I take the book, but I will give it back if you go away."

"Sure. After you've copied the formula down, of course. Don't look so innocent. I see the ink stains on the side of your hand and inside your two fingers. You've been writing plenty."

The girl leapt up, knocking the chair over, staring down at Percy. "It is mine. I only take what is mine!"

"Easy, girl, easy." Percy rose to her full height and looked down at the girl a good six or seven inches shorter than she. She up-righted the chair never taking her eyes off Schatzi. Her voice became stern.

"Sit down."

The girl complied, albeit unwillingly, then leaned forward in her chair. "How do you know it was me? How do you know?"

The chin jutted out again, defiant. Only the quivering lower lip revealed the fear she was feeling.

"I smelled your perfume downstairs in the outer office, where you work, and in Bogdanovitch's office the day the safe got broken into. Then I read your file. It wasn't hard to add two and two. Let me give you a tip, if you're planning a life of crime, nix the Chantilly."

"I like the perfume. Now maybe I can afford to buy more. Ya."

"You going to go somewhere and start your own chocolate business, now that you have your family's formula back?"

"I stay here in Queens. Soon my mother will join me. The Secret Army is helping her out of Belgium. She is at the top of the list."

"Just your mother?"

"My father and younger brother, they are dead in the war." Tears sprang to her eyes. "Now it is just my mother and I. I will sell to New York stores, like Carlotta did. Only I will use the real formula, not what she did to it now. *Verfälschen* is what she did."

"You're on a roll, sister. What's that word mean?"

"Bastard; not right. It is better to have three pure pieces of chocolate than thirty bastards, only to make the money. She was a bad woman."

"I'm sure there are others who agree with you, but not because she bastardized chocolate during wartime." Percy rose. "Okay, kid, give me back the blue book and we're done. I'll keep you out of this, if I can."

Schatzi rose warily. "That is it? You go and do not come back?"

"I go and don't come back." She reached out a hand for the book. "Only don't *you* come back to Brooklyn unless you're invited. Don't push your luck with me."

Chapter Thirty-five

Dear Diary,

Time to take care of Percy Cole.

Chapter Thirty-six

Percy dialed a number from inside the wooden phone booth at the bottom of the stairs of the Elmhurst station. The token booth had a 'closed' sign in the window, but several hardy souls were going in and out of the turnstiles. Probably like Percy, they carried a supply of nickel tokens, good for the subways and busses.

If you didn't have nickel tokens and the booths were closed, you couldn't ride the subway, unless you hopped over the turnstile. She watched a young man, who looked around him before doing just that.

Percy smiled. She used to do the same thing in her oh-so-distant youth. But that was then and this was now. She heard the rumble of the train arriving at the station and hoped the hopper made it to the platform in time.

Rendell answered on the first ring, like he'd been hanging around the chocolate factory's office waiting for her call.

"Hey, Rendell. Got anything for me?"

"Yes, ma'am, but first your father phoned and he's waiting for you to call him. I got a number for you."

"Shoot."

"Eldorado 5-9674."

She scribbled the number down in her notepad. "Got it. Anything else? Talk fast."

"Your brother called to say Goldberg should be out around one-thirty, two this afternoon. And he said for me to tell you, you were right on both counts. Hope you know what that means."

"I do. The workers earning their keep?"

"Yes, ma'am. Everybody but the Appelman woman showed up for work. None of the eight female workers are young, except for Regina Mason."

"She came to work?"

"Yes, ma'am. One cold fish. Most of the other women are in their late thirties, early forties, two older. The production line is going, but they expect to run out of chocolate by this afternoon."

Percy looked at her watch. "It's ten-thirty. You got the keys to the storage room, fridge, and freezer?"

"Yes ma'am."

"Don't give them to anybody unless you go with them and watch what they're doing. I'll call you back in an hour or two." She hung up and dialed the number for her father.

He, too, answered on the first ring. "Persephone?"

"Hi, Pop. Where are you?"

"Drugstore phone booth across from the Hall of Records."

"Keeping warm?"

"Better than laying under the Boardwalk at Atlantic City."

"I'll bet. Whatcha got for me?"

"I found her. Easy as one, two, three."

"I thought it would be. Where is she?"

"Would you believe it, over in Staten Island?"

"I believe it. What's her last name now?"

"Christensen. The orphanage is right across the street from the hospital, so I went there. I spoke with a nun, Sister Mary Margaret, who remembered Marianna Christensen well and tried to keep up with her. The child was adopted at six-years old by a Scandinavian couple who made boats over on Staten Island. Didn't have too happy a life. The sister thinks they only took her in to have someone to do housework. In any event, the father was a drunk and used to beat up the wife and kid. He died in a brawl when Marianna was eleven. The mother took in washing after that."

"Sounds right out of a Dickens novel."

"You still reading him?"

"Finished. Moved on to Virginia Woolf. Go on, Pop."

"The Sister and the girl would write letters from time to time. Never lost touch."

"The Sister the one who told the girl who her real mother was?"

"I asked and she said she finally told the girl a little over a year ago, even though there's a letter in the file saying Carlotta Mendez didn't want the child to know her name."

"One of these days it'll be against the law to reveal the woman's name, even to the child, when she says she doesn't want it known."

"Respect for privacy and all that? Well, Sister Mary Margaret blushed when she told me, not that nuns don't do that a lot, I expect, not seeing much of the real world."

"Might be they've seen too much. Could be why they left it. What else, Pop?"

"Marianna Christensen ran away when she was fourteen, fifteen, coming back home only after her adopted mother died about three years ago. She's still got the cottage her mother managed to pay the mortgage on. Any of this of help?"

"Yes, the fact she was in an orphanage until she was six-years old."

"Sister Mary Margaret doesn't know why. She remembers her as a pretty little thing who liked to sing and dance, do playacting, things like that. Smart, too, but no one wanted her. Sad that. One more thing, the midwife who delivered the baby was Iris Clancy, just like you thought."

"So she blackmailed Carlotta into giving her daughter, Regina, a job."

"More than likely, Persephone."

"Anything else?"

"Yes. On Leonard. When the officers came to his mother's door to tell her Leonard had died in the accident, she told them he wasn't married, that she was his only next of kin. That's why you didn't get notified."

"They don't check on things like that, Pop?"

"Apparently not or it got by them. Kathleen Donovan claimed his body and buried him."

"How'd you track this down?"

"I called her up and asked her if that was the case, Persephone. Seemed the simplest way."

Percy let out a chuckle. "You're where I get my learning from, Pop. That *was* the simplest way."

"She was proud of herself, too. I started to give her what for, but it don't matter. She's an unhappy woman, Persephone. Once you find out whether the body in the car was Leonard's or not, I wouldn't dwell on her part in this."

"Good advice. Pop, Jude called earlier to say Howie makes bail in a couple of hours. I need you to go over to the jail when he gets out. Stay with him, look out for him. Once he's free, he won't be as safe as he's been."

"That mean you were right about the phrasing of the will?"

"Jude just confirmed it. If something happens to Howie, the factory reverts back to the next of kin. Same thing if he's convicted of a felony."

"What about the cousin?"

"He's safe enough. Let me have that address in Staten Island. I'm heading for there now."

Pop gave her the address, adding the words, "You be careful, Persephone. She's already killed two people."

"That we know of. I've got the Mauser with me."

"You bundled up? Got your scarf?"

"Yes."

Percy gave out a small laugh. Her father ignored it.

"You have a good breakfast this morning? Your mother and I worry that you eat nothing but apples and those danged pistachio nuts."

"Filled up on oatmeal before I left. Hated it, but I knew what I had in store for me. Speaking of eating, don't let Howie eat or drink anything you don't give him."

"Sounds serious."

"It is. I'll try to call you from Staten Island. Love you, Pop."

"Love you more."

They hung up.

Percy exited the phone booth just as a group of teenagers, perhaps ten in all, clomped down the stairs, heading toward the train. Giddy on the idea of no school, the teens, mostly boys, were loud and rambunctious.

Four of the boys jumped over the turnstile, goading the rest to do the same thing. Another boy tried, missed his footing and much to the delight of the others, became tangled in the turnstile's arms. The other boys dropped in their tokens and were suitably razzed by the first four boys. The two girls put in tokens, as well.

A smaller boy, separated from the group possibly by shyness, watched the antics with a laugh. Like the girls, he put in his token, but stood off to the side of the grouping. The boisterous youngsters went down the stairs to the train platform, Percy on their heels.

Several levels beneath the surface the air was agreeably warmer, if not a little stale. The teens, still laughing and rough-housing, went to the back end of the platform where the last of the subway car would arrive.

Percy paid little attention to them, lost in thought over her next task. She sat on the hard bench in the center of the platform awaiting the arrival of the train back to Manhattan.

The trains were running on a holiday schedule, meaning every twenty minutes, instead of the usual five to ten. The waiting platform began to fill up with stragglers, people who would not or could not take a day off, no matter what the weather. Percy knew what it was like.

There was a soft rumbling sound, and movement of warm air coming out of the tunnel. The reverberating sound increased in volume. Percy stood and neared the edge of the platform. The IND train, dressed up in a bright red E sign and lit from inside, clattered on the rails and came to a stop with a high-pitched screech of the brakes.

There were fewer cars than usual, only five, and the train ended in the middle of the platform. The teens, seeing the last car was some twenty yards in front of them, scrambled toward it with hoots of laughter. Pushing at each other, they clamored aboard, moving in and out of one other like water sloshing in a glass.

If you could harness the energy of a sixteen-year old boy, you could light the city of Manhattan for a year.

Laughing at their antics, Percy decided not to take one of the many empty rattan woven seats, but grabbed an overhead leather strap. She tried to stay out of the way of the teens, who seemed to be everywhere.

The sliding double doors closed, and with a jerk, the train began to move. Picking up speed, the train went into a steady rhythm of clacking wheels, pitching from side to side on its route beneath the East River. It would be a full ten-minute ride to the first stop on the Manhattan side, Fifty-first and Lex.

Restless, Percy dropped her hand from the swinging strap and went to the back end of the car. She looked out of the window of the sliding door into the blackness of the subway tunnel.

Thanks to the spill-over light from the interior, she noticed the small standing platform built at each end of the cars. Normally, passengers could pass from car to car by going through the sliding doors via these connecting platforms. She had done it many times herself.

But as this last car functioned as the caboose, there were three chains linked across the iron railing from side to side. The chains served as a warning to passengers not to wander out or get too close to the back end of the train.

While musing, Percy felt crowded into, jammed against the door by a few of the teenagers. Someone had thrown a ball and, like the kids they were, they began to toss it around, jostling one another and anyone nearby in the process.

Before she could move, Percy saw the sliding door handle pulled at by a quick moving hand. The door slid open and she was pushed out onto the small platform.

Wind sucked at her. Noise assaulted her ears. Off balance, she reached out for something solid to grasp. There was nothing. She felt a strong shove between her shoulder blades. Percy toppled over the chains and into the blackness of the tunnel.

Chapter Thirty-seven

Tuck and roll. Tuck and roll, Percy screamed at herself in that split second she felt suspended in mid-air. Uncle Gil had taught her many things on the trampoline he bought his nieces and nephew one Christmas. At this moment, tuck and roll was the lesson she remembered vividly. Fighting gravity and propulsion, Percy managed to pull into a summersault before her body slammed into the unyielding concrete, gravel, and steel of the tracks.

In particular, her shoulders smacked against a wooden tie, elevated three or four inches above the ground. She felt the wind whoosh out of her and for an instant couldn't breathe.

When her lungs finally could suck in air, Percy struggled to a sitting position. She looked behind her to see the far away lights at the end of the train, round a corner and vanish.

She pivoted to face the front again and blinked. Blackness, nothing but blackness surrounded her. Percy rose on shaky feet.

All right, girl. Don't panic. Things could be worse. At least nothing feels broken and you're not dead. Yet.

Her hands flew to the top of her head.

Damn! My hat's gone. Where's my hat? My flashlight!

Trembling fingers reached inside her coat pocket and withdrew a small flashlight, one Pop insisted she carry at all times.

Thank you, Pop.

She clicked the light on. A strong, steady beam flew out from the cylindrical metal. He also insisted she put in fresh batteries once a month, no matter what the cost.

'You never know,' he'd say.

You never know, indeed, Pop.

Splaying the light up and down, she pivoted to get her bearings. Her fedora lay propped against a moist black tunnel wall. She stepped over the track, watching out for the third rail, and walked the two or three steps to retrieve the hat.

This reminded her of just how narrow the tunnel was in many places, wide enough for a train to travel through, with a couple of paltry feet on either side were often all that separated a train from the walls of the tunnel.

Percy felt her heart lurch in her chest.

What time is it?

She pointed the beam of light at the watch on her wrist.

Nine-fifty-three. We were traveling for around eight minutes. Give another two for my spill from the train and I've got about ten minutes before another train comes barreling through the tunnel right at me.

Percy shot the beam of light on the walls and ceiling of the square tunnel from top to bottom. Other than the occasional rivulet of water running down from the river above, there was nothing. Nothing. No recess, no door, no ladder, no freedom.

Ten minutes. I'd better get going.

Percy turned around, stepped back into the center of the tracks, and began the walk to Manhattan. She measured her footfall, going from tie to tie, not just for better balance, but so she could move faster. She stopped every now and then to glance at her watch. But always, she played the beam of light against both sides of the tunnel, looking for any possible escape.

There would be none, she suspected, as she was still under the East river or its banks. The only hope to escape to above via a ladder was to clear the river.

Breathing hard, she came to the place where she'd seen the train rounding the corner. She felt a slight rumble behind her in the distance. She looked at her watch. Nearly ten minutes had passed. Percy noticed that at the turn the tunnel was slightly wider. It gave her hope.

The rumble increased in sound and pressure. She could feel the ground beneath her vibrate. A train would be upon her soon.

Maybe I can press myself against the sides of the tunnel. It's wider here. Maybe the train won't take my face off.

Then she saw the metal ladder. An obscure, small ladder attached to the wall. She followed the rungs with her flashlight and saw the ladder went up the side for about thirty-feet and ended at the bottom of a horizontal rather than vertical door. She was still under the banks of the East River.

No escape yet.

Percy ran to the bottom of the ladder, just as she saw the headlight of the oncoming train. Barely a pinpoint at first, it grew larger and larger at an alarming rate.

She could now see from the oncoming light.

Percy shut off her torch and grabbed at the ladder. Rung over rung she climbed, losing her footing once and falling back down to the ground, striking her chin on hard, cold metal.

The light was almost blinding now.

She looked into the first window of the oncoming train. A man sat in the engineer's booth looking out onto whatever the light allowed him to see. Even if the engineer saw her, there would be no stopping tons of moving steel in time. The laws of inertia were not in her favor.

Fighting back the panic, she climbed more slowly but more carefully. The roar was deafening now. Fast moving air currents fought her climb to safety, but she continued.

The train was upon her.

She looked down at the few inches that separated her feet from the top of the racing train and held on for dear life.

Percy fairly bounced on the rungs, and hoped not to be dislodged by the vibration or airstream. Fortunately, it was only five cars that passed. If it had been the usual ten to twelve cars, she might not have been able to keep her grip.

Darkness returned.

Percy slowly felt her way down the ladder and dropped to the ground. She turned on her flashlight again. The walls were dryer now. Maybe she had cleared the riverbed.

Plodding on, she thought of her son, her beautiful boy, the child she lived for, and who needed her. She pushed aside the ache in her legs, and the lungs punished by foul and unclean air. She focused on counting the minutes. The pitch-black cavern went on and on, seemingly into oblivion.

The rustling of a small animal on the other side of the tracks gave her start. Aiming the light in that the direction, Percy saw a large rat heading in the opposite direction. The rat froze for a moment caught in the beam of light, its red eyes reflecting back to her. Then it scurried on its away.

Twelve minutes were gone and still she pushed forward as fast as she dared. The beam from her flashlight remained steady and strong.

She was in a rhythm now.

Gone was the fatigue and pain. She rounded another corner and the tunnel doubled in size. A second set of tracks ran through and into another darkened tunnel.

Oh God. Where does that tunnel lead? Is that where I should go? Should I turn right? Or go straight ahead?

She felt rising panic. Would she become lost in the twists and turns of the tunnels?

No, Persephone Cole. Pay attention. Follow the track you've been on since the beginning.

She felt another vibration coming from in front of her. She fought the panic again, trying to reason it out.

That's a train coming on the other tracks. If you stay where you are, Percy, you'll be fine.

Nonetheless, she stepped off the tracks and pressed herself against the tunnel wall. The oncoming train was another short one, and roared by a few feet away on the other set of tracks, continuing on its journey.

Percy stepped back onto the tie and moved forward. Everything told her she was nearing the station. Slightly fresher air, a larger, shared tunnel, and the addition of light, though scant, told her to keep going.

Sure enough the tunnel continued to widen. She stayed mid-track, avoiding the third-rail, an unseen but definite danger.

The live electrical rail can kill you with its 625 volts of electricity. It has killed before. It will again. But not today and not me.

Ahead and in the distance, she saw the faint glow of the 51st Street subway station. But how far away was it? One minute? Five? Ten? She didn't have ten minutes. She glanced at her watch. She had eight at best. She stepped up her pace with renewed energy, heading for the light and the safety of the station.

She felt the vibration of the train behind her through the ground before she heard it. She was getting acclimated to the underground. Like one of the rats who lived below, she couldn't count on her vision, so her other senses were heightened. Judging by the two run-ins she'd had with the subway trains, it seemed to her she had probably five or six minutes.

Percy broke into a fast run.

The closer she got, the stronger the glow ahead of her became. But as the light became stronger, the roaring noise behind her also became louder. The vibrating beneath her feet almost threw her off-stride.

The station platform on the right jutted out into the tracks, but was a good sixty feet away. Could she make it? Could she get to the platform in time?

Lungs burning, Percy saw an electrical panel set into the wall, probably used for maintenance. A short distance from the panel was a set of steep, narrow stairs leading onto the station platform.

She passed the panel as racing death almost overtook her.

Flinging herself upon the stairs, she felt a strong blast of stinging air. The train thundered by. Her hat blew off and danced across the platform, landing at someone's feet. The flashlight was thrown from her hand, bounced, and rolled to a stop near a trashcan.

Percy lay stretched out on the steps, as the train screeched to a halt. She lifted her head a bit. A small group of people spewed forth from the opening doors; just as many entered into the car afterward. No one noticed her. The doors closed and the train jerked forward slowly at first, but soon took on a goodly speed. It left the station, entering the tunnel's darkness once more.

Percy lay her head back down on the top stair, one hand extended before her. She couldn't move, not so much from shock as sheer exhaustion.

She heard a pair of feet cautiously approach and lifted her head once more. An elderly black man, dressed in gray overalls and carrying a broom, bent over, studying her.

"I don't know where you came from, miss, but I believe this is yours." He waved her battered fedora in front of her face.

Blowing the messy and tousled of hair off her face, she reached up with a grime-covered hand. Percy took the hat. She pressed it to her head, looked up at him, and winked.

"Thanks. I'll be up in a minute."

"Can I help you, miss?"

"I wouldn't say no."

He reached down with a strong, callused hand to grab her outstretched one. With his help, and using the nearby subway-tiled wall for support, she struggled to her feet. The man gave her a toothy, but confused smile.

"What were you doing in the tunnel, miss?"

"Got off at the wrong stop."

"You might want to wait for the next train, if you don't mind me saying, miss."

"Thanks. I'll keep that in mind."

Chapter Thirty-eight

On the twenty minute train ride down to the Battery, Percy had a lot of time to think. She was interrupted only once by a man who got on the train at 42nd Street playing a harmonica. After several tunes, he asked Percy for money. She gave him a subway token, and with an afterthought, made it two.

She'd cleaned up pretty well, all things considered. A visit to the station's ladies washroom, spotless due to the lack of patronage from the storm and the elderly black man's hard work, made it easier for her to look presentable.

There was nothing to be done about the rip in her coat or the streaks of soot, but a trip to the dry cleaners would sort everything out. Her hat could be re-blocked eventually. And being dark brown, it showed little of its encounter with the tunnels of the New York City subway system.

As for Percy, two hotdogs with extra sauerkraut and mustard from one of the station's venders, and a cup of strong coffee made her feel almost human again.

I'll feel like a truck ran over me tomorrow, but for today, if I keep moving, the soreness won't set in.

Percy got off at the Battery Maritime Building and made her way to the Whitehall Ferry Terminal. The twenty-five minute ride across the New York Harbor is free to Staten Island, but costs five cents for the return trip. The huge ferry, which can hold nearly eight-hundred people, transported only a handful that frosty Monday morning.

Percy stood inside the ferry's starboard side, as it glided by the Statue of Liberty. Lady Liberty, backlit by a startling blue sky, looked spectacular. Tall and elegant in the late morning sun, her crown sparkled with icicles, as if made of diamonds.

The sight brought a lump to Percy's throat, reminding her of what America was fighting for. Or maybe the lump came from the thought that her son's father was a man who shirked his patriotic duty to the point of killing someone and substituting the body for his.

Percy had considered enlisting herself, but with a young son and often the sole support of the family, it wasn't doable. She fought for freedom and right on her home ground, and sometimes it was just as dangerous.

She patted the German Mauser resting beneath her heavy coat in her jacket pocket. She could hardly feel the bulge under the layers.

I have so many bulges, it's hard to know what is where.

The ride over, Percy stood at the mouth of the ferry building. The snow clearing process was only in the beginning stages. Public transportation, other than the ferry itself, wasn't available. The other passengers dispersed, either walking to nearby destinations or having private transportation.

Now the lone person, Percy contemplated her options, which weren't many. The Christensen address was nearly a half a mile from the St. George Ferry Terminal. An easy walk most of the time, it wasn't something she cared to do in her state. Three feet of unshoveled snow, with drifts up to six feet high didn't help, either. Her only hope was hiring a cab. She scanned the white horizon for one.

"Hey, you. You!"

Percy turned her head toward the source of the gravelly voice calling out. It belonged to an older woman, bundled up and sitting atop a large but empty wooden wagon, wheels removed and converted to a sleigh. In front, a dark brown horse covered with a plaid blanket stood stamping his feet and pulling at the reins, seemingly anxious to get moving.

The woman guided the horse and rig around to the front of the building and pulled to a stop. She wore a beat-up gray hat tied onto her head by a faded pink scarf. Around her shoulders was a multi-colored crocheted shawl covering the upper portion of her gray coat. Calloused hands wearing brown, fingerless gloves held tightly to the reins. A long black skirt fell to the floor out from which peeked heavy, workman boots. One foot rested on the brake of the sleigh.

Percy's eyebrows shot up. "Lady, You're the second thing today straight outa Charles Dickens."

"Not me. I'm from Castleton Avenue. Lived there all my life. Where you going? Maybe I could give you a lift."

"573 Benziger Avenue."

"Going right by there. Twenty-five cents. Gotta feed my horse."

As if on cue, the horse whinnied and snorted, throwing off two nostrils of mist into the dry, cold air.

Percy let out a laugh, shook her head in amazement, and stepped off the curb to the waiting sleigh.

"You got it. I would have done it for thirty."

"So give me thirty cents. I'm not proud."

"How about I give you twenty?"

"How about you give me a laugh, we call it even?"

"Okay." Percy drew out the word, thinking for a moment. "'You only live once, but if you do it right, once is enough'."

The woman threw back her head and let out a hoot of laughter. "Mae West, right? You have to love a woman who can say things like that. Climb aboard. Like I told you, I was going by there, anyway."

"Thanks."

Percy lifted a leg high, heaved herself up on the running board, and climbed next to the woman. The woman clicked her tongue and snapped the reins. The horse lumbered forward, picked up speed, and went at a nice trot, hot breath ladling the air. It was several minutes before either woman spoke. The older woman turning to Percy.

"No point in traveling in silence. What's your name?"

"Persephone Cole. My friends call me Percy. What's yours?"

"Violet Castleton."

"Any relation to the Castleton Avenue you say you're from?"

"The very same. Land owned by my grandfather and his grandfather before him, right back to the Revolutionary War."

"Been meeting a lot of people lately whose grandfathers influenced their lives, for good and for ill." Percy blew on her gloved hands. "Brother, is it cold. You've been here a long time. You know a lot of people around here?"

"Like who?"

"The Christensens."

"That where you're going? The Christensens?"

"Yeah."

"Just the daughter left now. Joined a carnival or some such when she was just a kid. But she come back after her mother died. I don't know why. The place has indoor plumbing, but that's about it. Falling down around her ears. And still she sits there, looking out the window most days. That's when she's there. She isn't home much. Leastways, I only see her now and then." She glanced over at Percy. "There's some hot chocolate in that thermos by your foot. Clean cup by your hand."

"Thanks." Percy removed her cumbersome gloves and poured herself a cup of hot chocolate. She sipped, looking at the vista around her. "Looks like a fairyland around here."

"Snow covers a lot. Hides the ugliness. That's a junkyard you're looking at over there. We've been trying to get rid of it for years."

"And what do you do, Violet?"

"Call me Vi. Violet sounds like a flower and that's not me. But to answer your question, I harvest, sell, and deliver bales of hay for the livestock around the island. Finishing up a delivery when I saw you. Getting fewer and fewer calls as the years go by, though. Thinking of selling out, going to Florida."

"You won't miss your life here?"

"Hell, no. I'm sixty-four years old. Outlived my husband. Lost my boy at Pearl Harbor."

"Sorry to hear it."

"I thought he'd inherit the place, but there's nobody now. Might as well get my face warm. Probably take Toby with me." She gestured to the horse pulling the wagon. "He's a good horse. He could use the sunshine. Here you are."

Vi pulled back on the reins and stopped at the crossroads of Benziger and Bismark Avenues.

Percy sat the empty cup beside her and looked down a narrow street, with several houses spread out on either side. It had a bucolic look, but the houses, even covered with snow, needed maintenance.

"It's the middle house on the left, down where the smoke is coming out of the chimney. It isn't much more than a two-room shack. I heard she got hurt at that carnival, fell from a high wire, and walks with a limp. So she should be there. As W.C. Fields says, 'Ain't a fit day out for man nor beast'." Vi went into gales of laughter at her own interpretation of the actor's words.

"You know your movie stars, Vi," Percy jumped down. "Here," she said as she reached into the pocket of her coat and drew out a shiny quarter. "This is for Toby. And thanks."

"Well, thank you, Persephone Cole," Vi responded, pocketing the quarter. "The roads are clearer than I thought.

You shouldn't have any trouble walking back. You look like a sturdy girl."

Percy smiled. "That I am, Vi. That I am."

Percy watched woman and horse retreat into the distance, the animal's breath reminding her of the steam engine of a locomotive.

Percy turned and trudged down the street avoiding as many snowdrifts as she could. Her legs burned from the exertion of fighting the ice and snow, as did her lungs, an aftermath of her trials in the tunnel. Even in the fifteen degree temperature, she felt a trickle of perspiration slide down the side of her face. Her coat felt heavy and hot. By the time she arrived at the cottage, she was breathing like she'd run a race.

It was a fairly dismal and neglected looking place. If it hadn't been for the smoke rising from the chimney, Percy would have thought it was abandoned. Other than the roof, the house was in desperate need of attention. Exposed siding was long overdue for repainting. Raw wood shutters, splintered and swollen, were closed against the few small windows of the house.

A picket fence lined the perimeter of the small yard. On both sides, slats were broken or missing and the gate hung precariously on one hinge. The gate opened with difficulty, the bottom half refusing to slide across the uneven ice and snow. Percy lifted the gate up, almost pulling it off its rusty hinge.

Mercifully, the path had been cleared from the sidewalk to the front steps of the dilapidated porch and scattered salt was melting whatever ice lingered. Percy made her way up the walk, noting frozen clumps of weeds peeking out of the snow here and there within the tiny yard.

Percy climbed the steps with care, two of them shaky from rotting wood. She knocked on the front door, taking in a bent metal mailbox nailed next to the door, missing its flap cover, and the porch light missing a bulb.

After a minute, Percy rapped again on the door with more insistence. She heard an uneven clumping coming closer and closer. The door opened a crack a moment later and a shaky voice called out.

"Who is it? What do you want?" The female voice with its New York accent was thin and high-pitched, almost laughably so.

"I'm looking for Marianna Christensen. I have some good news for her." Percy spoke into the crack then pulled back, waiting.

"What's that? What kind of good news? Who are you?"

"My name is Persephone Cole. May I come in? It's cold out here."

Wordless, the woman backed up, opening the door wide onto the darkness of the cottage. Percy looked into the gloom, stamped the snow off her feet, and without hesitation, stepped inside.

Chapter Thirty-nine

The air was oppressively hot, made more so by the contrast to the cold outside. Percy removed her hat, her hair falling down to her shoulders. She unbuttoned her coat and loosened her scarf while she allowed her eyes to adjust to the lack of light.

Once she could see in the dimness, she looked around the one room functioning as kitchen, dining room and living room. Aged and peeling wallpaper, the original color no longer recognizable, clung haphazardly to grimy walls. A dark sofa, pillows askew, its legless, right side propped up on magazines, sat in front of two milk crates serving as a coffee table. A lone floor lamp wore a tattered shade tilting precariously to the side. Its low watt bulb gave barely any light at all.

A tapping, almost a scraping sound distracted Percy. At the left rear of the house was a door, probably to a bedroom. The scraping sound seemed to come from the other side of the door.

The woman, young if Percy had her pegged right, stood facing her but was backlit by a fire going in a large fireplace against the back wall of the kitchen. In front of the fireplace, sat a long rustic table surrounded by four mismatched chairs.

The fireplace seemed to double as a stove, as well as heating. Above the crackling fire, a kettle hung on a cast iron hook that could swing in and out of a fire.

The woman took two steps backward, with a pronounced limp.

"What is it, lady? What kind of good news do you have for me?"

The thin, high-pitched voice was hardly more than a whisper. Percy couldn't see the features of the woman's face but noticed thick glasses poking out below ragged bangs. Long, unruly, dark hair covered the sides of her face.

"You are Marianna Christensen?"

"Yes," she said, nodding.

"You have proof?" Percy tried to study the features of the woman, an almost impossible task. Not much more was revealed than a nose.

"Of course. Why shouldn't I be who I say I am, lady?"

Marianna Christensen turned away abruptly, and limped to the fireplace. She picked up a fire poker and potholder. Using the poker, she caught the hook and swung the kettle out of the fire and toward her. With the potholder, she grasped the kettle's handle while saying,

"I was about to make some tea, lady. Would you like some?"

"No thanks. You were adopted in 1926 by Adele and Neal Christensen?" Percy came closer, separated from the woman by the bare and roughly hewed kitchen table.

"Yes, they were my adopted parents, but they are both gone. I am alone now."

The woman turned to face Percy, kettle in hand. The scratching at the bottom of the door increased and a small yip could be heard on the other side of the door. Percy looked from the door into the woman's face.

"Why don't we let Poopsie out, Lola Mae, or should I call you Helena Wilson?" Percy drew the Mauser out of her coat pocket and pointed it at the woman who was standing stock still.

"What are you talking about? I am Marianna Christensen. I don't know who those other people are. You're a crazy lady." The voice became even higher in pitch, a thin wail. "I'm going to call the police."

"Ah! You have a phone. I'll bet it's probably in the other room, a room filled with more of life's niceties. This outer room is just a façade like the outside, right? Staging for a woman who has developed theatrical illusion to a fine art."

Holding the gun on the other woman, Percy crossed to the bedroom door and opened it. A small Pomeranian dog came bounding out and headed for Marianna Christensen. The woman ignored the dog that yipped a greeting then sat wagging his tail looking up at her.

"I must say, you've hidden your shock of seeing me very well. But then, you are a consummate actress. Put down the poker, Marianna, and hang the kettle back on the hook."

The woman stared at Percy. After perhaps thirty-seconds, she let out a deep sigh, hung the kettle back on the hook, and leaned the poker against the fireplace bricks before she spoke.

"What now, Percy Cole?" Marianna's voice had lowered to a pleasant pitch with a neutral, cultured accent. She looked at the woman detective and removed her glasses.

"Why don't you take off the wig?" Percy stepped to her end of the table. "I'll bet it's hot in here with it on. I know it feels that way to me." She pulled the scarf around her neck off, while using the gun in the other hand to gesture for the woman to sit down across from her.

"And take a load off. You've had a busy morning, Marianna, what with riding back and forth on the subway, and pushing people off of trains."

Marianna shrugged and yanked at the wig to reveal platinum blonde hair gathered up in a hairnet. She tossed the glasses and wig on the table then turned to the dog.

"I knew you were going to be my downfall, Poopsie, but I couldn't bear to part with you."

She bent down, picked up her pet, turned the dog's face to hers, and nuzzled it. Walking to the table, minus the limp, she sat down.

"You are my Sherlock Holmes and I am your Professor Moriarity. Which one of us will survive the fall from the falls? Every pun intended."

Marianna assumed an easy, relaxed persona. Percy, however, did not let down her guard, still pointing the gun directly at the other woman.

"That was pretty clever of you, following me around, pretending to be a teenage boy. You had me fooled."

Marianna bowed her head in acknowledgement with a smile. She then reached down at her side.

"Easy, easy," Percy said when the girl made the unexpected move. "Don't try anything cute. I'm a little annoyed with you and might shoot."

"It's just a lift inside my shoe that helps me with the limp. See?" Marianna slowly reached inside her shoe and pulled out a piece of thick fabric from the heel. "It isn't very comfortable, but a limp is a great way of distracting your audience. Well, Percy Cole, I thought I fooled you. As you say, I know the art of illusion. I've been fooling a lot of people for a long time."

"To your credit, you did fool me for awhile. But Sonja Henie was never a gymnast. She was an ice skater and skier. That was a foolish mistake."

"I was trying to justify my muscles, and Sonja Henie's name was the first that came to me. I've trained as an acrobat and weight-lifter since I was fifteen, but I don't know many other women who have. And I didn't want Lola Mae to be tied in with anything like a carnival or circus, like I was. She had to be a helpless southern belle."

"That one mistake started me thinking. I asked myself just exactly who is this Lola Mae Lawton? So I did a little investigating. Or rather, Pop did. There is no Lola Mae Lawton. There never was. You're not from the south, and you're certainly no helpless female. I could tell by the way your clothes fit and the way you moved you were a very athletic girl. And that strength is how you managed to strangle Carlotta and put her body in the vat of chocolate."

"I'm as strong as a lot of men." Marianna paused for emphasis. "Like you."

"Did you know she wasn't dead yet? She died of drowning in the chocolate."

"I didn't know, but thanks for telling me. That's poetic justice for you."

"Once I disallowed everything you said about yourself, I was left with the fact that you needed to live next door to Howie, what with him working at the chocolate factory. He was your number one patsy. You must have been planning this for what, a year?"

"Longer. Ever since Sister Mary Margaret told me who my real mother was." Marianna reflected. "It's too bad about Howie. I really liked him, but a girl's gotta do what a girl's gotta do. I had to have a fall guy." She stopped speaking and smiled. Percy picked up the conversation.

"And by inventing a husband who was on the road all the time, one you could join occasionally, it gave you a lot of freedom. You could come and go as you pleased to assume the other identities. Like Helena Wilson, girlfriend of patsy number two, Ronald Bogdanovitch."

"Oh, yes. Ronald. Such a randy guy. He was easy." Marianna stroked the dog's head and neck, almost out of habit. "How did you tie me in with him? I'm curious."

Percy reached in her pocket and pulled out an envelope from the Hudson Hotel. She opened the flap and took out several long blonde hairs.

"Let's start with the hair taken from the bathroom in the apartment Bogdanovitch set up for you. I found another one in the factory's office. If you look under a microscope – which I did - you can see not only are they the same, but at the tip of each strand is a small growth of blue-black hair. I'm betting it's the same color hair as Carlotta's. It's an unusual color as you, yourself, said about my son's hair."

"I'm beginning to realize I have to be careful what I say and do around you."

"You're not the first to think so."

"What else?"

"Next you left a bowl of water in the hotel room, something someone might put down for a pet. And all three women were the same age, same build. Last and most importantly, Lola Mae and Helena had no past. They showed up out of nowhere and vanished into nowhere."

"True. Such is a vagabond life." She lifted up the long haired dark wig next to her. "How'd you know this was a wig?"

"The only way one woman could continually have different color hair is to use wigs. Thanks to the Goldbergs, it's not a foreign concept to me. When an Orthodox Jewish woman gets married, she shaves her head and wears a wig."

"We use them a lot in show business, too. But I'm glad I don't have to do this anymore." She grabbed a hank of her over-bleached hair. "It's time consuming and peroxide is hard on the hair."

"I guess in order to be Helena, you had to use your own hair."

"Had to; sleeping with someone can be messy. And Ronald liked blondes. A Betty Grable fetish."

"So you bleached your own hair and got a job as a cigarette girl at his favorite bar. It wasn't hard for you to use him to get into Carlotta's business, I'm assuming when she wasn't around."

Marianna gave a soft laugh, while stroking the dog's fur. "He was such a dope and he loved flaunting me after the fact. He even had his way with me on her desk. He'd fallen asleep afterward, but then I'd put sleeping pills in his whiskey."

"That's when you got into her safe."

"There were many worthwhile things I learned in my six-years in the carnival. Opening safes was one of them. It can be a lucrative sideline for a traveling carnival."

"And when you opened the safe, you found your birth certificate, and her papers, including her will and financial earnings. You ever wonder why she kept your birth certificate? Maybe she cared more than you think."

Now a throaty, self-deprecating laugh emerged from Marianna. Hard eyes focused on Percy from across the table.

"Not bloody likely. When I told her who I was, do you know what she did?"

Percy shook her head slowly.

"She spit on me. Spit on me!"

"That must have been rough."

"She said she kept the birth certificate as penance, a reminder of the most terrible, sinful thing she'd done in her life. That's what I was to her."

"So your plan was what? Pay her back for the miserable life she forced on you?"

Marianna looked away then brushed her cheek against her pet's fur. The features of her face softened, but her voice kept the same hard, matter-of-fact edge.

"She threw me out like so much garbage. So yes, I wanted to pay her back. She was a cold-hearted woman and insanely jealous of Ronald. I decided to use him to get to her."

"Did he know who you really were?"

"No. Like most men, he only saw what he wanted to see. But as Helena I used him to access her business, see what was there for me. When I got into the safe, I found out that dear mama was much richer than I had suspected. And the will was phrased right, leaving everything she had to her next of kin. I didn't have to change it."

"So the wording of the will worked as long as it looked like somebody else did her in. Like Howie."

"Exactly. According to the law, I can inherit from my mother, even though she gave me up for adoption. Once the cops found my birth certificate and read the will, I knew it would only be a matter of time before they located me. I've been waiting."

"It might have been a long wait. One of the employees broke into the safe after you did and stole the certificate, hoping to use it to blackmail whoever was Carlotta's kid. Don't look so alarmed. I've got it right here." She patted a pocket of her coat with the hand still holding the scarf.

Marianna gave Percy a fleeting smile. "Well, you just can't trust anybody these days, can you?"

"True enough. Why the rope? Why did you tie the rope around her neck only to throw her into the chocolate?"

"I'd been down in her cellar before and saw a coiled rope tucked away in a corner. That night I knew she'd be downstairs in the cellar, as she usually was, mixing the concoction. She was so busy concentrating; she didn't even hear me come up behind her. I threw the rope around her neck, and threatened to hang her from one of the beams in the ceiling. I wanted to see her sweat."

"And did she?"

"No. She thought I only wanted her money, which she had no intention of giving me, I might add. That's when she spit on me. So I strangled her. Pulled the rope so tight, my hands actually got rope burns."

"Then what?"

"Then I thought, why not bury her in what she loved the most? So I dragged her body upstairs and threw it into the empty vat. I went back down and grabbed all the chocolate I could find. I surrounded her body with it, that chocolate that meant more to her than anything or anybody in the world. Before I left, I turned the flame up as high as it would go. Burn, witch, burn."

"You have a flair for the dramatic."

"Thank you. Then I went back to Lola Mae's apartment and became her again, waiting for the police or someone like you to show up. I needed to be on the spot, to make sure Howie hung for this. Did you like the story about the young 'gentile' woman pounding on Howie's door the week before? I threw that in as a distraction."

Percy chose not to answer that question, but said, "It must have been hard, keeping up three separate lives."

"Not really. When I was Lola Mae, I got to be in a bright, lovely apartment. Howie was fun and taught me a lot about cooking."

"I'll be sure to tell him the next time I see him."

"And when I was Helena, well, you could say I was off my feet a lot. Say what you will about Ronald, he knew how to please a girl. I was sorry to have locked him in the freezer like that, but he was getting in my way. Now that Carlotta was gone, he wanted for us to come out into the open. I couldn't have that. Lola Mae and Helena had to disappear."

"So you could go back to being just Marianna Christensen. At least for awhile."

"That's right. Then take the money and run. Off to somewhere for an extemporaneous existence. Have you ever been to Brazil?"

"Nope. And don't get too attached to the idea, yourself." Percy waved the gun at her. "I have to hand it to you. Interesting characters, Marianna, Lola Mae, Helena, a teenage boy. The smaller, standoffish one, right?"

"Attitude is everything, Percy Cole. You should know that."

"You are one talented girl. And you speak so well. Words like extemporaneous just roll right off your tongue."

"You're not the only woman who can read a book and learn. Of course, you finished high school. I left in the eighth grade. Now don't *you* look so alarmed. I had to do a little research on you, see what I was up against, ask a few questions. I may have gone to the School of Hard Knocks, but I graduated summa cum laude."

She leaned forward, worrying the dog's collar.

"You and I have a lot in common, Percy Cole."

"Not really."

"Sure, we do. We're both smarter than anyone suspects. We know what's what. I'm now worth over a quarter of a million dollars. Keep your mouth shut and we can split it. Think of what you could do for your son with that kind of money. We could be partners."

"Forget it. Your partners tend to freeze up on you."

"That's a shame. That means I'll have to kill you instead."

In one quick move, Marianna removed her hand from the dog's furry neck holding a small derringer. It was pointed directly at Percy's heart.

"We're at a standoff, Percy Cole."

"So I see." Percy gestured to the small gun with a nod. "Very clever."

"Oh, this?" Marianna gave a self-deprecating scoff. "A trick I picked up along the way. I always keep it attached to Poopsie's collar, with the safety on, of course. Hand over the birth certificate." She reached out a hand. "I'll have to plant it somewhere the cops will find it then we can all go about our business."

Percy shook her head slowly. "I don't think so."

Percy stared at her, the Mauser never wavering. Marianna returned her stare with an amused smile, an almost amused glint in her eye.

"Why Percy, don't you trust me?"

"Not as far as I can throw the Empire State Building."

"In that case, it's a Mexican stand-off. Who's going to shoot who first, Percy Cole? It would be a shame to make Oliver an orphan, but this is kind of fun. After all, I have nothing to lose. You, on the other hand, have everything. Should we both fire at the same time and see what happens? On the count of three. One – two -"

"Hold on, Marianna. Let's not get carried away. Maybe we can work something out."

Percy set the Mauser on the table and shoved the gun toward Marianna. It stopped dead center. Marianna looked confused, but Percy assumed a relaxed position, as relaxed as Marianna's had been moments before. The detective gave her a smile.

"See? I can be reasoned with."

Marianna looked doubtful. "Just like that? I don't believe it."

Percy shrugged and in doing so, accidentally dropped the scarf from her hand. It fell to the floor. While bending over to pick it up, Percy reached inside the sleeve of her right boot.

She pulled out a Jim Bowie knife and threw it at Marianna's hand holding the gun. The sharp blade flashed as it pierced the soft part of the woman's hand between her thumb and forefinger. Marianna's wounded hand released its hold and the gun clattered to the floor. The knife landed next to it.

Marianna uttered a sharp cry of pain and clutched at her bleeding hand. The frightened dog jumped off its owner's lap and backed into a corner of the room whimpering. Leaping up, Percy ran to the other side of the table. She retrieved the derringer and knife from the floor then stood over the woman who moaned.

"That's a trick *I* picked up along the way." Percy looked down at the woman rocking back and forth cradling her hand.

"Wrap this around your hand to stop the bleeding," Percy said. She dropped her scarf in Marianna's lap, while snatching up the Mauser from the center of the table. "Then stand up, Marianna. We're going to go into the other room and find that phone to call the cops."

Chapter Forty

Percy pulled Ophelia into the space at the curb in front of her lower east side apartment building. This was a close-knit neighborhood. Car owners who lived here tried to leave designated parking spaces. This was the Cole spot.

Percy turned off the motor and sat, thinking. The past few days had been busy and she was exhausted.

A rap on the window on her side of the car startled her. She looked over and saw the smiling face of her friend, and sometime suitor, Detective Ken Hutchers. He took a long drag on his cigarette then threw the butt into one of the many puddles of melted snow.

Percy opened the car door and alighted, reveling in the warmer temperature that had released the tri-state area from the recent grip of frigid, arctic air.

"Hey, Hutchers."

"I see you got your car back."

"Yeah, Rendell organized to have it dug out yesterday. Then the big overnight thaw happened. If they waited a day, they could have saved themselves the trouble."

"Ain't that always the way?"

"Yeah. Pop drove it back last night, since I've been spending my time at police stations filling out reports. Man, you cops do more writing than policing, as far as I can see."

"You're telling me. Nice weather we're having," he said looking around.

"Sure is. Must be at least forty-five degrees. Maybe I'll go swimming."

They both laughed and leaned against the side of the car next to each other. Percy relaxed for the first time in three or four days. She looked at the man who had that effect on her.

"What's up?"

"First off, the lab results for the strawberry jam tested just like you said. Loaded with arsenic."

Hutchers turned and grinned at Percy. She smiled back at him.

"I figured if 'Lola Mae Lawton' dropped biscuits and jam off to Howie in jail, there would be more to it than an act of kindness."

"Good thing your father confiscated the basket first and Howie didn't have any of that jam he professes to love."

"Yeah, he can be a pig."

"Anyway, the D.A. thought about getting her for the attempted murder of Howie, but --"

"But why bother?" Percy interrupted. "I mean, you could get Marianna Christensen for the attempted murder of me, if you wanted. Pushing somebody off a moving train is not good for their health."

"Other than the few bruises on your cheek, Perce, you seem to be okay."

"You should see the bruise across my shoulder blades from landing on that railroad tie."

He moved closer. "Is that an invitation? Because I'd love to."

"Cool it, buster. Somebody could walk by at any time."

Her voice was stern, but she nonetheless smiled. As if on cue, a man and woman with three kids hurried down the street, caught sight of Percy, and waved. Percy waved back. They then went up the stoop and into her apartment building. She turned back to Hutchers, gesturing to the young family disappearing into the building.

"Some of our invited guests. The Coles and Goldbergs are throwing a party for Howie, early, so kids can be a part of it." She changed the subject. "The scuttlebutt is Marianna confessed to doing in Carlotta, Bogdanovitch, and her adopted father when she was eleven."

"That man was no loss to the world." Hutchers gave Percy a knowing look.

"But you have to admit, it isn't a normal reaction for a kid, even one that gets beat up regularly."

"But she might not have turned out the way she did, if she's had some decent upbringing."

"Spoken like a true father."

"I try. Even though I only see my kids on weekends, I try."

A sadness swept over The New York detective and settled down on him. Percy reached out and touched his arm lightly.

"Come on upstairs, Hutchers. I can promise it will be lively."

"Thanks, but I got to get going soon."

He took out a packet of cigarettes from his coat pocket, flipped one out, and offered it to Percy. She shook her head.

"Given it up. Bad for your health."

"Says who?"

"Nobody yet, but they will."

Hutchers shrugged, took out the cigarette, and lit it with a match. There was an awkward silence. Percy studied the man by her side.

"Okay, so why the big stall?"

After a long pull on the cigarette, he spoke.

"We got back the dental comparatives today. I wanted to tell you in person."

She took a deep breath, drew her body away from the car, and stood tall. "So how did it play out?"

"The dental x-rays taken of the corpse right after the accident and the ones taken from Leonard Donovan's dentist, they match. The body in the car is now officially listed as Leonard Donovan's."

Percy turned away from him, lost in her memories and feelings.

"So Leo is really dead. No scam."

"No scam. You were probably right about his wallet being thrown from the scene and somebody finding it. I'm sorry, Perce."

"Thanks." She shrugged then tensed up. "I'll have to tell Oliver. I don't know how he'll take it."

"Tell him what he needs to know and answer any questions. Then be there for him. That's my advice."

"That's pretty much what Pop said. I think mothers try to solve all the problems of the world for their children. Fathers can be more realistic."

"Until their girls are old enough to start dating. All bets are off then."

Percy chortled. "You always know how to make me laugh, Hutchers. Thanks."

"That's what friends are for. Speaking of friends, Howie is free and the new owner of a chocolate factory because of you. I hope he appreciates it."

"He does."

"Here's a bonus. Lieutenant Griffin's got a red face from arresting the wrong person. The papers have crucified him."

"So I read."

"Yeah, but he still wound up taking credit for most of your work."

"That's the way it goes."

"Tell me, do you get free candy from Howie for the rest of your life?"

"I'd better. I gave him the blue book with the formula in it, so it should be pretty tasty stuff. It's in Spanish, but he had it translated."

"And just where did you get that book, Perce?"

"Slips my mind. I've been to a lot of places lately."

"Uh-huh." He raised one eyebrow and studied her. "You know, that book might be considered evidence."

"Come on. It's just Carlotta's recipe for chocolate. Not much else in it. But I'm sure Howie would be willing to share it with you flatfoots, now that he's copied the formula from it. Like some other people," she added under her breath.

"You're one for the books, yourself, Perce," Hutchers said with a laugh. "Did I tell you about the two men we arrested a few days ago?"

Percy shook her head without looking at him. He went on.

"Middle of the night. Driving with two flat tires. Got pulled over for endangerment and damned if they weren't half naked when they were told to step out of the car. Nineteen degrees, no shoes, and in their skivvies. Said their trousers and shoes were stolen by a big woman wearing a fedora. Ring a bell?"

He turned to Percy with a grin. She feigned taking a moment to think, then shook her head again. Hutchers let out a laugh, while throwing his cigarette butt into another puddle.

"I didn't think so."

"I should get upstairs." Percy made a move toward the stoop of the building then turned around. "You sure you don't want to join us?"

"Nah. But here, this is for you." He withdrew a small heart-shaped red box from inside the breast pocket of his coat. "Happy Valentine's Day."

"Why, thank you, Detective Ken Hutchers." She took it in her hand and turned it over. "Hershey's Chocolates? And with Howie owning his own chocolate business now?"

"I figured you been eating enough of his stuff. Give you a variety. Before you told me, I thought all of it was just, you know, chocolate. But you say the taste is different, so I guess it's different."

"Oh, I say so. And Hershey's Chocolate just might be my favorite. But, let's not tell Howie."

She came toward him and placed a gentle kiss on Hutchers' lips. Without moving, he returned it just as gently. She pulled away and looked at him with a grin.

"I'll see you around, Hutchers."

"Yes, you will. Maybe I can take you out for your birthday. I hear that's coming up."

"You bet."

Chapter Forty-one

Percy climbed the stairs to her apartment, listening to the hub-bub that got louder with every step. It sounded like everyone on the east side was there, but how often do you get to attend an all out bash in these troubled times?

Between the Coles and Goldbergs, every dime and ration coupon they could raise had been spent on Howie's Welcome Home Party. But knowing the neighbors as she did, Percy knew each one of them would contribute a potluck dish to the occasion. Good people all, as Pop said.

She stepped inside the hallway of the apartment where it was wall to wall humanity having a wonderful time. Smells of lasagna, roast pork, and brisket of beef made her mouth water. Bursts of jovial voices and raucous laughter peppered the air. Glenn Miller's rendition of "I've Got a Gal In Kalamazoo" filtered out from the kitchen. Percy heard Mother singing along with it in a loud, but thin voice.

Mother's been at the sherry again.

Percy's name was called. She looked over the sea of heads and recognized her sister's hand above the crowd waving frantically at her. Sera called again, jumping up and down.

"Percy, Percy!"

Sera pushed her way through the throng and breathless, stood in front of her older sister. Her face shone bright and freshly scrubbed, devoid of the usual pound and a half of makeup she wore. Eyes sparkling, Sera wore a smile that almost broke her face.

"Percy, I was so afraid I wouldn't see you before we left."

"Left? Where are you going? And who's *we*?"

Before Sera could answer, a young private first class came to her side wearing a dress uniform. Percy recognized him right away.

"Bobby? Bobby Evans? I don't believe it. I thought you were overseas."

"He was, but he's back. For eight whole days," replied Sera.

Wordless, Bobby smiled and wrapped an arm around Sera.

"And we're getting married, Percy," Sera said in a rush, snuggling into Bobby's chest. "Day after tomorrow at City Hall. Say you'll come. Say you'll come," Sera begged.

Stunned, Percy stared first at one happy young person then the other. "Married? But I thought you two broke up."

"Oh, we did," said Sera, with a dismissive wave of her hand. "But that was months ago. He asked me to marry him yesterday and I said yes. Isn't that grand?"

"Sure, sure," Percy stuttered.

"We've got to go, Percy," Sera said, looking at her watch. "We're late now. Bobby's parents are throwing us an engagement party for all his friends and relatives. I'm sorry."

Sera managed to look contrite for a moment before going on.

"But this is the only night his whole family can get together. His uncle, who's a staff sergeant, goes back to France tomorrow morning. He can't even be here for the wedding. Isn't that sad?"

Sera looked at Bobby, who shrugged amiably, but still hadn't said a word. Then they both looked at Percy and grinned like two Cheshire cats out of Alice in Wonderland. Sera snatched at Bobby's hand and gave him a tug toward the door.

"See you later," Sera said into the air.

As Bobby passed Percy, he looked up at her and whispered. "I love her desperately, you know."

"Glad to hear it," Percy yelled to their departing backs.

The barking of two dogs captured Percy's attention. At her feet Freddie the dog, appeared and sat up on hind legs in a greeting. She swooped him up in her arms. Right after, Oliver, carrying Poopsie, collided into her. He looked up.

"Mommy," Oliver said with surprise. Then his eyes became wide in dismay. "This isn't my fault, Mommy. I put the dogs in my room like you said. Somebody opened the door and let them out. Nobody stepped on them yet, but I couldn't carry both of them. Freddie got away."

With her free hand, Percy cupped the back of Oliver's head and guided him to her bedroom door. She opened it and pushed him gently inside. Closing the door, she set Freddie on the floor and turned to Oliver. So serious, so responsible, in some ways the oldest soul she'd ever met – that was her son.

"I'm sure you did, Oliver, and it's all right. Somebody probably opened the door thinking it was the bathroom. We'll keep the dogs in here and I'll lock the door, okay? This way nobody can get in and the dogs can't get out again. Now put Poopsie down and let's go get something to eat."

Reluctantly, Oliver set the smaller dog on the floor.

"Can't we keep Poopsie, Mommy? He doesn't eat much and Freddie and he play together all the time. Can we? Huh?"

"We've already had this discussion, Oliver. Poopsie is Uncle Howie's dog now. Poopsie and Howie have been friends for a long time. Besides, Uncle Howie's lonely with his roommate off fighting the war. You don't want him sitting all alone while you have two pets to yourself, do you?"

The boy struggled with the idea for a moment. "I guess not. And Uncle Howie says he takes Poopsie to work with him every day. But he doesn't give him any chocolate, though. He says he read somewhere chocolate's not good for dogs."

"Well, then I guess you'd better not give any to Freddie, either."

Oliver's mother bent down to ruffle her son's hair. Then she took his hand and led him to her desk. After sitting down in the chair, she hoisted the boy on her lap. Her voice was soft as she leaned her chin down on the top of his head.

"Oliver, you're getting to be a big boy now."

"Almost nine!"

"That old? My, my. I thought it was more like eight and a half."

"Eight and seven months. I counted them."

"Yes, that's a big boy. How would you like to go out for Chinese food tomorrow night? Just you and me? I want to talk to you about something."

Oliver craned his neck and looked up at his mother. The sweetness of him tightened her throat.

"You mean just you and me? Nobody else?"

"I do."

"Not grandpa or grandmother or Aunt Sera?"

"Nobody but you and me."

"Oh, boy! Can I have eggrolls?"

"As many as you want."

"Wow! Lucky me."

"Lucky me, too, Oliver. Lucky me."

The boy climbed off his mother's lap and turned to her.

"Are you going to tell me about my father?"

Percy was silent for a time. Finally, she spoke.

"I am."

He stood looking at her then licked his lips. His voice held a slight tremble.

"He's not coming back, is he, Mommy?"

"No, son. He's not. There's been an accident, a terrible car accident, and he..." Percy broke off, not wanting the say the words that were so final. "He didn't make it, Oliver. It happened a long time ago. Come here." She pulled him back on her lap, enveloping him in a hug then covering the top of his head with kisses. "I'm sorry, Oliver, so sorry."

He hugged her back, more tightly than she could have imagined. His muffled voice was small but clear.

"That's why he didn't come back to us, right Mommy? He couldn't."

With only a fleeting hesitation, Percy said, "That's right. He couldn't." She pulled him away from her and looked directly in his face. "But you've got me, and grandmother, grandpa, Aunt Sera, Uncle Jude, Uncle Howie --"

"And Freddie." Oliver interrupted, looking down at the pet that sat staring up at the two of them. Large brown eyes searched their faces aware, as a dog often is, that something serious was happening.

Percy choked on a pent up sob or laugh; she wasn't sure which. "That's right. You've got Freddie. So many people love you, Oliver. Never forget that."

Percy kissed her son lightly on top of the head again and pushed him off her lap. "Now let's get out to the party and have a good time, okay? Later on you can ask me any questions you have about this. At any time and as often as you want, okay?"

"Okay." His face took on a somber look. "But are we still going out for Chinese food tomorrow?"

"You bet we are. And not just tomorrow. We'll go next week, too. Whenever you like. You and me. Now go find Freddie - the kid - and play or something. Are you sure you want to keep the dog named Freddie? It's not too late to change it. We've got Fred Rendell senior, Freddie junior, and now Freddie the dog. That's a lot of Freds."

"Oh, yes ma'am. But Freddie's a good name. I like it."

Chapter Forty-two

There was a whoop and a spurt of laughter coming out from the parlor. Percy pushed her way through the crowd gravitating toward Howie's laugh.

"Hey, Howie. How's it going?"

"Hey, Percy!" Howie wheeled around at the sound of her voice then fairly shouted to the crowd in the room. "Look, everyone. My savior has arrived, the heroine of the hour. Let's hear it for Percy Cole!"

Applause filled the air. Embarrassed, Percy gestured for everyone to stop. Friends and neighbors laughed at her apparent shyness and, none too soon for Percy, went back to their conversations.

"Hey, your hands are empty," Howie exclaimed. "Someone go get the lady a glass of red wine and a meatball sandwich," he shouted out.

An older man Percy knew from across the street smiled, saluted, and made his way through the crowd in compliance. Howie leaned in with a wicked expression on his face.

"Or would you rather have some lobster? I left some on the other side of the Peacock screen for you, just in case. It fell off the truck this morning, courtesy of Alf. I told him those days were gone, but I confiscated part of the load for tonight's party, including some Chianti. He promised he'd be better from now on."

"You believe him, Howie?"

"I think there's good in the man, after all."

"You believe there's good in everybody."

"I'm giving him a chance. And I made Vinnie his boss. He'll toe the line or answer to him. Vinnie's tougher than I thought. He's sure tough on me, even though he's supposed to be my assistant. He'll keep all of us in line."

"I been out of the loop for a couple of days answering questions for the cops in three boroughs, but it sounds like Vinnie's got some backbone," Percy said, as her neighbor thrust a glass of wine in one hand and a meatball sandwich in the other. "I heard Carlotta's cousin signed the papers to inherit her estate and took off for Chicago again."

"He didn't even stop by the factory. Maybe everything that happened scared him off."

"Could be." *Or maybe he didn't care about anything other than what went into his pocket.*

Almost as if reading her mind, Howie said, "It's sad. No one seems to mourn the loss of Carlotta Mendez. Hardly anyone was at her funeral besides me."

"I don't think she had a knack for making friends."

"Maybe not. But nobody deserves to be buried alone."

"Howie, never change. You're one of life's good guys." She took a bite out of the sandwich, red sauce running down her chin. "Man, this is tasty. You make this?"

Her friend nodded with a smile then became serious. "Percy, I don't think I told you how grateful I --"

"Don't make me hit you, Howie," Percy said in between chews of food. "You thanked me plenty. I know you're grateful. Enough already."

"You're a good friend, Persephone Cole. If it hadn't been for you and Jude --"

"Where is Jude?" Percy interrupted her friend again, looking around her.

"He was around a minute ago. He mentioned something about going to the preliminary hearing for Lola Mae, I mean, Marianna. It was set for tonight in Brooklyn."

"Wants to make sure she doesn't get out on an insanity plea, I'll bet."

"She might be insane, Percy. Look at all she's done. What sane person does that?"

"An amoral one who's looking for a lot of dough, and doesn't mind framing a friend and neighbor to get it, that's who."

"Maybe." Howie shrugged and looked away. "It's sad though."

"Then let's change the subject. What do you hear from Ralph?"

"He's coming home on leave in a month. I can't wait. Did you see the chocolate heart-shaped Valentine's Day cake I made in your honor? A one-of-a-kind."

"Not yet."

"Three layers of dense chocolate. I got this idea to take the chocolate formula and put it in a cake mix. So far, rave reviews on the ones I made yesterday and the day before. I'm thinking of making only chocolate cakes and brownies from now on. Leave the candy to Schatzi. She's a nice girl; deserves a break, I think."

"Of course, you do."

"Anyway, some big restaurants are interested in carrying my cakes, like Sardi's. I brought them some today and they loved it. I'm branching out in a whole new direction."

"Sounds like it. Congratulations." She looked around her. "Where are our parents?"

"The Moms are in the kitchen, but you don't want to go in there. At least, not yet."

"Why not?"

"They're having one of their 'discussions'.

"Uh-oh."

"It seems *my* mom tried to reorganize *your* mom's spice cabinet. Then *your* mom tried to put Spam in *my* mom's brisket of beef so it would stretch farther. All out civil war."

"Those two have been having battles like that for years. It's part of what makes them tick."

"Dad fled to the apartment downstairs about ten minutes ago, but he has to be up early to open the store tomorrow. He was making gefilte fish for the party since four am this morning. You should try it. It's good."

"I will. Where's Pop?"

"The last time I saw him was when he stepped out on the back porch for some air. I'll bet he's still there."

She looked around, and raised her voice over the din.

"I think I'll go find him. The party sure is in full swing."

"It's a doozy. Been going on for nearly two hours, Percy. The whole neighborhood is here and then some. Glad you finally showed up."

She turned to leave when Howie's voice stayed her.

"And Percy, once again, please let me thank --"

"Oh, shut up," Percy interrupted him with a growl. She pressed her way through the mob but shouted over someone's head, "Say that one more time, and I'll slug you."

Howie laughed and blew her a kiss. "I'm going to say it as many times as I want, so slug away."

Ten minutes later, after meeting and greeting half the neighborhood crammed inside the apartment, Percy made it to the small porch at the rear and opened the back door. Protected somewhat from the elements by an overhang, it was almost as warm as inside the apartment.

In one corner of the four by six foot porch was the Cole washing/wringer machine. Empty clotheslines strung with clothespins danced in the evening breeze.

In the other corner Pop sat in his worn rocking chair, his place of escape with a cigar when he could afford one. With the weather warmer than it had been in weeks, Pop was wearing only a wool sweater over his white shirt. His special occasion tie, a blue and green hound's-tooth design, dangled from his neck. He looked somber and deep in thought.

"Pop, you okay?"

"Persephone." His persona changed abruptly, his tone bright and loving. "Come on out, my girl. I've been waiting for you to come to the party. How was Staten Island? You were there a long time."

"What are you doing out here, Pop? Something wrong?"

Pop looked surprised. "Nothing's wrong, Persephone, nothing at all. In fact, everything's right."

"You mean Sera and Bobby getting married? They told me on their way out. Who would have figured?"

"Come on over here and take a seat next to me." He tapped the three-legged stool next to him.

Percy took the two steps that brought her to her father's side and sat on the stool. He took her hand and caressed it, but said nothing.

"Pop, are you okay?"

"I am. Just reflecting. Robert Evans is a good lad. Wants to be a teacher, you know. Bright future. They've known each other since grammar school. Been seeing each other on and off for four years now."

"Yeah, but I thought it was more off than on, Pop."

"We all know love can take some strange turns. But the long and short of it is, Robert asked Serendipity to marry him, and she said yes. The Coles and Evans, we're giving them two nights at the Astor Hotel as a wedding present. The rest of his leave they'll stay at a friend's cabin on Long Island."

He fell silent, wrapped in an air of contentment. Percy, however, grappled with how she felt.

"I can't believe it. I go to Staten Island to sign a deposition and all hell breaks loose back in Manhattan."

"Our Serendipity knows what she wants. Always has. Him. I suspect that's why she's been a bit on the wild side. But no more."

"I guess that means when the fleet's in, they'll have to make other plans."

"Now, you behave, Persephone. She's a good girl at heart."

"It wasn't what she was doing with her heart that had me worried, Pop."

They both laughed before her father spoke again.

"Those days are over now. Serendipity and Robert will get married. After the honeymoon, he'll return to his troop, and she'll continue living here until the war's over. When he comes back, she'll have a full and happy life with him."

Percy thought for a moment then let out a chuckle. Her father looked at her, puzzled.

"Seems like you can't get rid of your daughters even when we get married."

"We wouldn't have it any other way." He stroked her hand lightly. "Mother and I are blessed."

"Speaking of Mother, I hear she and Mrs. Goldberg are in the kitchen going at it hammer and tongs."

"Their children are well and happy, finally. Now those two can go back to doing what they do best." He leaned in conspiratorially. "Sparring with one another."

Percy sat for a moment, while Pop lit a cigar. He let out a deep sign of contentment.

"It's been a day of revelations and changes, but all good." Pop studied Percy's face for a moment. "Anything you want to tell me, daughter? Anything going on with you I need to know about?"

Percy hesitated for a split second. "Nothing that can't wait until tomorrow. You enjoy your cigar." Percy stood, squeezed her father's hand and dropped it. He looked up at her with a grin.

"Mother gave me a box of them for Valentine's Day. When the all clear sounds, Persephone, go into the kitchen and see the broach I got your mother. It's small, but it's gold and got a ruby in it. A real one."

"Where'd you get that, Pop?"

"Had it on lay-away since November. Finally paid it off this week. Mother cried like a baby when she seen it. Says she'll never take it off."

"I'll bet she won't. Happy Valentine's Day, Pop."

Chapter Forty-three

"Morning, Rendell. Or should I say, good afternoon?" Percy stepped from behind the Peacock screen and into the office.

"Yes, ma'am. It's a quarter after twelve. Lots of phone calls while you were out. Two new possible jobs. I told them you'd be in touch. Your brother, Jude, phoned a short while ago. Said to call him."

"Have a donut." Percy tossed a small brown bag on his desk. "The bag absorbed most of the grease. Too bad."

"Smitty's Donuts?" He stopped his filing to read the side of the bag then reached inside with his one good hand. Percy winked at him good-naturedly.

"You bet. They're the best."

"I thought they only had a store in Brooklyn."

"You thought right, Rendell. I was there for Marianna Christensen's sentencing."

Rendell watched Percy remove her fedora, shake out her mane of hair, and sit behind her desk before he spoke.

"The radio said the jury came back pretty fast."

"It was short and sweet. They weren't out fifteen minutes. Death by electric chair." She paused. "Any coffee?"

"I made a fresh pot just a minute ago, ma'am."

Percy rose from her chair and stepped to the small file cabinet that doubled as the coffee set up. She poured herself a cup, while Rendell went on.

"I want to thank you for taking me on permanently, ma'am. What with the new baby on the way, Sylvia and me, we --"

"I did it for myself, Rendell," she interrupted then took a long, satisfying gulp of coffee. "In two months time you know more about this office than I do. You type faster than me with only one hand, and you make a good cup of coffee. Just keep it up. No need to mention it again."

"No, ma'am."

Her assistant turned away with a smile. The phone rang. Rendell put down the remnants of his donut, brushed off his hand, and picked up the phone.

"Cole Investigations. Fred Rendell speaking." He turned to Percy. "It's your brother again. You in?"

"I'm in."

She stretched across the short space that separated their two desks and took the receiver, the cord being just long enough to reach.

"Jude, I saw you in court not an hour ago. What's up?"

While she listened, Rendell picked up the telephone base, and set it at the end of his desk closer to Percy, and returned to his filing. Percy hardly noticed. She was busy listening intently to the conversation on the other end of the line and did so for the better part of a minute. Then she continued to sit in silence.

"Yeah, I'm still here," she finally said to her brother. Putting her hand over the mouthpiece, she turned to her assistant.

"Rendell."

At the tone of her voice, the man stopped what he was doing and looked at her.

"Take lunch. Be back in an hour."

He nodded, shut the file cabinet drawer, and left the parlor, closing the door behind him. Percy waited a beat before she removed her hand from the receiver and spoke again.

"When did this happen?" She listened. "They weren't watching her? Nothing?" She listened again. "No, I guess they didn't. I didn't figure she was the type to hang herself, either. One of these days, they're going to take things like belts and shoelaces away from condemned criminals. Not that it's going to do Marianna any good. Okay, okay. I'll shut up and let you talk. What?"

She listened then rose, more thrown than agitated. "What you do mean, she left me her diary and a letter? Why did she do that? I'm the reason she got caught." Percy sat back down or rather fell into the chair. "What does it say? Okay, okay. So you don't know. Tell me what you do know. She left instructions for them to be sent to me? Now?"

She heard the front doorbell ring followed by a loud, impatient knock.

"They're at the door. I'll call you back if I need to tell you anything. Thanks, Jude."

She replaced the phone and hurried out into the hallway, yelling toward the kitchen. "It's all right, Mother. I got it."

She opened the door to see a young, skinny teenage boy dressed in a brown uniform, complete with cap.

"You Percy Cole?"

Said with an air of boredom, he looked directly at her, raising his eyebrows. She nodded. Satisfied, he thrust a clipboard at her.

"Sign here, lady."

Percy scribbled her name on the proffered document and returned it to the waiting boy. Out of the worn, leather pouch slung over one shoulder, he removed a small brown paper package neatly tied with a string followed by a white letter-sized envelope, both addressed to her. Meanwhile, Percy reached into her pocket for a dime. They exchanged items and the boy finally smiled.

"Gee, thanks, lady. They usually give me a nickel."

"You could give me change."

Pretending he didn't hear her words, he grinned, touched his cap in a salute, and clomped down the stairs.

Percy returned to her office, sat down, and placed the book-shaped package on her desk. After sitting for a full minute, she sliced open the top of the envelope with her letter opener. She read the handwritten note not once, but twice before fully absorbing it.

Dear Percy Cole,

If you're reading this, it means I'm already dead. The State's offer of the electric chair didn't surprise me, but that's not how I'm planning to die.

I'm glad Howie took Poopsie and will give him a good home. That almost makes me sorry I tried to frame my neighbor, because the dog is the only living thing I ever loved. Not one person measured up to his devotion.

As for you, you gave me a run for my money, but I never thought you would outsmart me. I guess if we were Holmes and Moriarty, I'm the one went over the falls, just like in the books.

Speaking of books, I'm sure you noticed the bookshelves in my room at the cottage when you called the police that day. Many of them are rare or first editions. I have left instructions for the contents to go to the New York City Public Library on 42nd Street. Maybe it's the two lions guarding the entrance, but I've always been drawn to that place. Any peace I've had I found there.

However, with your permission, I would like to leave my copy of "The Little Engine That Could" to your son, Oliver. I always liked your boy; I never faked that.

The book's not worth more than a couple of bucks, if that, but it meant a lot to me. There was a time in my youth when it gave me more hope than anything else in my life. I won't tell you what I traded for the book's ownership back then, but the world can be a wicked place. I found the truth of that more often than not.

I am also sending you my diary. I trust you to dispose of it and not let it get into the hands of people who may want to study the 'criminal mind'. What I've written is deeply personal and I don't want to share my thoughts with anyone. I know I can count on you to honor this last wish.

No matter what I did, I hope you will remember me with some measure of understanding.

Most sincerely, Marianna Christensen

Chapter Forty-four

Percy sat for a time thinking. She got up and went to the small fireplace in the parlor part of the room and lit a fire. After waiting for it to catch, Percy returned to her desk and picked up the brown package. Without unwrapping the diary, she tossed it onto the flames, prodding it with the poker until it was consumed. Only then did she return to her desk, reading Marianna's letter again and again.

Ten minutes later there was a soft knock on the door and her mother entered. She leaned around the screen, her nose lightly dusted with flour.

"Persephone, who was at the door?"

"Just something for me, Mother." She turned around in her chair and gave her mother a brighter than normal smile and changed the subject. "What are you baking?"

"An apricot-sweet potato pie."

"Sounds different, but good." Percy added, folding the letter and replacing it inside the envelope.

Instead of leaving, Mother stepped into the section of the parlor partitioned off as the office. As she rarely did this except when called upon to be the temporary secretary, Percy was surprised. She watched her mother sit down in Rendell's vacated chair, and smooth out her apron as if she wanted to say something, but didn't quite know how to start.

"You look like something's on your mind."

"Persephone, dear, I've done something you might not like, but I felt it was the right thing to do, so I did it." Mother straightened her back and faced Percy with an almost defiant look. "I was only thinking about Oliver's well-being."

"Oliver seems to be the subject of a lot of people's thoughts recently. What did you do?"

Mother took a deep breath and plunged in. "Two days ago I wrote to Kathleen Donovan and sent her some pictures of Oliver, grandmother to grandmother. I invited her to come for a visit."

Mother went on in a rush, not allowing Percy to interrupt.

"After all, he's her grandson, too. And my thinking was, Persephone, my thinking was, that if she just *saw* the boy, saw what a sweet, loving child he is, she might want to be a part of his life. She might not be such an unhappy, miserable old woman." Mother took a deep breath and reflected. "Of course, she might not come around, but I wanted to give her a chance, a chance to --"

"Be a bigger and better person?"

"Don't you dare make fun of me, young lady, or say I didn't have the right. I'll --"

"I'm not making fun of you, Mother."

"After all, Oliver is an important part of our family. Look how much we love him and..." Mother broke off and stared at her daughter in disbelief. "You're not upset with me or think I was wrong to do that?"

Percy tapped the envelope containing Marianna's letter against her free hand.

"No, Mother, I'm not upset. I might have been yesterday, but not today. Redemption, that's what you're offering Leo the Louse's mother. Redemption. And if someone had offered a little to Marianna Christensen somewhere along the line, her life might not have taken the turn it did. So if Kathleen Donovan wants to be in her grandson's life and it makes Oliver happy, I'm all for it."

Percy opened her desk drawer, dropped the envelope inside, closed the drawer slowly, and locked it with a key. She turned to her mother.

"But don't expect me to be nice to her at all costs. She can be a real pill."

"Now, Persephone, I think we should give her the benefit of the doubt."

"Everyone deserves a second chance. Let's not mention this to Oliver just yet, though, in case she runs true to form and doesn't show up. I don't want him to be disappointed."

"No, of course not. Thank you, Persephone, for agreeing to this. I don't know what else to say."

"Then say 'I'm going back to the kitchen to bake my pie now, Persephone' and let me get back to work."

Mother rose to leave, but hesitated, turning to her daughter. Percy looked at her in an open and guileless manner. The older woman smiled.

"There's a part of you that's glad I wrote her, isn't there?"

"I wouldn't go that far."

"I would. You can fool others, but I know you are a very sweet, loving person."

"If you say so, Mother. Just don't let it get around the neighborhood. It can be bad for business."

~

About Heather Haven

After studying drama at the University of Miami in Miami, Florida, Heather went to Manhattan to pursue a career. There she wrote short stories, novels, comedy acts, television treatments, ad copy, commercials, and two one-act plays, produced at several places, such as Playwrights Horizon. Once she even ghostwrote a book on how to run an employment agency. She was unemployed at the time.

Author of the Alvarez Family Murder Mysteries, *Murder is a Family Business*, *A Wedding to Die For*, *Death Runs in the Family*, and *DEAD….If Only*, Heather is currently working on the fifth book of the series, *The CEO Came DOA*.

In *Death of a Clown* and as the daughter of real-life Ringling Brothers and Barnum and Bailey Circus folks, Heather brings the daily existence of the Big Top to life during World War II. Embellished, of course, by her own murderous imagination, this stand-alone noir mystery was inspired by her trapeze artist/performer mother and her father, an elephant trainer.

Corliss and Other Award-Winning Stories is an anthology of her own favorite short stories, short-shorts, and flash fiction.

Heather lives in the foothills of San Jose with her husband of thirty-plus years, and two cats, Yul Brynner, King of Siam (Yulie) and Elphaba, Queen of the Nile, (Ellie).

Also by Heather Haven

•*Death of a Clown* – A noir mystery

The Alvarez Family Murder Mystery Series

•*Murder is a Family Business* – Book One

•*A Wedding to Die For* – Book Two

•*Death Runs in the Family* – Book Three

•*DEAD….If Only* – Book Four

The Persephone Cole Vintage Mystery Series

•*The Dagger Before Me* – Book One

•*Iced Diamonds* – Book Two

•*The Chocolate Kiss-Off* – Book Three

Read on for a sample of
Murder is a Family Business!
Book One of
The Alvarez Family Murder Mysteries

Murder is a Family Business

Chapter One
The Not-So-Perfect Storm

"God, surveillance sucks," I griped aloud to a seagull languishing on a nearby, worm-eaten post, he being my only companion for the past few hours. He cocked his head and stared at me. I cocked my head and stared at him. It might have been the beginning of a beautiful friendship, but a nearby car backfired, and he took off in a huff. Watching him climb, graceful and white against the gray sky, I let out a deep sigh, feeling enormously sorry for myself. I eyeballed the dilapidated warehouse across the parking lot hanging onto the edge of the pier for any signs of life. I didn't find any.

I knew I was in trouble earlier when I discovered this was the only vantage point from which I could stay hidden and still see the "perpetrator's place of entrance," as I once heard on *Law and Order*. That meant I couldn't stay in my nice warm car listening to a Fats Waller tribute on the radio but had to be out in the elements, hunkered down next to a useless seawall.

For three lousy hours, rambunctious waves from the San Francisco Bay made a break for freedom over this wall and won. Salty foam and spray pummeled my face, mixed with mascara, and stung my eyes like nobody's business. Then the wind picked up, and the temperature dropped faster than the Dow Jones on a bad day.

Speeding up Highway 101 toward Fisherman's Wharf, I'd heard on the car radio that a storm was moving in. When I arrived, I got to experience it first-hand. Yes, it was just winter and me on the San Francisco Bay. Even Jonathan Livingston Seagull had taken a powder.

I concentrated on one of two warehouses, mirrors of each other, sitting at either side of a square parking lot containing about twenty cars and trucks. "*Dios mio*, do something," I muttered to the building, which housed the man who had caused me to age about twenty years in one afternoon.

I struggled to stay in a crouched position, gave up and sat down, thinking about the man I'd been following. I was sure he was a lot more comfortable than I, and I resented him for it. Two seconds later, I realized the cement was wet, as well as cold. Cursing my stupidity, I jumped up and stretched my cramped legs while trying to keep an eye on the door he had entered, lo those many hours before. With me being the only one on the job, I couldn't keep an eye on the cargo bay on the other side of the warehouse, but I felt pretty safe about it being a non-exit. Without a boat or a ship tied there, it emptied into the briny bay. The perp, thankfully, didn't look like much of a swimmer, even on a nice day.

I tried to focus my mind on Mr. Portor Wyler, said perpetrator, and the singular reason for all my misery. I kept coming back to this burning question:

Why the hell is a Palo Alto real estate mogul driving 42-miles roundtrip two to three times a week to a beat-up, San Francisco warehouse on the waterfront?

After that, I had an even better one:

What the hell am I doing here? Oh, yeah. Thanks, Mom.

My name is Liana Alvarez. It's Lee to my friends, but never to my mother. I am a thirty-four year old half-Latina and half-WASP PI. The latter, aforesaid relatives, drip with blue blood and blue chips and have been Bay Area fixtures for generations. Regarding the kindred Mexican half of me, they either immigrated to the good old US of A or still live in Vera Cruz, where they fish the sea. How my mother and father ever got together is something I've been meaning to ask Cupid for some time.

However, I digress. Back to Portor Wyler or, rather, his wife, Yvette Wyler. It was because of her I was in possession of a cold, wet butt, although I'm not supposed to use language like that because Mom would be scandalized. She has this idea she raised me to be a lady and swears her big mistake was letting me read Dashiell Hammett when I was an impressionable thirteen year-old.

My mother is Lila Hamilton Alvarez, of the blue blood part of the family, and CEO of Discretionary Inquiries, Inc. She's my boss. Yvette Wyler has been a friend of my mother's since Hector was a pup, so when Mrs. Wyler came crying to her, Mom thought we should be the ones to find out what was going on. That didn't seem
like a good enough reason for me to be where I was, assigned to a job so distasteful no self-respecting gumshoe I hung out with would touch it, but there you have it. Leave it to my mother to lay a guilt trip on me at one of my more vulnerable times. I don't know who I was more annoyed with, Mom or me.

Furthermore, I had no idea what my intelligent, savvy, and glamorous mother had in common with this former school buddy, who had the personality of ragweed and a face reminiscent of a Shar-Pei dog wearing lipstick.

Whenever I brought the subject up to Mom, I got claptrap about "loyalty" and "friends being friends." So naturally, my reaction to the woman made me aware of possible character flaws on my part. I mean, here Mrs. Wyler was, one of my mother's life-long chums, and I was just waiting for her to bark.

But the long and short of it was pals they were. Discretionary Inquiries, Inc. was on the job, and I was currently freezing my aforementioned butt off because of it; thank you so much.

Computer espionage in Silicon Valley is D.I.'s milieu, if you'll pardon my French. The Who, What, Where, When, and How of computer thievery is our livelihood. To elucidate, high tech companies don't appreciate staff making off with new hardware or software ideas, potentially worth millions of dollars, either to sell to the highest bidder or to use as bribery for a better, high-powered job with the competition. If you haven't heard about any of this, it's because this kind of pilfering keeps a pretty low profile in Silicon Valley. Upper management of most companies feel it's important not to give investors the shakes nor the techies any ideas. Ideas, however, are what techies are all about, and it's a rare day when somebody isn't stealing something from someone and using it for a six-figured trip to the bank, whether upper management likes it or not.

Until the recent change in copyright law, each individual company dealt with the problem by filing civil lawsuits against suspected counterfeiters. It was a long and arduous process often resulting in nothing more than a slap on the wrist for the guilty parties. Now that there are federal statutes with teeth, which include prison sentences, these companies are anxious to see the guilty parties pay to the fullest extent of the law. It's at this point that Discretionary Inquiries, Inc. is brought into the act.

D.I. is the Rolls Royce of high-tech investigation, if I must say so myself, with a success rate of over 94 percent. To say business at D.I. is brisk is an understatement. D.I. often turns away work. For me, it's exciting and challenging; I love working with the FBI's counter-intelligence division, the IRS, the U.S. Customs Service, and the "hi-tech units" of police departments.

My particular specialty is being a ferret, and I hope I'm not being too technical here. I sniff out means and opportunity *after the fact* until I have enough evidence that will stand up in court. Yes, I am a perfumed ferret, resplendent in Charles Jordan heels, Bulgari jewelry, and Versace dresses. I sit in cushioned office chairs and have high-powered lunches drilling stricken staff members who "can't believe what happened," until I enlighten them as to how it can and did. Then everybody's happy, and I receive a nice, fat bonus when the job is done. Sometimes I'm allowed to throw a bone to the local newspapers or one of the television stations, depending on how spiteful the wounded company wants to be, so everyone loves me. And, it is my dream job.

This was my nightmare. I closed my eyes and willed it all to go away. It didn't. Just then, the sky darkened, and a gust of wind whipped up at least half the water contained in the Bay. This water joined forces with a maverick wave with a nasty disposition and impeccable timing. They both came at me like a blast from a fireman's hose. I lost my balance, and found myself flat on my back in a very unladylike position, as my mother would say.

I gurgled and spit out about a half-gallon of salt water hoping the Bay was as clean as the mayor boasted. My hair was plastered to my scalp and face in long, wet, strands that went nicely with the quivering blue lips and streaked mascara.

I got to my feet and tried to zip up my black leather jacket. The teeth caught in the fabric of my sweater and refused to budge despite any amount of coercion from numb fingers. My wool slacks clung to my legs and lost whatever shape they previously had. To finish it off, my new suede boots bled their color in puddles around my feet.

"Well, at least it isn't raining yet," I said aloud, trying to remember what I'd learned about positive thinking the previous month. I had attended a three-day seminar at the Malaysian Institute of Advanced Studies in "Self-Excellence and Positive Thinking" sponsored by the Ministry of Culture. I'm not sure what I got out of it, other than great food, but the Institute has a rather unique approach to carrying out daily tasks with "dedication and integrity," as stated in their brochures.

This approach is being written up on about a billion dollars worth of software right here in Silicon Valley. D.I. is their very own personal firewall against thievery, so I wanted to give these Malaysian theories a chance.

I saw the lights go out from under the door of the warehouse and wondered if it was a power outage, or was Wyler preparing to leave? Whatever, my body tensed with renewed alertness or as much alertness as I could renew. At that moment, of course, a bolt of lightning struck. Its point zero was so close by my soggy hair stood on end, and my nose twitched from the electrical charge. The flash of light illuminated everything, including the white-capped waves of the Bay hurtling in my direction. The lightning was followed by a clap of thunder, which sounded like a herd of longhorns stampeding over a tin bridge.

As if that wasn't enough, the walkway I stood on began to quiver, and I knew it was going to do something Really Big at any moment. That's when the heavens opened up. Sheets of rain, driven by the wind, hammered at my skin, and I could barely open my eyes.

"That's it! Stick a fork in me, I'm done," I yelled to the world at large. I reached inside my drenched shoulder bag for my cellphone and prayed it would work. It had been acting up lately, like everything else in my life, but I hit speed dial and ran to a nearby Plexiglas phone booth. The booth no longer contained a phone, only sodden newspapers littering the floor. Fighting the assaulting rain, I pushed the door closed and heard someone pick up on the first ring. Things were looking up. My cell phone was working.

"This is Lila," said a well-modulated voice.

My mother annoys me when she is well modulated, but now that she sounded dry on top of it, I found it maddening.

"It's me, and I feel like Noah without the ark. Get the dove ready. Find me an olive branch. The rains have come, and I am gone."

"Yes, dear. Ha ha. Now what is the matter?"

"What isn't the matter?" I wailed, forgetting I was annoyed with her. "I'm cold; I'm soaked through, and I was almost hit by a bolt of lightning."

"Where are you, Liana? Try to be more *succinct.*"

"Where am I?" I was so stunned by the question that I took a deep breath and decided not to have a tantrum. Lowering my voice several octaves, I enunciated each word. "I am where I have been for three miserable, boring, useless hours, in accordance with your wishes. Succinctly, I'm in a phone booth catty-corner to the warehouse. The lights went out maybe thirty seconds ago just as a storm hit full force. It's raining too hard to see anything more than a foot away. I'm drenched; I'm tired, and I'm freezing." The octaves began to climb again because while I was wiping the water from my face, I poked a finger in my right eye. "Son of a bitch!"

"Watch your language," Lila rebuked, ever the lady. "And don't be petulant, Liana. It doesn't become you. So, what you are saying is, you don't know whether or not Wyler is still inside the warehouse," she said, getting to the issue at hand.

"*Exactamente.* What I do I know, is it's a monsoon out here, and I'm going to catch pneumonia if I stay out in it much longer."

"Oh, stop being so dramatic, Liana. It's just a little water," the woman who gave birth to me chided. So much for mother love. "It's too bad you've lost him so late in the proceedings, though. We were doing so well," she added.

I loved the way she included herself in all of this. "Well, don't tell me you want me to go into the warehouse and look for him," I said, with an edge to my voice. An involuntary shiver ran through me, as I felt a movement of the wet papers at my feet. This wind even comes through Plexiglas, I thought.

"Absolutely not! We agreed to follow him from a safe distance, not to make contact. If we lost him, we lost him. Go on home."

"Oh." I felt the air go out of my balloon of martyrdom. "Sorry about this," I added. This may have been my third tedious day following a man who made Danny DeVito look tall, dark and handsome, but I was a professional and trained to do the job. Although, to be honest, I wasn't quite sure what that job was. His wife thought he was cheating on her. Okay, that's understandable given who she was, but once she caught him in *flagrante delecto*, what then? California has a no-fault divorce law with a fifty-fifty property split, pants up or pants down.

As far as I could see, this wasn't quite the same scenario as demanding the return of stolen property, intellectual or otherwise. I mean, what was he going to "return" here? If Wyler dropped his drawers elsewhere, literally, could he just return his private parts, figuratively, to the little wifey with a vow to never do it again?

When I thought about it that way, I guess you could make a case for it. However, if Lila considered a philandering husband in the same category as computer espionage, and if D.I. was heading in that direction, I was going to get out of the business and become a nun.

"It can't be helped," Lila replied, interrupting my mental wanderings.

"What can't be helped?" I said, still lost in my own thoughts.

"Pay attention, Liana. I'm telling you to go home. Make sure you log all the information you've got on the computer when you get to the office in the morning." She added, "We'll go over it tomorrow with Richard. By the way, have you been able to come up with the owner of the warehouse?"

"You mean in my spare time?" I retorted. "No, I've done some digging, but I can't find a company name yet. I think we're going to have to bring in the Big Guns."

"Hmmm, strange," Lila pondered. "By 'big guns,' as you've put it, I *assume* you mean Richard." Mom has an irritating way of underlining certain words of a sentence with her voice. I don't mean to complain, but it can be almost as exasperating as her modulations. And then there's her overall aversion to the use of slang words, which is too bad, because I use them all the time. Dad's side of the family.

Aside from Dashiell Hammett, my formative years were influenced by any 1940s movie on television I watched. That was whenever I wasn't being thrown outside to play. When I was ten years old, much to my mother's dismay, I fell in love with Barbara Stanwyck's portrayal of Sugarpuss O'Shea in the movie *Ball of Fire*. I imitated "jive talk" every waking moment until I got hustled off to a craft summer camp. The camp may have curtailed my jiving, but to this day, Miss Stanwyck is one of my favorite actresses, along with Selma Hayek, who I just loved in *Frida*.

Mom continued her train of thought about the warehouse, oblivious to my inner musings.

"At first, I didn't think it was important enough to tie up Richard's time, but now I'm curious as to why something as simple as finding out the ownership of a building should be so difficult. Maybe we'll ask his department to see what they can discover tomorrow. We'll talk later. Go home."

With that, she hung up without even so much as telling me to drink some hot tea when I got there or to be careful driving in this weather. It was at times like these I wondered if Mom and Medea had maternal similarities I didn't care to think about.

I threw the phone in my bag and leaned against the Plexiglas, reluctant to go out again into the storm. All of a sudden, I felt movement again at my feet and looked down.

Under the papers was a small lump, a moving one! I drew my breath in, as I opened the door to the phone booth. Water rat! There was a rat in this phone booth with me! I stepped out in the rain backward, keeping my eyes on the mass of papers. Then I thought I heard a plaintive cry. I leaned my head back into the booth ignoring the rain beating down on my back like small pebbles.

"Kitty?" I said. "Kitty, kitty, kitty?"

A meow sounded again. I pulled the wet papers from on top of the lump to reveal a small, orange and white kitten, drenched to the skin. It turned amber eyes up to me and let out a silent meow as it cowered in the corner.

"Oh, my God! Look at you." Reaching out a hand, I picked up the trembling creature. "What a little thing. And so wet. Come here." Like an idiot, I looked around for the owner until I caught myself. I tried to unzip my jacket to slip the kitten inside but the teeth still wouldn't release one of my best cashmere sweaters. The jacket's pockets were huge, so I wound up sort of stuffing the kitten inside, as gently as possible, of course. It turned itself around and stuck its head out with a puzzled stare.

"Well, I can't just leave you, and it's pouring out there. So you stay inside until we get to my car." With that pronouncement, I pushed its small head back inside the dry pocket and left my hand inside for protection and company. The kitten moved around a little and then settled down, leaning against my open palm.

Half walking, half jogging to my car in the torrential downpour, I glanced back in the direction of the warehouse and began to play the "on the other hand" game with myself.

On one hand, Wyler has to be in the warehouse. But it looks dark and deserted. Did he somehow get by me? No, no, he can't have!

On the other hand, when I was lying flat on my back swallowing half the Bay, maybe he did. Stranger things have happened.

Oh, come on, I other-handed myself again. I had the only entrance and exit under constant surveillance for the last three agonizing hours, and I was only indisposed for less than a minute. How likely is it he got away? He must be there. On the other hand, and now I was up to four hands, why aren't the lights on if he is?

This might not look so good on my resume. Uh-oh! I should check for his car. If I let him get by me, Lila will never...wait a minute!

I began to see a silver lining in all those damp clouds.

If Portor did get by me, Lila will never let me live it down. Following this line of logic, she would probably never, ever ask me to do something like this again.

I continued this new train of thought sloshing through puddles up to my ankles and almost broke out in a dance like Gene Kelly in *Singing in the Rain.*

The movements of the kitten in my jacket distracted me, and I wondered what I was going to do with it when I got back to the car.

Well, I reminded myself, *I couldn't just leave it back there to drown.*

That settled, I removed the keys from my bag, pressed the beeper to unlock the doors and slipped into its dry, comparative warmth.

This classic '57 Chevy convertible was my pride and joy, the last extravagant gift from my father shortly before his death. It contained a rebuilt engine, in addition to all the latest gewgaws offered in newer automobiles. Dad had outbid everyone at a vintage car auction for this stellar rarity still wearing the original white and turquoise paint job. He gave it to me for my thirty-first birthday, a reward for surviving a rotten marriage and a bitter divorce. I never knew what the price tag was, but the insurance premiums alone are enough to keep me working until I'm around ninety-seven.

The kitten stopped moving, and I panicked.

This is all I need, I shuddered, *a deceased kitten in my jacket to complete an already ghastly day.*

However, it rubbed up against my hand, and I could feel the fleece lining had dried it off. Then it popped its head out to stare at me with that "now-you've-gone-and-done-it-so-I'm-your-responsibility" look. It was a little unsettling.

"Well, I see you're okay, little guy, but what am I going to do with you?" I challenged, trying not to look it in the eye. Seized with an idea, I thought of my friend who was a vet and would probably take the kitten in, warm-hearted chump that she was. I checked the time. Six-thirty. She would still be at the clinic. "Let's take you to see your new mommy," I cooed. I started the car and drove down the Embarcadero now black, wet and abandoned in the storm. I felt as if I were in a film noir; there didn't seem to be a soul out besides this wet feline and me.

After the earthquake of '89, nearly everyone in San Francisco had prayed the freeway would come down, and the beauty of the bay would be revealed again. When the cement structure was razed, it revitalized a previously neglected area of the city, and man oh, man, do I wish I had been an investor in some of that waterfront property. Everybody who was anybody wanted to be in this area: living, working, shopping, walking, jogging, or running along the Bay, all the while talking or texting on cellphones. That was the latest form of multi-tasking.

The amazing part was they were willing to pay through the nose for the privilege of being crowded into this strip of territory along with a never-ending stream of tourists. Even with the foggy summers, it's probably worth more per square inch than any other place in the states.

I only drove for a couple of blocks when I began to have the gnawing feeling I had some unfinished business. I decided to check and see if Wyler's car was still around or if he had given me the slip. Ever since I started trailing him, I'd noticed he'd always left the car about three blocks away from the warehouse on a side street instead of parking right in front of it. That, in itself, I found very suspicious. He didn't strike me as a man who was into exercise for exercise's sake.

Turning on my brights, I hung a U-turn and drove back to where he parked earlier. I spotted the lone black Mercedes, a solitary car on the block. Noting the time, I hesitated to drive away. Something told me I should return to the warehouse and search for him even if Lila had given me direct orders not to make contact. I turned off the motor shivering in my wet clothes and listened to the sound of the rain drumming on the roof of my car, while I chewed at my lower lip for a time.

Oh, well, I thought as I started the engine, *this won't be the first time I haven't paid any attention to what Lila said. Or the last, either.*

I turned the car around and drove back to the warehouse. At this point, I didn't care if I blew my cover or not. I needed to know.

As far as I could see, which wasn't much, the parking lot was deserted. The lot was around one hundred and twenty feet deep stopping at the thick and ineffectual four-foot high cement wall on the Bay. A narrow walkway leading to piers directly behind each warehouse ran alongside the cement wall. Amber-colored, low-watt lampposts lit the air above the walkway between the two warehouses and the parking lot and served more as symbols than actual illumination. About five feet inside the perimeter, telephone poles lay on their sides to keep vehicles from hitting the warehouses or the seawall.

Given my vision was *nada* even with the headlights on, I relied on my memory and hoped nothing had changed within the last half hour. I aimed the car towards what I calculated was the warehouse door and waited for the feel of the wheels hitting the pole. When I felt the resistance, I stopped the car, turned off the engine, but left the lights on.

Pulling some Kleenex and a headscarf out of the glove compartment, I wiped my face with the former and tied the latter over my head to contain my dripping curls. Underneath the passenger's seat, I found a flashlight, small but powerful, and a not too dirty hand towel. With all this movement, the kitten began to wiggle inside the jacket. I hauled the critter out and wrapped it in the towel. All the while, I spoke in what I hoped was a good version of the reassuring tone of voice was used on *The Crocodile Hunter* the one time I had watched it in mute horror. Of course, this wasn't a crocodile, but the same theory should apply.

"You stay here for just a couple of minutes, little guy. I'll be right back." I placed the mummy-wrapped cat on the seat, opened the door and slid back out into the downpour. I aimed the flashlight at what I hoped was the entrance to the warehouse and was rewarded by the glint of the metal door. I ran to it, found the handle and pulled with all my might. Major locked. Rivulets of water streamed down my face, as I searched for another way to get into the building.

A far off flash of lightning struck, and out of the corner of my eye, I thought I saw something on the ground in the walkway near the water's edge. It was hard to tell by the three-watt bulb of the lamppost, so I trotted towards it, aiming the flashlight ahead of me. The closer I got, the faster I ran, because it looked like a shoe, toe pointing upwards.

Breathing hard, I rounded the corner to see what connected to the shoe. It was Portor Wyler. He lay flat on his back, arms opened wide, unseeing eyes staring up into the falling rain. The front of his once white shirt had turned a pinkish hue, blood diluted by the downpour. Three small reddish holes formed a "v" in the center of his chest.

I know I screamed, but a clap of thunder must have drowned me out. I felt the shriek reverberate inside me but never heard it. I also must have been backing up, because I tripped over one of those damned horizontal telephone poles and fell backward, flinging the flashlight up in the air. It landed near my head with a sobering, clunking sound. I retrieved it, got up, and leaned against the building fighting for control.

When I could move, I stumbled back to the car and grabbed my cellphone off the front seat. The first two times I punched in 911, nothing happened. After banging the phone against the steering wheel, I finally got a connection. My teeth chattered from shock, cold, and fear, but I gave a lucid enough report to the dispatcher before the phone went dead again, as dead as Portor Wyler. Frustrated, I threw it into the back seat as hard as I could. I turned back to face a kitten that had managed to get out of his shroud in my absence and was staring up at me, wide-eyed. I reached a shaking hand out, and it rubbed its body against my fingers. This small bit of friendship overwhelmed me, and I bit back tears.

I couldn't get the picture of Portor Wyler's face out of my mind. His mouth had been frozen open in an "oh," as if he'd been as surprised as me that he was dead. Funny what you notice when you see death for the first time.

~

Contact me. I'd love to hear from you.

Heather Haven, writer
San Jose, California 95135
http://www.heatherhavenstories.com/
Heather's blog at:
http://heatherhavensays.blogspot.com/
https://www.facebook.com/HeatherHavenStories
Twitter@HeatherHaven
Heather's author page at Amazon:
http://www.amazon.com/Heather-
Haven/e/B004QL22UK/ref=sr_tc_2_0?qid=1372537066&sr=1-
2-ent
Email me at: Heather@HeatherHavenStories.com

The Wives of Bath Press

The Wife of Bath was a woman of a certain age, with opinions, who's on a journey. Heather Haven and Baird Nuckolls are modern day Wives of Bath.

www.thewivesofbath.com

Made in the USA
San Bernardino, CA
04 September 2015